W9-CHT-114

ARAB
SUMMER

ARAB SUMMER

SASHA DEL MIRA SERIES, #3

A THRILLER BY

DAVID LENDER

THOMAS & MERCER

The characters and events portrayed in this book are fictitious. Any similarity to real persons, living or dead, is coincidental and not intended by the author

Text copyright © 2013 by David T. Lender
All rights reserved.
Printed in the United States of America.

No part of this book may be reproduced, or stored in a retrieval system, or transmitted in any form or by any means, electronic, mechanical, photocopying, recording, or otherwise, without express written permission of the publisher.

Published by Thomas & Mercer
P.O. Box 400818
Las Vegas, NV 89140

ISBN-13: 9781611097832
ISBN-10: 1611097835

For Berny Schwartz

ALSO BY DAVID LENDER

Trojan Horse

Trojan Horse is a love story built around a thriller about a Wall Streeter who falls in love with an exotic spy and then teams up with her to stop a Muslim terrorist plot to cripple the world's oil capacity.

The Gravy Train

The Gravy Train is the story of a novice investment banker who helps an aging Chairman try to buy his company back from bankruptcy, pitted against ruthless Wall Street sharks who want to carve it up for themselves.

Bull Street

Bull Street is the story of a naive, young Wall Streeter who gives a jaded billionaire the chance for redemption, as they team up to bring down an insider trading ring before they wind up in jail or dead.

Vaccine Nation

Vaccine Nation is the story of an award-winning documentary filmmaker who is handed "whistleblower" evidence about the US vaccination program, and then races to expose it before a megalomaniacal pharmaceutical company CEO can have her killed.

CHAPTER 1

Eighteen months ago.

SASHA DEL MIRA SMILED AT the baker as she took the loaf of bread he handed her over the counter. *"Danka, Herr Gustoven,"* she said, turned and stepped back into the throng of people in the shop. It was Saturday morning, 9:00 a.m., and the shops in Old Town in Geneva were already crammed with tourists. Sasha knew the shopkeepers loved the traffic, but it was locals like Sasha who filled the cash registers on their Saturday-morning rounds for their weekend essentials, walking directly to the counters with purpose instead of milling around and gawking like the foreigners. She worked her way to the door, hearing French, English, German and Italian being spoken. A typical spring Saturday. Near the door she encountered a man poring over a Michelin guide. Two girls, perhaps seven and ten years old, stared up at him.

"Please, Daddy," the younger one said in American English.

"In a moment, Sandy," the man said without looking up from the guide, "I'm looking for something."

Sasha stopped in front of the girls. "Can I help?"

The older girl looked up with relief in her eyes. "Oh, thank God. You speak English. Are you British?"

"No, raised across the lake from here, mostly. My English tutor was British." She smiled. "Can I help?" she repeated.

"Daddy said we could have treats, but we don't speak the language."

"There's a universal language for that," Sasha said, and motioned toward the display cases filled with neat rows of pastries, cakes, pies, strudel and torts. "May I show you?"

The man finally looked up from his Michelin guide. He smiled at Sasha and nodded to the girls. They followed Sasha to the display case. "Just point," she said. The younger one pointed to a Napoleon, the older one to a custard torte. Sasha raised her hand. *"Bitte, Frau Gustoven."* The gray-haired matron behind the counter smiled, then crouched behind the case and observed where each girl now pressed her finger against the glass. She retrieved the pastries, wrapped them in baker's paper and passed them over the counter. Sasha handed them to the girls and turned to see their father holding out a handful of Swiss francs. She pulled out seven francs and handed them to Frau Gustoven. *"Vielen Dank,"* Sasha said. *"Guten Tag."* Sasha turned to leave, said to the man, "Enjoy your stay in Geneva." The man thanked her.

Her errands finished, Sasha left the fragrant warmth of the shop and stepped outside into the cool April air. She shifted her grocery bags into one hand and pulled the collar of her blazer up around her neck against the damp breeze off Lake Geneva. She walked across along Place du Bourg-de-Four, relishing the familiar feeling of the uneven cobblestones under her feet, taking in the 16th-and 17th-century limestone facades of the shops. Swiss locals in sports jackets with ties, walking with stiff formality, intermingled on the sidewalks with the tourists in their brightly colored parkas, Polo khakis, $200 Nikes and backpacks. Sasha smiled, loving it, and continued onto Rue de la Fontaine to descend the hill from Old Town to the center of Geneva.

When she reached the Pont du Mont-Blanc she picked up her pace. Daniel would be home from the gym soon. She wanted to arrive before him, get breakfast started and lay out the dishes as part of a peace offering. She forgot who had once dispensed to her that newlywed advice, "Never go to bed angry at each other," but it rang loudly in her ears now. Then she was laughing to herself over it, because now, after six months, it felt like they were an old married couple. On reflection, the argument last night could have been avoided if only she'd held her tongue. Telling Daniel he'd had too much wine as she pulled him into the foyer to leave the Delarches' apartment, loudly enough to be overheard, wasn't politic, particularly since she'd had too much wine herself. They'd ridden home in a taxi in silence. This morning, Daniel had left for the gym without a word. Sasha figured a cheery hello and the table set for breakfast would put things back on an even keel.

She walked up Rue du Mont-Blanc and had entered Rue Ami-Lévrier, hurrying now, when she noticed a man was walking behind her, seeming to match her pace. She slowed to let him pass. He slowed. She felt a bolt of alarm and slid her hand into her handbag, felt for the grip of her 9mm Beretta Cheetah. *The American from the baker's?* She took a sharp breath, stopped and turned. It was a portly man in a sweat suit. He widened his eyes at her abrupt movement, then smiled, said, *"Guten Morgen,"* averted his eyes and walked past.

Sasha could feel her pulse in her temples as she watched him turn the corner onto Rue des Alpes. She exhaled. She remembered Daniel's constant admonishments of her for being paranoid. *Or just careful?*

She continued down Rue Ami-Lévrier, then opened the door to their apartment building.

"Hello, Miss Sasha," François said from behind his security desk when she entered and crossed the lobby to the elevator. She checked her watch on the elevator, tapping her foot. Upstairs, she hurried, hoping to get breakfast well on its way before Daniel returned home. The ingredients for their goat cheese, sun-dried tomato and caramelized onion omelets were all prepared and waiting when she heard Daniel enter. She brushed her hair back from her eyes, looking up at him as he crossed the dining room into the kitchen. His tan from their two weeks in St. Maarten made him gleam like a sun god, warming her.

"Sorry I got so pissed off," he said.

"My fault, darling, I had too much wine." She smiled back. Her rising desire and hunger for him told her it wouldn't require breakfast for them to make up. She turned off the burner, reached out to Daniel as he took her in his arms and kissed her.

A half hour later, she cradled her head on her elbow in bed next to him, running a finger over his chest. "That was a better way to break the ice from last night than I'd planned."

He leaned over and kissed her. "I wouldn't have complained about breakfast, but..." He grasped her hand. "... I agree with you." He kissed her, then stood up. She watched him cross the bedroom to the bathroom. He'd hardened and slimmed his body over the last year. She felt a rise of desire for him again.

She said, "Retirement's been good to you." He stopped and looked over his shoulder at her. "When I met you, you were lamenting your love handles and your 40s metabolism. Working out regularly agrees with you."

He smiled and walked into the bathroom. She rolled onto her back as she heard him turn on the shower. Sasha sighed, content. This was her man. How could she ever imagine anyone else in her life?

The next Saturday, Daniel left for the gym, Sasha on her rounds to her usual shops in Old Town, as had become their routine. When Sasha returned home and pulled on the door to their apartment building, she found it locked. She peered in and saw that François was away from his security desk. *Probably a bathroom break.* She fished out her keys, opened the door and walked to the elevator. Upstairs, she noted that the light at the far end of the hall was out, and saw light emerging from beneath the rear door to their apartment, where they'd created their master bedroom suite by knocking out the walls to take over the other apartment on their floor. *Is he home already?* She opened the main door and called from the foyer into the bedroom, "Daniel?" No answer. She dropped her handbag on the dining room table and was in the kitchen putting the groceries down on the island when she heard Daniel's key in the lock. As she crossed back through the dining room into the foyer, she saw Daniel smile as he entered.

"Hi," he said.

As she opened her mouth to respond, she heard the crunch of something underfoot on the hardwood floor from the master bedroom suite. She froze, her scalp tingling. Her gaze darted toward the master bedroom, then back to Daniel, who dropped his gym bag and rushed toward her.

It happened fast.

A man—Arab complexion, bearded and wearing a Western business suit—strode a few paces into the room and raised a gun with a silencer attached. Her instincts told her to dive through the doorway back into the dining room, but before she could move, Daniel yelled, "No!" and threw himself in front of her. She heard the muffled sound of the silenced gunshot and the slap of the bullet into Daniel as one. She leaped sideways into the dining room, her brain now barking commands. She rolled, righted herself, thrust her hand into her handbag and pulled out her Beretta, then turned with the gun raised. She heard the gunman's footsteps advancing across the marble floor of the foyer and fired one, two, three, four times into the sheetrock wall between the dining room and the foyer. She heard a grunt and a crash as the man must have toppled a piece of furniture.

Daniel! She lunged on one knee through the doorway into the foyer, her Beretta raised in firing position. Daniel lay in front of her on his back, a halo of red on his chest. The gunman was sprawled on the floor by the door with a shoulder wound, the gun dangling uselessly from the hand on his injured arm. She saw him lean forward, struggle to sit up, then reach across to the gun with his other hand. She fired again, hitting him in the stomach and putting him down. She ran to him, kicked the gun from his grasp and heard him gurgling, blood now coming from his mouth. She rushed back to Daniel.

Oh my God, no! His eyes were open, staring straight at the ceiling. She clasped his face in her hands, turned his head to look directly into his eyes. *Nothing.* She felt his jugular. She couldn't tell whether the throbbing she felt was her own heart pounding or Daniel's pulse. She took in a huge gulp of air, pressed her lips to his and exhaled. Again. And again. She lost track of how many times, her mind frantic, her heart wailing. She kept on until she was gasping for breath. Still Daniel stared, his eyes wide open but lifeless. She forced herself to look at the wound. It was directly over his heart. And now she felt the dampness through her jeans where she knelt over him, saw the pool of blood encircling them both. Her mind told her he was gone, but her heart wouldn't accept it. She ran to the phone and dialed emergency.

"My husband has been shot. He's not breathing. Send help. Fifth floor, number nine, Rue Ami-Lévrier. Please hurry!" She hung up and ran back to the foyer, picked up the Beretta from next to Daniel and crossed the room to the gunman. He was still breathing, coughing up blood. She leaned over and stared into his face. "Who sent you?"

He didn't answer, his eyes glazed. She pressed the Beretta to his temple. "Who sent you?" she said again, this time in Arabic.

Now his eyes focused on hers and held her gaze. The man shook his head.

"Who?" she repeated in Arabic. "Tell me and I won't kill you."

He put his chin to his chest to look down at the bullet wound, said faintly, "I'm already dead." Then he smiled, as if mocking her, and motioned for her to come closer. She bent down, her face so close to his she could smell his blood, the garlic on his breath.

He whispered to her.

Her hands trembled with rage as she stood, aimed at the man's heart and fired.

She dropped the Beretta and ran to Daniel, fell to her knees and cradled his head in her arms, her heart feeling like it was exploding. She moaned, rocking him as she cried, then gave in to her horror and anguish and wailed. "No!" she heard her soul crying out.

Sasha wasn't prepared for how she would be affected by the last 200 yards of the mile-long drive to the summit of the hill. It was when her Mercedes took the last turn in the winding drive, bordered by towering evergreens and stone walls deteriorating from neglect, that the Countess Del Mira's 15th-century chateau came into view. All 15,000 square feet of it, ivy-covered blocks of limestone, muscular oak timbers holding forth within, presiding over the 400-acre estate. She drew in a short breath and held it. She swore she'd never return, and yet here she was.

She directed her driver to enter the circular drop-off area in front of the chateau, the Belgian block covered with debris, pine needles and leaves. She had him stop the car under the portico before the curved limestone facade and the massive arched front door. She felt a swell of emotion in her chest, a mixture of nostalgia, anguish and tenderness. How many hundreds of times had she stood next to the Countess—Christina, her guardian—beneath the sparkling chandelier on the polished marble floor of the entrance hall, greeting Christina's guests at her elaborate parties—counts, dukes, oil barons, politicians, OPEC ministers, wealthy jet-setters and the usual assortment of poseurs?

"Around the side, please," she said. The driver took her to a parking area beneath a patio on the side of the chateau. "Here," she said. The driver got out and held the rear door for her. Sasha carried her satchel up the steep stone steps, careful not to lose her footing on the moist moss and pine needles. She swept aside more pine needles and leaves with her shoe to create a reasonably dry area on the slate patio to place her satchel. Then she walked to the limestone railing and looked out over the pines and deciduous trees—just beginning to sprout with leaves—and down the hill to the valley below that extended to the town of Vevey and Lake Geneva beyond it. It was here—the last place she'd stood,

25 years ago, before walking down the steps to a different black Mercedes, Yassar in the backseat waiting for her, to take her to Saudi Arabia and a new life. She walked to the limestone railing, turned to face the house and rested her backside on the railing, just as she had that day. *Why did I come back here?*

Her emotions took her back to that day, at 16 years old, resting on the railing and staring back toward the house, at nothing, her mind and heart in turmoil. She replayed the previous conversations she'd had with Christina.

Sasha had implored her; she was all Sasha had, and Sasha was all Christina had. Except, Sasha realized, for the opium. She'd stormed out of Christina's bedroom in anguish. Then, five minutes later she'd regrouped, still unable to accept what was happening to her. She gritted her teeth and stomped back up the stairs.

As she strode back into Christina's bedroom, Sasha said, "So, now, after years of gradually selling the paintings, then working your way through your antiques, your jewelry, finally mortgaging the chateau and spending it, you're, in effect, selling me."

Christina was seated in front of her makeup mirror. "Your propensity for drama will get you in trouble one day, child," she said, putting on eye shadow.

"I asked you before. How much is Yassar paying you? What's the going rate for a 'companion' for the son of an oil prince?"

Christina now turned from the mirror to glare at Sasha. She pulled a wisp of hair off her face, said, "My financial affairs are none of your business."

"I won't go."

"We're covering the same territory, child. Yes, of course you'll go. Because you have no choice."

"Haven't I?"

"No. My money is gone, and you don't have any. I didn't raise you to get your hands dirty. So what's your alternative?"

Sasha kept looking into Christina's eyes, seeing no compassion, no love, nothing, but refusing to believe it. She felt tears coming, tried to stop them and just as quickly decided she didn't care. She clenched her hands into fists and shouted through tears, "Damn you! Damn you, Christina, how can you? You've raised me. This isn't how it's supposed to be."

Christina's face was expressionless, unreadable.

Sasha said, "When people—families—run into trouble, they stick together. Who cares if we'd be poor? We'd be together."

Christina smiled. "That's a quaint thought. Really very sweet. But ridiculous. As I said, I didn't raise you to be poor. And I'll be damned if I'm going to make a fool of myself, and you, by dragging you around like some Dickensian waif."

Sasha felt as if someone were clamping his hands around her heart, squeezing it. She again looked into Christina's eyes, at her dilated pupils, and saw only the opium. "You don't care," she said and ran from the room. She descended the stairs and burst out onto the patio.

A few minutes later, sitting on the railing and staring off at the house, she saw Christina behind the French doors inside the library. Christina posed as was her way, one arm across her stomach, her hand cupping the other elbow as she held her cigarette aloft. She took a long pull on her cigarette, then arched her chin upward and spewed a geyser of smoke at the ceiling. She seemed to hesitate, then opened one of the French doors and stepped out onto the patio.

"Don't think I don't care, child. I care enough. And at least I've given you an understanding of what zest means. I've taught you to actually experience life, which is more than most *real* parents can say. But I've done all I can for you. Now you're on your own." She stepped back inside, latched the door and disappeared into the library.

Sasha, sitting on the cold limestone of the railing, now felt as she had that day: dizzy, as if she would tumble over backward. Her eyes focused on the French doors—the windows dirty from years of neglect, the room inside obscured. It was on this spot all those years ago, heartbroken, that she'd summoned her defiance and anger to empower her. It was then she decided that the only thing to do was to make the best of her situation until she could see a way out. Save enough money to make that happen.

That, and never allow herself to need anybody again. As that came into her mind, Daniel came back to her in a rush of emotions. She fell to her knees on the cold slate and sobbed. *Oh, Daniel.* All those years she'd kept her young girl's hopes alive of finding a soul mate, buried until finally she found Daniel. And now that he'd been taken from her she felt dead inside. Except for the all-consuming ache. *Who am I without Daniel? Who was I before him?* She knelt there and wept.

Finally, she got to her feet and walked to her satchel. She unzipped it and removed the statue of Ganesha, the Hindu god, the boy with the head of an elephant, her Remover of Obstacles, then the simple wooden *puja*. She placed the statue on the puja, then the photograph of Daniel, and finally the urn containing his ashes. She lit a stick of incense, placed it on the puja, and then knelt on the damp stone and offered her prayers to Ganesha for Daniel's safe passage.

When she finished she stood, answering her earlier question, *Why did I come back here?* She carried the urn to the railing, removed the top and scattered Daniel's ashes over the side, watching as they drifted down into the valley below. Christina was right: Sasha's experiences here had made her into the person she now was. As such, it was where Daniel's spirit could experience what had molded hers.

She turned, walked back to her puja, placed it and the other items back in her satchel and descended the steps. Her driver held the door of the Mercedes open for her. She paused in front of it, then turned to look back at the chateau, knowing it was the last time she would do so. She entered the backseat and sat. Closing her eyes, she whispered a final prayer to Ganesha for Daniel. Then she lowered her chin to her chest and let the darkness that now inhabited her rumble up from deep inside. "Let's go," she said.

Prince Yassar, the Finance and Economy Minister of Saudi Arabia, sat in his office. His cell phone rang.

"Yassar, it's Sasha."

He brightened. "Sasha, what a pleasure, my dear—"

"No, it's not. I have terrible news."

Yassar felt his fingers tense around the phone.

"Daniel's been murdered. I should say assassinated. A single gunman was waiting for us in the apartment. He shot Daniel, then I killed the shooter myself."

Yassar felt his limbs go weak. "Are you safe?"

"I think so."

"Where are you?"

"Still in Europe."

"Come home. To Saudi Arabia."

"It isn't home."

Yassar could hear the resignation—no, hopelessness—in her voice. He said, "Yes it is. You're loved here. I know this is a horrible blow, but let me help you through it." Yassar listened carefully, trying to assess how she was dealing with it.

"Yassar, dear Yassar, I know you love me. And I love you, too. You're the only father I've ever had. You know that." He heard her sigh. When she spoke again she sounded cold, detached. "But Saudi Arabia isn't my home. I don't feel I've ever had a home."

"Sasha—"

"I'm a wasted life. I've done nothing."

"Don't talk this way. You've had a terrible shock. You're not thinking clearly."

"Yes, I am. I'm staring reality in the face. What have I done with my life? A precocious little dilettante until my teens. Then, God, a concubine. The only money I've ever made is on my back. I've never known who my parents were. And God knows Christina let me down horribly."

Yassar felt a weight on his chest. "As did I."

Sasha didn't respond right away, let his words hang there for a moment. Finally she said, "That was a long time ago, and once I came to understand your culture, I learned not to look at it that way. We don't need to revisit that."

"Please, just come home. Let me help you."

"No. I'm dropping out for a while to sort out my life. Goodbye," Sasha said and hung up.

Yassar felt a surge of guilt. All those years ago, what had he done to her? Would it ever stop haunting him?

Two days later, Sasha sat on a marble bench on the portico to Swami Kripananda's ashram in Ganeshrada, India. She'd sat here every day during her time here as a child. She remembered one such moment over 35 years ago.

Mirabai knelt on the portico ten feet from Sasha, a dented metal bucket next to her, scrubbing the marble with a nearly toothless brush and humming one of the mournful tunes that she and her fellow devotees of the guru, Swami Kripananda, chanted every morning. Mirabai was almost finished with this, her *seva*, her assigned daily chore in the ashram, polishing the floor and the shrine to Hana, Swami Kripananda's teacher. Sasha saw that Mirabai was conscious of the two guests seated behind Mirabai on another bench.

Mirabai sat up, pausing to inhale the mountain air, perfumed by lotus and jasmine, and looked out over the valley beneath the ashram, at the grass, trees and a few cows that grazed and roamed unimpeded. Sasha saw her smile. She knew Mirabai loved this place, loved her seva.

Sasha heard the guests talking.

"Really, Sandra, I don't know whatever possessed me to come here," said the woman who Sasha would later learn to call Ophelia.

Sandra looked at Ophelia, inhaling the air. "Perhaps you'll see here what Christina was attracted to. You can feel the spirituality."

Ophelia rolled her eyes. "More to the point, whatever possessed a bona fide Italian countess—my God, she's a Del Mira—to throw it all away and come to a place like this?"

"She hasn't thrown it all away. It's sitting back there in Switzerland waiting for her."

"A week or two is a fashionable diversion. But, honestly, it's been *six months*."

"Perhaps it was her feelings for the girl, wanting to raise her with some base in spirituality." Sandra nodded toward Sasha, where she squirmed on her marble bench not 20 feet away. "I believe that's she over there—Sasha."

"Has she adopted her?" Ophelia squinted at Sasha. "What is she, four? Nobody's quite sure how Christina came by her in the first place, are they?"

Mirabai continued her scrubbing, polishing and meditating. A minute later she backed up to the square at the feet of the women, stood and turned to face them. Ophelia's jaw opened and her eyes went glassy. Sandra smiled, then embraced her. "Christina."

"I'm known as Mirabai here," Christina said. "But you may call me what you wish. Welcome to Swami Kripananda's ashram."

"Wonderful to see you," Sandra said, squeezing Mirabai's hand.

"And I'd like you to meet Sasha." Mirabai held her hand out toward Sasha, who rested on her back on the bench with her feet in the air. "Sasha, come meet my friends." Sasha stopped doing acrobatics at the sound of her name. She leaped to her feet, looking directly at Mirabai. "Finished with seva?"

Mirabai smiled. "Yes, child." She said the words proudly.

"She's beautiful," Sandra whispered.

Mirabai's eyes gleamed. "Yes." She turned back to her friends. "Beautiful and special. Swami Kripananda's monks say she possesses the grace of the guru, for it is always she who is invited to sit at Swami Kripananda's feet during special prayers."

A second later Sasha laughed, clambered from the portico into the gardens and started toward the dirt path to the monks' quarters.

"Oh!" Sandra said. "She's just a child. Should she be left all alone?"

Even Ophelia stood with alarm. "Yes, surely, Christina," Ophelia said.

"She'll be alright," Mirabai said. "She's quite independent. When I'm done with my seva each morning she goes to listen to the monks tell stories."

Sasha reached the path, hurtling down it with joy in her heart, in too much of a hurry to put on her sandals, her sarong and black hair flying behind her. She had removed her sandals to walk on the holy ground of the temple, and the dirt felt cool on her bare feet this early in the day. She leaped over an exposed root in the path, the spot of many falls. *Jump past the owee-fall-downy place.* This was her favorite part of the day. After morning chants, then breakfast, then seva with Mirabai, she would always dash to sit at the knees of the other swamis, the guru's monks, who told the children the stories of Vishnu, Lord Shiva, Parvati and the other Hindu gods, recounting their battles and failures and triumphs. Today she would hear her favorite story, the one of Ganesha, the boy created by Parvati out of clay who became a god. Ganesha, the boy god with the head of an elephant, the Remover of Obstacles.

Sasha stood up from the bench now, glancing at the path she'd taken on those mornings as a child. Christina had left any consciousness of Mirabai behind by the time they got to Bombay, even before they'd reached her chateau in Switzerland. But the deepest part of Sasha had never left the ashram. She felt the grace of Swami Kripananda and smiled. She'd come to the right place to begin grieving, and to begin finding herself.

CHAPTER 2

Present day.

RASHID AL-ABDEL SQUINTED AGAINST THE dust swirling on As Sinaah Boulevard. His back was pressed flat against the steel roll-down doors covering the glass of a retail shop, all of which were closed for this day of demonstrations in the center of Buraida, the capital of Al Qasim Province in north-central Saudi Arabia. Even with the wind the air was oppressive, over 110 degrees and smelling of perspiration, the ever-present dust and the hot tar of the street.

Protesters—estimated at 70,000 strong—attended the funeral of Faisal Ahmed Abdul-Ahad, one of the organizers of the "Day of Rage" protest a week earlier. Faisal had been shot to death during that protest by security forces. Today had begun peaceably, protesters throwing flowers on the funeral bier of Faisal. Now it was getting ugly: they walked, chanting, "Down with Abdul," arms upraised, many stomping on photographs of King Abdul. One man dragged a figure of King Abdul through the crowd, burning in effigy. Others used the flames to ignite photographs of the monarch. When the security forces drove up in armored personnel carriers, many of the protesters began throwing rocks at them. Now they chanted, "Terrorist!" "Criminal!" and "Butcher!" led by voices over megaphones.

Rashid was sweating, his nerves, all his senses rubbed raw after an hour of this. He was having trouble keeping his eyes on Saif, who was talking to the members of the Umma Islamic Party, the first political party in Saudi Arabia since the 1990s, founded by a group of ten activists and lawyers, all present today. Rashid pushed away from the steel doors of the shop with his palms, fighting his way into the moving throng, forcing himself against the tide to draw closer to Saif. At the curb he raised himself on tiptoes trying to see Talib and Hassan, who had also been assigned to protect Saif during the protest. He couldn't spot either of them. He stepped off the curb into the street and worked his way toward Saif. As he approached he heard the men talking, barely making their voices out over the noise of the crowd.

"Our primary demand is an end to the al-Asad absolute monarchy, and establishment of a representative government, as called for by Islamic law," one of the UIP founders was saying.

"Unfortunately, we don't expect to change things overnight. There are no rubber bullets, no water hoses, no birdshot in Saudi Arabia," another said, pointing to Faisal's funeral bier.

Saif was nodding his agreement. He said, shouting above the crowd, "What about anti-Shiite discrimination? Prisoners held without charge? Torture?"

"Of course. Also among our demands," another said.

"Who are you?" another asked.

Saif said, "Saif Ibn Mohammed al-Aziz."

"Al-Mujari?" the first man asked.

Saif didn't answer. He smiled.

Rashid now saw a column of gray Mercedes SUVs nose their way around the armored carriers through the crowd on the traffic circle, 20 meters away. They stopped and men began piling out. *Secret Police.*

Another of the UIP founders said, "We are peaceable. We aren't looking for trouble."

Saif said, "You call this not looking for trouble?" He waved his arm toward the crowd occupying the park and extending up As Sinaah Boulevard.

Rashid saw a group of Secret Police burrowing through the crowd, followed by a column of armed security forces. They headed directly toward the circle of the UIP members talking to Saif. Rashid felt a flash of alarm. He stepped closer to Saif. He watched over Saif's shoulder as the men parted the crowd. Ten meters away one of them pointed toward the UIP group, then turned back and said something to the men behind him. They continued on. Rashid grabbed Saif by his collar, yanked him backward and spun him into the crowd. He forced Saif's head down, crouched out of sight and pushed Saif toward the other side of the street. "Secret Police, coming toward us," Rashid yelled. Saif twisted out of his grasp and glared at him, but continued to work his way through the crowd. Rashid glanced back to see the Secret Police and security forces encircling, then manhandling the UIP founders. He exhaled with relief, stepped forward to catch up to Saif, grabbing him by the shirt sleeve and dragging him through the crowd.

Tom Goddard got off the elevator on the 15th floor at CIA headquarters in Langley, Virginia, where he'd been summoned for a meeting with the Director of the CIA, Harold Ross. As Mid-East Section Head, Tom'd been on the hot seat for the better part of 20 years, in the crucible because of the constant conflicts in the Arab states, and given the strategic importance of the region.

Not to mention the attempt two years ago by the Islamic fundamentalist group, the al-Mujari, to sabotage the world's oil business. Even with all that, he'd had a bitch of a time pulling the previous day's meeting together. A whole building full of professional spooks who were supposed to be the most paranoid guys in the world, you'd think all Tom needed to say was something like, "We've got a problem again," and they'd all come running. Whatever, he'd gotten his meeting, finally. Ralph Rivera, Tom's liaison from the National Security Agency. Three of Tom's Intelligence Analysts, Johannsen, Fleischer and Duckman. Terry Holcombe and Rich Stageford, Section Heads from North Africa and Western Europe. His boss, Section Head Coordinator Terry Jenkins. And the surprise guest Jenkins had invited, the man himself, Harold Ross.

Tom recalled his pleasure at seeing Ross, who'd been seated at the head of the table when Tom walked into the conference room, Ross staring at the briefing memo Duckman had passed to him like he was wondering what to do with it.

Tom had been introduced to Ross and his wife, whose name he couldn't recall, a few years ago at one of those bullshit dinners the Agency threw now and then—he couldn't remember the occasion—Ellen on Tom's arm. Tom admired the guy. He was a great spook, somebody they all looked up to at the Agency, and he was enough of a politician that he'd survived a long time in the top job. It was perfect that he had attended the meeting. The shit had already hit the fan in Tom's region again and now it was threatening to splatter everywhere else, and yesterday he had the director poised to hear about it.

So today he obviously wants to do something about it.

The 15th floor was about as plain vanilla as every other floor in the building—off-white walls, fluorescent lighting, coffee-colored carpeting, work cubicles extending behind the reception desk, windowed offices and conference rooms around the perimeter—only the women researchers and analysts were better looking than anyplace else in the building. Tom wouldn't have noticed until a year or so ago, when Ellen left him. Now he took in those glorious 20-and 30-year-olds, realizing they were just exotic art to him, too old to do anything about them. Besides, he wasn't sure he was up to working that hard at it anymore, even for a mature, low-maintenance woman in her 40s.

As he approached Ross' office he thought about buttoning the top button on his oxford shirt and hitching his tie up against it. He considered his rumpled tweed jacket and Dockers, the usual. *Why bother?*

After Ross' assistant motioned Tom in, Ross smiled, leaned forward in his seat and said, "Good to see you again, Tom."

Yeah, the man's a politician. Probably had to be shown a photograph yesterday to be reminded who this Tom Goddard was who had called the meeting.

"Close the door, please," Ross said, pointing to a chair in front of his desk. Tom sat down, taking in Ross' office. It was remarkably spartan, particularly for a politician. None of those handshake photos with other politicos on the walls. Simple furniture like in Tom's office. Photos of what must be his wife, kids and grandkids on the credenza behind him. Lots of papers and folders on his desk. Ross said, "I just got back from a meeting with the president's national security advisor. Your intelligence on Saudi Arabia was the primary topic. You're going prime time."

Tom inclined his head.

"I need you for a follow-up meeting tomorrow here in my office with a couple of people. You don't need to know who for now. I don't need you to do anything special but be ready to talk like you did in our meeting yesterday, and answer any questions."

Tom nodded. "No problem."

"Stick to the facts and don't go too crazy interpreting things."

"I'm not sure what you mean by that."

"I've read your file," Ross said, tapping a two-inch-thick folder on his desk, "and as long as you don't start anything with your 'unconventional approach' to things we'll both be in good shape." Tom was trying to guess what that meant when Ross said, "I mean improvising like you used to do when you were a Station Chief in the field in Riyadh, running Saudi agents. And like you did two years ago as Section Head during that al-Mujari mess. I'm not being critical. In my mind that's a great strength. I want no-bullshit guys like you when we're in a tight spot." Ross paused for a moment and just looked at Tom. "But don't get creative tomorrow, okay?"

"Was that supposed to be a pat on the back or a kick in the ass?" Why was Ross telling him to rein in himself in this upcoming meeting? And why the mystery about who else would be there?

Ross said, "Let me give you a little insight into my job, and what my life is like. I'm a Republican, and I've survived three different administrations as director, one with the Democrats, having been passed from George W. Bush to Obama, and now to Ron Paul's administration. Almost 20 years. And even after Paul dropped dead, I was still accepted by Santorum after he was sworn in. Know why?"

"No, but I have a feeling you're going to tell me."

Ross smiled. "I'm an old spook, but my real job is being a politician. I have to be a tough son of a bitch in one of the toughest of worlds—Washington politics. Without guys like me running interference for the Agency, each presidential administration would stick its fingers into our business and muck everything up. No continuity. Covert agents exposed. Allies hung out to dry. Programs that took years, even decades to come to fruition dropped in the middle because some candy-asses who advise the man who occupies the White House don't have the balls to follow through. It's a bitch that it needs to work this way in Washington, but I've survived this long only because I let each administration know only what it needs to know, and hold the rest of what the Agency knows over its head, with some tantalizing hints. Or threats. You following me?"

Tom nodded.

"Don't talk much, do you?"

Tom shook his head.

Ross smiled. "You're an old spook, too, and I guess keeping our mouths shut is the only way we get there, huh? Old, I mean."

Tom nodded.

"Okay," Ross said. "I guess I can give you a taste of what we're up against here." He sat back in his chair as if settling in. "As I see it, the Saudis have two major reasons we're interested in them. First, they're the largest producer of oil and they have the largest oil reserves in the world. Second, they're the site of Islam's two holiest shrines. Let's talk about the first one.

"We—the West, and by that I mean primarily the US—are in a comfortable standoff with the Saudis. Maybe a better way to say it is we're swapping one thing for another. We rely on the Saudis to keep the price of oil reasonable by pumping more than the world needs, so supply outpaces demand. And that also means the Saudis, as the largest member of OPEC, drive OPEC's position. Every US president since forever has felt a moral commitment to political reforms within Saudi Arabia to help out the average Saudi schlub. But that hasn't happened, largely because we don't want to piss them off with that kind of moralistic rhetoric as long as they keep oil prices low. And in exchange, we keep our mouths shut about what they're up to in their kingdom, and sell them our military hardware so they can keep their neighbors and the average Saudi schlub at arms' length."

Tom said, "More the average Saudi schlub, because these days he's their greatest threat."

"Exactly. But all the crap the White House spouts about human rights agendas and moral imperatives is something we can't let divert us from our real focus. We start letting Rick Santorum poke his finger in the Saudi royals' eyes and we're looking at a major problem that could cascade into the economy with paralyzing implications."

Tom didn't envy Ross the nature of the world he operated within.

Ross went on. "If we're too candid with the new president's staff about what's really going on inside Saudi Arabia, we're likely to screw everything up." He stared Tom in the eye. "I'm not going to be subtle, here. We out the Saudi royals and we're in big trouble. Any of it: Exposure of the full extent of suppression of the Shiite minority. The fact that people still disappear in the middle of the night. Torture of dissenters. Corruption. The royal family in every major corporate or government position. You name it. Stuff Santorum could use as a soapbox. We can't let that happen, can we?"

Tom didn't move.

"Which gets us to the second reason we're interested in the Saudis: they're the center of the Islamic world. Anything that happens over there is influenced by that fact, big-time. So keeping the lid on the tensions between the Shiites and the Sunnis is critical, because they're a volatile mix."

"You're preaching to the choir."

"The guys who'll be here tomorrow will be highly sensitive to anything you say." Ross paused and continued to stare Tom in the eye. "So stick to the facts in your briefing memo, no more."

"But there are—"

"Just your memo. I can't have you going rogue on me. Are we clear?"

Tom felt an almost imperceptible movement of his neck, and Ross nodded back, message received.

"Tomorrow's meeting is strictly Need to Know. In your case, that means nobody else needs to know, and that includes Jenkins."

Tom nodded again.

"Good. And another thing." He looked Tom up and down. "You own a suit, don't you?"

Tom nodded.

"Wear it. And a white shirt and tie, and a pair of hard shoes, shined. You'll need to look the part."

CHAPTER 3

AT 7:50 A.M. THE NEXT morning, Tom sat in a room ten minutes across town from CIA headquarters. Sitting here reminded him of the old days as a Station Chief, killing time, waiting for a covert meeting with a field agent. He glanced from his *Washington Post* to his watch, discreetly, from habit and long experience at not appearing to be waiting for someone, even though he was upstairs in a room at the Staybridge Suites. *Twenty minutes late.* He smiled. *Just like her.*

A few minutes later he heard a knock on the door, walked over and opened it. The same long black hair, petite 5'4" frame, full breasts and dancer's legs that went all the way down to the ground. Dressed casually in jeans and a sweater. *Still beautiful.* Tom smiled.

"Hello, Sasha."

"Hello, Tom, you're looking well."

Sasha took him in. *Still handsome.* He wore a tailored blue suit—pressed, of all things—and his tie was snugged up against his starched white collar. Even that unruly mop of sandy hair looked reasonably tamed. He directed her to a table set for breakfast for two. She sat down.

"You look like you just stepped out of a Ralph Lauren shop window."

He smiled, those impossibly blue eyes of his turning up at the corners. "Big meeting later today."

"I don't think I ever told you my nickname for you before we were introduced was 'the scruffy American.'"

He laughed.

She said, "Quite an introduction, as I recall. You swooped in on me at my table, remember?"

"Of course. The Sea Wall Café and Lounge at the Baron David de Duval Hotel in Nice. I was stalking you."

"Yes, but not for the reason a man normally stalks a woman."

He shrugged. "You had it figured out." He paused, leaned toward her. "How are you?"

She felt the ache, looked down at the table.

He said, "I was sorry to hear about Daniel. I liked him. I'm sure that was horrible for you. How're you doing?"

The air had gone out of her lungs. She had to pause to inhale before she looked back up at him. His eyes were sympathetic, sincere. She was surprised her throat didn't well up with emotion. "Better now than I was. It's a process."

After they helped themselves to the hot-and-cold buffet set on room service tables, she asked herself, *Why am I dragging this out?* He'd given her a few chances to say why she'd asked to see him. *I'm closed up.* When they started eating breakfast she still hadn't gotten to it.

He said, "I tried to find you after I heard about Daniel." He paused. "So what have you been up to?"

"I've been living in an ashram in India for the last 18 months."

She didn't look up from her fried eggs—she'd taken four from the heated servers, hadn't eaten one in 18 months. *Get it over with.* "I'm sure you want to know why I asked to see you today." She felt a flutter of nerves, then pushed it away, looked him in the eye and said, "I want you to help me find a murderer named Saif."

Tom didn't react. He took a moment before saying, "Who's this guy, Saif?"

Sasha hardened her eyes. "Come on, Tom, don't stonewall me. Saif Ibn Mohammed al-Aziz. I knew him 20 years ago. Just before the al-Mujari recruited him. He was high enough up in the organization two years ago that you must have scads of intelligence on him. I know I don't have any security clearance now, but you recruited me once and you can do it again. I want to go back undercover and get him."

"Why?"

"Daniel. Saif ordered the hit."

Sasha thought back to the Geneva police's forensics report that she'd seen. The shooter had taken three bullets, one at close range in the heart, which the report said had to be the last, because it would've killed him instantly. She was certain someone as diligent as Tom would have reviewed it before meeting with her. He must have, because he put it together. He said, "The shooter told you it was Saif, then you did him, right?"

"And now I want Saif."

Tom put a spoonful of oatmeal in his mouth, took his time chewing and swallowing before saying, "Must've been some ashram."

Sasha made her tone matter-of-fact as she said, "This is about good versus evil."

Tom looked at her skeptically, said, "Good versus evil notwithstanding, we're not in the assassination business."

"What about two years ago?"

"That was different. We were under attack. The president signed a directive authorizing it."

"What if I just brought him in? So he could stand trial, make an example of him. Show his people what their aspiring leaders are really like."

"Bullshit."

"Okay." She clenched her jaw, narrowed her eyes. "You're right. The man had my husband murdered. I want him dead. More than that, I want to do it myself."

"We aren't in the revenge business, either. Besides, if you could get close enough to him to kill him, he'd have you killed first."

"No, he won't."

"What're you talking about? He tried it once, he'll do it again."

"He didn't try it once."

"What?"

"I returned to the apartment in Geneva first. If he'd wanted me dead, his shooter would have stepped out of the bedroom and shot me. He didn't. He waited for Daniel to get home, then made his move."

"He wanted to be sure to get both of you."

Sasha shook her head. "You trained me. Trust me, I've had 18 months to replay it thousands of times. Even if he wanted us both, any professional would have made me the first target. Daniel had just closed the door. He was pinned, nowhere to go. I was in the doorway to the dining room, free to duck out of the way. Take out that target first—me—then the one who can't move out of your line of fire."

He nodded, thinking it over. He said, "Tell me more."

"The shooter came out of the bedroom. I froze. Daniel ran to me. The shooter didn't fire until Daniel was in front of me. Heart shot." She choked on the words, recovered as she kept going. "I dived and rolled to my handbag on the dining room table. I fired through the wall. We'd renovated the apartment and it was just two layers of sheetrock and those silly tin beams. A 9mm cut through it like paper."

"So that's how you got him?"

"Yes, but he was lying by the apartment door, running to escape, not coming to finish me."

"It doesn't make sense."

"Yes, it does. Saif was sending a message. Even if his man had gotten away he'd have left one. He wanted me to know."

"A message? What?"

"It was a long time ago, after that awful business with Ibrahim, after you and I lost contact. Saif and I were lovers. I know him. I'm sure he believes I betrayed him and his cause two years ago by helping you and Saudi Arabia. He probably wants to break my spirit, to make me suffer and die of a broken heart, just as his parents did, betrayed by Saudi Arabia."

Tom didn't respond. He was still meeting her gaze but his eyes seemed unfocused, as if he were turning it over in his mind. *What's he thinking?*

The reporters and cameramen were almost finished setting up for the press conference in Prince Yassar's office, adjacent to his quarters in the Royal Palace in Riyadh. Prince Yassar tried to imagine what they were thinking. He confessed to himself he couldn't. Reporters and camera crews had been allowed inside the ballrooms for diplomatic functions, but to allow access to the personal office of one of the highest-ranking members of the Council of Ministers was unprecedented. He saw them eyeing the polished marble floors and walls, the Persian rugs and his gold-trimmed walnut desk as if they were from another planet. Yassar and Reem Assouf, the woman who would share the press conference with him, were already seated at the conference table in front of microphones. Reem was draped in a black *abaya* and wore her *hijab* headscarf and veil covering her hair and face. Yassar wore his traditional Saudi robe and headdress. Facing them were 30 reporters from the Saudi Arabian and worldwide press, including the *London Times, The New York Times* and *The Wall Street Journal. Good.* They would help Yassar make a colorful display of the event. All the better to stuff it in the faces of his cousins, make it harder for them to stem the tide of change.

Yassar looked over at Reem and smiled. She was petite, perhaps 5'2" and less than a hundred pounds. *So tiny, and yet so formidable.* She was largely responsible for the social milestone they were here to discuss today, something that would seem silly in the West, but was radical in Saudi Arabia: women going to work in lingerie shops.

Yassar's Communications Director nodded to him. "We're ready," he said.

"Very well," Yassar said. "Shall we begin?" He cleared his throat. "Thank you for coming. Since the subject we are discussing today is based on a new openness and social progress in Saudi Arabia, I thought it appropriate to welcome you into my personal office to formally announce it. I am Prince Yassar, a member of the royal family and Saudi Arabia's Finance and Economy Minister. It is my pleasure to announce that effective today, my ministry is formally enforcing the royal decree issued by King Abdul two months ago, ordering that sales personnel in shops in Saudi Arabia selling lingerie and other garments that are only for women must be female. This represents the first time that Saudi Arabian women have entered the private sector workforce, and a major step in our government's Saudization efforts to put Saudi Arabians into jobs in our country. I am pleased to introduce Reem Assouf, the woman who is largely responsible for this achievement. Reem?"

Reem said, "Minister Yassar is being modest. I introduced the idea and pushed for it, but it was Minister Yassar who made it possible by putting his support behind it. He worked for over two years to convince social conservatives among his fellow ministers, many of our influential sheiks and other religious scholars that this was a desirable change. Without his efforts we could not have succeeded."

"It is Reem who is being modest," Yassar said. "She got my attention with an 80,000-strong Facebook community dedicated to this change. A novel approach for a seismic shift in our culture." He turned to Reem and smiled. "We'll take questions now," he said.

"My first question is for Ms. Assouf," Barton James from *The New York Times* said. "Are you a practicing Muslim?"

"Absolutely. I am Sunni, married, with two children."

James asked, "Doesn't Islam prohibit women from working outside the home?"

"Not according to modern interpretations of our religion. In fact, Saudi Arabian women have held jobs in medicine and education for decades."

Another asked, "Minister Yassar, how many jobs do you expect this to create for Saudi women?"

"Over 28,000. And the majority of those jobs are currently held by foreigners."

Another reporter asked, "How will these women get to work? I understand Saudi Arabian women are prohibited from driving, and must be accompanied by a man in public."

Reem looked over at Yassar, said, "Yes, those are both true, and so we must look to Minister Yassar for some additional reforms, or at least for better public transportation."

Yassar said, "One step at a time."

"Soon," Reem said, "we hope."

The press conference went on for half an hour. Yassar signaled it was over by saying, "Thank you all for coming. My ministry is already compiling a list of other jobs women will be permitted to hold. We expect to be making additional announcements in the coming months." With that, he stood, looked at Reem and extended his hand toward the door to his private chambers. She preceded him out of the room. Once inside his private chambers, Reem said, "If we weren't in Saudi Arabia I'd give you a hug."

Yassar said, "Perhaps one day that will be an appropriate gesture. For now," and he extended his hand, "this will have to do." Reem shook it and clasped her other hand over his.

"I can't thank you enough for what you've done for us."

"My pleasure," Yassar said, and showed her to the door. *If only she knew.* Yassar had used every ounce of his persuasive abilities to cajole his cousins into agreeing with this step, and still they'd backpedaled after he convinced King Abdul to issue the royal decree two months earlier. It had exhausted him. As did the list of issues assaulting him daily.

Two years. That's how long it had been since his successful collaboration with the Americans and their allies in thwarting the al-Mujari's terrorism against the oil industry and the Saudi government. In his exhilaration at the virtual beheading of the al-Mujari's top echelon, including the assassination of Sheik bin Abdur, Yassar had believed that Saudi Arabia would by now be on the path to a revival. But even before the death of King Abad, his fellow royals had become complacent with the primary provocateurs of social dissent in the country removed. The kingdom had returned to its old ways with a vengeance, treating the country's oil income as the cash flow from a family business. Even more profligate spending by the royal family, less money for social programs, virtually ignoring Yassar's "jobs creation" programs for the average Saudi, and a shorter fuse and harsher response regarding any civil protests. His cousins on the Council of Ministers continued to nod in agreement as Yassar urged them, but it didn't take him long to realize they were simply "yessing" him into irrelevance.

He saw the other Arab nations being forced to adopt more democratic approaches as a harbinger of troubles to come in Saudi Arabia. It could very easily completely unravel for his royal cousins, lead to a violent overthrow of their regime. It would result in chaos, spell the end for all of the programs he had worked so hard for over the last dozen years, programs that would rebalance their budget, give the Saudi people well-paying jobs, and restore the spirit of a once-great culture that could become greater still. So much for his plans to make the Saudi royal regime a model for the Arab and Islamic worlds.

He glanced at the clock, sighed and thumbed an eyebrow. *Fifteen minutes.* He expected his upcoming meeting with King Abdul to be a waste of time: more of the same. He breathed deeply, took a moment to ground himself. Then: *Not this time.*

He turned to his computer and clicked on his contacts. He found the number, picked up his phone and dialed.

Saif sat in a darkened corner of a mosque in northeast Buraida. He kept off to the side of his brother-in-law, Sheik Qahtani, not wanting to be conspicuous. This was Qahtani's moment. A chance for Qahtani to prove to the twelve assembled imams and Koranic scholars from the seven southern Saudi Arabian provinces that he was, in fact, the Mahdi. It was the sixth such meeting Saif had organized, and by far the most important. Most of the Shiite population in Saudi Arabia resided in the six northern provinces, and they had fallen in line easily with Qahtani's Shiite message. The support of the primarily Sunni southern provinces was harder to win. Particularly since Riyadh Province, the most influential, was home to the city of Riyadh, Saudi Arabia's capital, and to the Sunni royals. The group of bearded men in black robes, dusty from their journey north, sat around Qahtani on the cool marble floor, their hushed voices reverberating off the 40-foot domed ceiling of the mosque. It was going well, and Saif felt a sense of calm, in part because of the atmosphere in the mosque. Not that it made him feel unusually close to Allah. It was because the minimal light filtering in kept the place dark and cool, a respite he always welcomed from the harsh Saudi elements outside. *No heat, no sand.*

Saif focused his attention back on the group as he heard Qahtani say, "The prophet Muhammad said, 'The world will not come to an end until the Arabs are ruled by a man from my family whose name is the same as mine and whose father's name is the same as my father's.'"

One of the scholars looked skeptical. He said, "The Mahdi's aim must be to establish a moral system in which all superstitious faiths have been eliminated."

Qahtani said, "In the same way that students enter Islam, so unbelievers will come to believe."

Saif smiled. Qahtani spouted the second half of Umm Salama's prophecy right back at the old man. Qahtani must've been staying up late at night, studying. Saif was coming to believe that Qahtani had convinced himself that he was, in fact, the Mahdi. Was it the power of Saif's suggestion through two years of focus on the prophecies, or had Qahtani always believed it? Saif wasn't sure he cared. It was working.

Qahtani went on. "The Mahdi will return with a company of his chosen ones. He and his enemies' armies will fight one final apocalyptic battle where the Mahdi and his forces will prevail over evil."

One of the other imams said, "The Mahdi is the protector of the knowledge, the heir to the knowledge of all the prophets, and is aware of all things."

Qahtani responded, "The dominion of the Mahdi is one of the proofs that Allah has created all things; these are so numerous that the Mahdi's proofs will overcome everyone and nobody will have any counter-proposition against."

The silly game of reciting prophecies back and forth—proof of nothing, but all-important to the participants—was almost at an end. *Volley, return.* It was like the tennis matches he watched while at university in England. That seemed like forever ago. Not just in time, but from another life. A time when his father, then a member of the wealthy merchant class and a respected importer of oil drilling equipment, was able to afford to send Saif to university. A time in Saudi Arabia when a father was able to have the ambition for his son to achieve more than he had in his lifetime.

Saif remembered the day when the reality that was no longer true smashed him in the face.

It was upon his return from university, a graduate from Eton in economics, an educated young man who would help bring Saudi Arabia into the 21st century. The ride from the airport in Riyadh to Buraida took five hours. Five hours of baking in the Saudi heat in a bus with broken air-conditioning, smelling diesel exhaust, tasting the omnipresent dust, yet still excited to be home. He had to admit English ale was a delicious discovery, English girls were wonders, many of whom would have sex with you on the first date, and visits to London strip clubs were extraordinary experiences. But Saudi Arabia was home, and those days in England were behind him. Now it was time to use the knowledge he'd gained to do something with his father's business. Modernizing. Expanding the product line to import other types of equipment. Opening new offices.

The bus entered his neighborhood on the outskirts of northeast Buraida and he paid attention now, looking out the window to take in the low-slung concrete and cinderblock rows of shops in muted grays and browns. He smelled the aromas of halal meat grilling on skewers on the grills of the street-side vendors, mixed with the scent and taste of the Saudi dust from the unpaved streets. As he entered his own street, the spaces between the buildings grew, now homes with side yards between them, many with fenced-in pens for goats and sheep. His heart raced as he approached his home. *A little disheveled looking. Could use a coat of paint.* Things Saif could take care of within a week.

When he carried his bags through the door, his mother greeted him with a howl of delight. As he hugged her, he saw over her shoulder that his father was home, seated in the living room in his upholstered lounge chair. "Father!" he said and rushed to him. When his father stood to receive him, Saif saw that he'd lost weight and even seemed stooped. Had he been sick? A major change in the eight months since Saif had last seen him. When Saif hugged him, slapped him on the back and kissed him on the cheek, his father felt unsteady on his feet. "Home so soon from work today?" Saif said, smiling at him.

"Yes, well," his father said. He shot a glance over Saif's shoulder at his wife. Saif turned and saw his mother retreat into the kitchen.

Saif felt a rumble of dread. "What's wrong?"

His father pointed to the chair adjacent to his and sat. "Business has not been good," his father said. "In fact, we've lost most of it."

"How could that happen?"

"We lost most of our customers to another company. All our higher-margin product lines. Drill bits, specialty valves, pumping equipment."

Saif's limbs felt heavy. "But that's where all the profits are."

"Yes, very little profit left now."

"But your customers. Why did they leave you? You had such long-term relationships."

"Politics."

"What do you mean?"

Saif's father shrugged and looked at the floor.

Two hours later Saif learned the full story when his older brother, Farid, who worked with his father in the business, arrived. "It's the royals," Farid said, squinting with anger. "They've been systematically moving in on any international trade that just happens to be too profitable."

"But why?"

Farid scowled at him. "Because they can. They set up their own company and told Father's customers they would do business with them now. The royals only left us the dregs. Now our business consists largely of selling drill pipe."

"A pure commodity."

"Exactly. The lowest-margin product in our business. So now we just limp along."

It was Saif's first realization that he hadn't returned to the Saudi Arabia he'd expected.

That was 20 years ago. Saif's chest constricted as he thought of the ensuing two years, watching his father crumble and die. Then a year later his mother withered and died, undoubtedly from a broken heart. His own heart now felt like it would burst from the pain. Since then things had gotten steadily worse. The al-Asad royals had succeeded in mismanaging the country's economy, and squandered its oil billions on their self-indulgent lifestyle and the military toys they bought from the Americans. He clenched his jaw, reenergized by his anger.

Saif was certain that the old days could return in his lifetime. Days when their Muslim traditions and laws governed behavior in the kingdom. Days before the West's increasing influence gradually dissolved the Saudi Arabian culture, before decency and trust gave way to a ruling class that would destroy an honest merchant's business. He was closer than ever before to bringing about a return to those days. Only two years ago he had been frustrated, working his way up through the al-Mujari to become a confidant to Sheik bin Abdur, only to be blocked by Abdul and Waleed, forced to wait his turn. Forced to watch as Abdul and Waleed steered the sheik in the wrong direction. The plan they launched had been too ambitious: cripple the rest of the world's oil supply, overthrow the Saudis and all the other Western "puppet" regimes in the Muslim world, bring the infidels to their knees by controlling the only remaining producing oil wells in the Middle East. It was just too broad to work, even though the execution of it was beautifully simple. They hired only a few top-notch computer hackers, keeping the plan contained from leaks, and attacked the world's oil infrastructure. The hackers infiltrated the computers of the largest software vendors to the oil industry. Then they deposited logic bombs in the software that controlled the industry's operations, carried in trojan horse programs they inserted into routine updates sent online. They should have been less greedy, starting by going after the al-Asad royals, taking over Saudi Arabia and its oil production first, then moving out in stages. Even controlling just the Saudi Peninsula would have allowed them to have their way with the West. Just as the addict will pay any price for his heroin, so would the West for its oil. But by overreaching they had failed, and the net result was the murder by the West of Sheik bin Abdur, the al-Mujari's leader, and most of his top lieutenants.

Now the return of the old days was within reach. *Just a little more time.* He focused his attention on the group encircling Qahtani in front of him. The imams and scholars were nodding in agreement. Saif would have his army. An army of restive Saudi citizens who were out of work, stripped of their rights, poorly educated and weary of an indifferent al-Asad regime. An army that believed that the Redeemer of Islam was among them.

Saif watched as Qahtani, followed by his entourage, left the mosque for a meal prior to returning for evening prayers together. Saif drove to his home on the outskirts of Buraida, arriving just before evening prayers. He entered his house—his father's house, the house of a once-wealthy merchant that now was home to the families of his brother, Farid, and his, eight people in total. Saif greeted his wife, Noor, felt a spasm of guilt as he kissed his five-year-old daughter, Indira, and hurried into his study, the tiny room that had been the servants' quarters in his father's more prosperous days. He locked the door. He rolled out his wool prayer mat and turned it west, toward Mecca.

Prepared, he sat down in front of his desk, opened the drawer and pulled out his tablet computer. He felt another stab of guilt, thinking of little Indira. Saif led her in prayers this morning and knew Indira would have wanted to share evening prayers with her father as well. But five times a day was too much for Saif. Even before he'd gone to London to university he'd believed he could be just as committed a Muslim by honoring Allah once or twice a day. He plugged in his ear buds and switched on the Fire. He scrolled in the carousel to the movie *Robin Hood, Prince of Thieves.* He was three-quarters of the way through, just at the point the genius, Alan Rickman, as the Sheriff of Nottingham, erupts into his near-demented rant, exhorting his men to crush Kevin Costner as Robin Hood, his men leaving inspired by the intensity of Rickman's charismatic leadership. As the movie resumed play from where he had paused it the day before, Saif remarked on the brilliance of these Americans. With his tablet computer and Netflix subscription, he could log onto the Internet from anywhere in the world and instantly access almost any movie. More importantly, he could watch 27 movies in which Rickman appeared. Rickman, a superb actor who could be either hard or soft, but particularly showed his genius as a maniacally driven leader of men. A leader who exhibited the passion and commitment that could only be expressed through the ferocious intensity of his three most magnificent portrayals, the Sheriff of Nottingham in *Robin Hood*, Hans Gruber, who similarly inspires his men in *Die Hard,* and Severus Snape, a being who strikes fear in all who encounter him in the *Harry Potter* series. A fearsome and courageous leader that Saif had witnessed—no, absorbed, from the third row, including being sprayed by Rickman's spittle in his fervor—live on the stage of London's Royal National Theatre as the charismatic Henry V. A performance that stirred Saif to believe he possessed similar greatness within him if only he could school it properly to bring it out.

He'd settled in to watch the movie just as he heard the evening call to prayers droning from the minarets at the local mosque, taking in yet another lesson from Rickman.

CHAPTER 4

AFTER BREAKFAST WITH TOM, SASHA had her driver take her back to the Willard, her hotel in Washington, DC. Entering the lobby, she didn't bother to put her hair up, cover it with her scarf and wear her sunglasses as she had on the way out. It wasn't that she didn't care, it was just that, at the moment, she felt fatalistic. If Saif hadn't taken his shot at her 18 months ago, he wouldn't now. *And if he does, so be it.*

Back in her room, she dropped her handbag on a chair and threw herself on the bed. She knew Tom as well as she knew anyone, but she hadn't been able to read him. On the plus side, he'd seemed curious about her knowledge of Saif. He wasn't just curious, he was focused, intent. As if his mind were piecing it into whatever else he knew, things she couldn't be aware of. Then when they'd parted after breakfast, he'd asked her where she was staying and for how long. When she'd said it depended on his answer, he'd nodded.

She felt a wave of dread. *God.* What was she doing? Trying to talk Tom into helping her put herself in a life-threatening situation. She felt a tremor in her chest. *Second thoughts? Fear?* She'd sworn to Daniel, to his memory, that she'd make certain he hadn't died needlessly. She'd had 18 months to decide that was more important than her own safety. But was she getting cold feet?

Or was it another form of that dead feeling inside that now dominated the ache? Swami Kripananda told her that feeling was part of her path. She'd need to experience it, live through it, see what came up for her afterward.

Would what came up for her afterward matter? *Maybe.* The way she felt right now, whatever came next in her life would only matter if she righted this wrong. And she only saw one way to do that. Like she'd said to Tom: good versus evil. *Get Saif.*

She let out a sigh. What if Tom said no? Yassar would never help her do it, never put her life in jeopardy, even for this. And if Tom didn't agree, she didn't see how she could do it on her own.

She felt another tremor, this one anger. If Tom wouldn't help her, she'd have to figure out a way anyhow. *But Tom will come through*, she told herself. She recalled that intense look in those blue, blue eyes of his as she talked about Saif. Yes, she had something he needed.

When Tom arrived at Ross' office after breakfast with Sasha, Ross' assistant asked him to wait outside. Tom noted four serious-looking guys in suits standing around. They wore earpieces with wires extending down into their collars. *Secret Service.* That meant a couple of big guys were inside meeting with Ross. Tom wasn't one to get nervous over important meetings, but after a while his collar started to feel tight.

After forty-five minutes the assistant's intercom buzzed and she sent Tom in. Ross introduced him to Secretary of State Warren Harmon, National Security Advisor James Francis, and Chairman of the Joint Chiefs of Staff John "Rusty" Baldridge.

Tom knew Harmon by reputation. He was a right-wing Southern Republican, a self-righteous evangelical Christian, and vocal about it. He was taller in real life than he looked on television. Older, too, and stuffed into a three-piece suit that fit him 20 pounds ago. Harmon didn't wait for any other preliminaries. He said to Tom, "As I'm sure Harold told you, we had a briefing on your memo on the situation in Saudi Arabia yesterday. We've spent most of our time here talking about what our options are. Before we decide anything, we need to know if your intelligence is any good. You sure you've got your facts lined up?"

"I wouldn't have written the memo if I didn't."

"What're your sources?"

"Our people on the ground in Saudi Arabia, NSA eavesdropping and satellite imagery."

"You have people inside the al-Mujari?"

Tom glanced over at Ross, who showed no change in expression. "Some. And some of our intelligence is from the Saudis' Secret Police, some from informants."

Ross said, "All this is standard practice, and most of our facts are corroborated by at least one other source. This is good intelligence, Warren."

Harmon never looked away from Tom. He said, "Okay, let me hear it from the horse's mouth. Impress me."

Tom cleared his throat. He felt his pulse pick up. "Let's call it the summer after the Arab Spring. One we don't want to let get too hot. Arab Spring. Ben Ali in Tunisia overthrown by populist uprising. Same with Mubarak in Egypt. Libya, with a little help from us and our friends, gets rid of Qaddafi. Over a dozen other Arab states have at least some level of civil unrest challenging their governments."

Harmon said, "But those are good things."

Tom said, "Three governments overthrown, all run by bad guys who kept the average Joe held down. Tunisia and Egypt through revolutions, Libya through civil war. Civil uprisings in Bahrain, Syria and Yemen, major protests in Algeria, Jordan, Iraq, Kuwait, Morocco and Oman. Minor protests in Lebanon, Mauritania, Sudan, Western Sahara, even Saudi Arabia."

"Old news," Harmon said.

Tom said, "Iran still with its nuclear program. And making noises on and off about cutting off oil shipments through the Strait of Hormuz—"

"After spending over $1 trillion in Iraq, we aren't likely to get ourselves involved in something like that again," Harmon said. "And after Ron Paul's election agenda—Occupy Wall Street values, the 99% versus 1%, no foreign wars, no US role as world policeman, no military presence abroad—it's never going to happen."

Tom said, "I think we've got a big problem in Saudi Arabia."

"Why?" Harmon said. "It's a stable regime. One of our closest allies. In fact, we sell them all our current military hardware. This Arab Spring thing's been going on for years. Why all of a sudden should we be worried about the Saudis?"

Tom was thinking, *What the hell is Harmon's agenda? He gets Ross to bring him here to hear what I have to say and starts taking potshots at everything that comes out of my mouth? What's going on?*

Ross looked at Harmon and said, "Go on, Tom."

"We can't afford for the Saudi royals to topple. The al-Asad family has been in charge for over 90 years. After King Abad died, Crown Prince Abdul took over, but even though Abdul is a moderate, and works through the Council of Ministers, nothing's really changed over there in decades. It's still a we/they society.

The al-Asads still have their gold-domed Royal Palace, Boeing jets and diamond rings for their multiple wives and concubines. Half the workforce in the country is still foreign workers, a third of the populace is illiterate, most Saudis are out of work. They've still got over $100 billion in debt and they're running deficits every year to pay for their social welfare programs to keep the Saudi people from blowing the lid off the country. But their grip is slipping. Protests over labor rights, release of prisoners, and for equal representation in key government offices have been held in a half dozen cities, some with 100,000 protestors. Saudi Secret Police have used live rounds in containing some of them and a number of protestors have been killed. Women have protested for voting rights and the right to drive, and have gotten arrested and flogged for it. Add to it the Shiite versus the Sunni Muslim thing. Blood hatred going back centuries. The al-Mujari whips the Shiites into a frenzy and puts the Sunni Saudi royals in the crosshairs."

Harmon was making faces. "The al-Mujari is in shambles," he said. "All their top people, including Sheik bin Abdur, were killed two years ago. You know that better than we do—you ran that operation."

"I've said it before, and I'll say it again. The al-Mujari is like jock itch: you can suppress it, but you can never actually get rid of it. Right now we have the perfect conditions for the same thing to happen in Saudi Arabia as happened in Tunisia, Egypt and Libya, and is happening elsewhere right now in the Arab states. The al-Mujari almost pulled it off last time, but we stopped them. We may not be so lucky next time."

Harmon said, "So where's this going, Tom? This whole discussion seems to be wandering around."

Tom turned to respond to Harmon but Ross put his hand up to stop him. Ross stared at Harmon from behind his desk for a long moment. Finally Ross said, "You know, Warren, I have a pit bull at home. He's a really sweet dog, but sometimes he plays too hard. The trainer told me that when he gets too aggressive, I should say to him, 'Enough.'" Ross paused, continued to look at Harmon. "Enough, Warren, please. Let the man talk," he said. He turned to Tom and said, "Go on."

Tom said, "The al-Mujari has reorganized. There was enough of a core left of the organization and conditions were ripe to support it."

Ross asked, "What are they up to?"

"For the moment they seem to be zeroing in on the Saudi royals," Tom said.

Harmon was squirming in his chair.

Ross asked, "How so?"

Tom said, "We've intercepted multiple transmissions talking about something planned in the next month or two. The conversations are networked from all over the Saudi peninsula, so there's major coordination. We've been tracking training operations for the al-Mujari in northern Saudi Arabia and in Yemen."

"How long?" Ross asked.

"Four months," Tom said.

Ross said, "Sounds like a prelude to terrorist activity."

"We don't think so," Tom said. "The al-Mujari has aligned itself with the Ikwan, the Muslim Brotherhood and the Islamic Revolutionary Party, other Islamic dissident groups with large followings, both Shiite and Sunni. Based on that and the chatter the NSA is listening to, we think they're training and organizing for a move against the Saudi government."

Ross said, "So they've reorganized. Who's in charge?"

Tom said, "Saif Ibn Mohammed al-Aziz. He was recruited into the al-Mujari in his early 20s, came up through the ranks and has been there for 20 years. Now he's a major force. Saif's brother-in-law, Sheik Qahtani Ibn Muhammad al-Najd, is a cleric. Saif has convinced his followers that Qahtani is the 'Redeemer of Islam,' who the Islamic prophecies call the Mahdi. The Mahdi's supposed to be the new spiritual leader of the Muslims who'll rid the world of all nonbelievers. Saif is the operational guy, the brains who's calling all the shots. Qahtani is the spiritual leader. Saif is dragging Qahtani around by his nose, although he's positioning it for the masses that Qahtani's the head of the organization in order to recruit the Muslim faithful to the cause. Now we're worse off than we were before under Sheik bin Abdur, the al-Mujari's former leader, who believed his own bullshit."

Ross was nodding.

"Now we've got a shrewd one in Saif who doesn't care if it's all bullshit: we think he's working Qahtani and his followers to provoke an uprising that will overthrow the Saudi royals and allow him to grab power for himself."

Ross said, "So is this just some Islamic mumbo-jumbo or should we be scared?"

"Petrified," Tom said. "I am."

Ross looked over at Harmon.

Harmon said, "Is everything you know about this fellow Saif in your memo?"

"Pretty much. He's young, charismatic and he's demonstrated he's clever enough to know what buttons to push with his use of his brother-in-law, Sheik Qahtani."

"You think he can pull off organizing a full-blown revolution?"

Tom could feel Harmon's gaze boring in on him. He didn't hesitate. "I've seen dumber guys pull off worse."

Harmon seemed taken aback. He paused for a moment, then said, "And it's clear in your memo? This thing looks pretty long."

"Twenty pages, with a two-page Executive Summary."

"Even the summary's too long. Draw me a map. In grammar school English, since I'll be briefing the president and the National Security Council," Harmon said.

Tom said, "Saudi government toppled, the al-Mujari takes over. Oil disrupted, then the price goes to $200, maybe $300 a barrel. The Saudis either take over or annex Iran. The Saudis become a fundamentalist Muslim terrorist regime funded by 25% of the world's oil reserves, armed by Iranian nukes. That do it for you?"

Harmon pursed his lips. He ruffled the corners of the pages on the briefing memo. "Are you aware of the implications of this if we take this up through diplomatic channels with the Saudis?"

The guy was finally starting to piss Tom off. "Yeah. And also aware of the implications if we don't do anything about it. If a revolt leads to disruption of Saudi oil production, there's no way to replace over nine million barrels of oil a day in the world supply that doesn't result in all kinds of mischief."

Rusty Baldridge leaned forward in his chair. Even out of uniform in a business suit he looked like a four-star general. As big as a football tackle, hands as big as baseball gloves, crew cut showing scars on his scalp. He said, "The Saudis are armed to the teeth, with a lot of our hardware. About three hundred aircraft, mostly our F-15s, armored vehicles, artillery. But they aren't prepared for an all-out Libyan-style revolution. Any revolt would be a hand-to-hand combat affair in the streets, where their hardware won't do squat. And we couldn't help them out. We pulled out all our troops almost a decade ago. Force on our part could only be a last-ditch option. If we absolutely had to, we could go in there and occupy the oil fields to turn the spigot back on, but we'd need to launch a full-scale invasion to do so."

Harmon said, "You're getting way ahead of yourself, Rusty. And that's never going to happen unless, God forbid, everything else fails."

Tom said, "Even if we did it, that would mean occupying Muslim holy soil. It would be a declaration of war on a billion Muslims, and incite a Muslim-West conflict that would make the jihad that bin Abdur launched two years ago seem like some playground scuffle."

Tom shot a glance at Ross again. No reaction.

Francis, the national security advisor, asked, "But we aren't looking at an immediate threat to US interests, are we?"

Tom said, "I'd say we're a few steps away, but things could escalate quickly."

Harmon said, "We're looking at a situation that calls for good old-fashioned diplomacy. I've gotten to know King Abdul over the last two years, and he's met President Santorum at least once." Harmon looked over at Baldridge. "I don't see any reason for an immediate alert, do you, Rusty?"

Baldridge said, "*Alert* is too strong a word. We'll brief our commanders on the situation and dial up our preparedness a notch."

Harmon said, "Alright. The president and I should be able to see King Abdul within the next few months."

Tom felt a bolt of alarm. *Is he kidding me?* He said, "If I may, I think the situation could come to a head sooner than that, and it may be dangerous to wait that long."

Harmon glared at Tom, said, "I think you're wrong. We've been after the Saudis for a while now on cutting the little guy in on their oil prosperity, ramping up their social programs.

Not only do we have a moral responsibility to see those things happen, we've now got a tangible reason to see them done. No, this is a matter that we'll be handling through diplomatic channels." Harmon looked over at Francis, said, "This is a situation that needs to be defused by the Saudis themselves. We'll inform the president, and I'll put in a call to King Abdul." He looked over at Ross. "Keep us informed, please, Harold." He turned to Tom, said, "Good work," stood up and left, with Francis on his heels.

Ross walked over and closed the door, turned back and said to Tom, "Diplomacy, my ass. So how do we really fix this?" He walked back to his desk and sat down.

Tom glanced at Baldridge and then back at Ross.

Ross said, "You can talk candidly. We're on the same side here."

"The simplest solution would be to do what we did two years ago. Take out Saif and Qahtani."

Baldridge said, "A Special Ops SEAL team could get in and out before anybody knew about it."

Ross said, "In your dreams. You heard Harmon. He wouldn't support it and Santorum wouldn't authorize it. Saif and Qahtani haven't done anything yet, certainly not to us, to justify deadly force under US law. If we did it on our own we'd get crucified. Can we get the Saudis to do it?"

Tom said, "Not likely. Islamic brother against brother. They'd have to get a sheik to issue them a *fatwa*—a religious exemption—which they'd never get unless the al-Mujari committed some atrocity against Islam that the Saudis could prove."

Ross said, "Alright, so what channels have you got to get some attention to this at a higher level in Saudi intelligence? And without it getting leaked out to Harmon, or running into him and the president going directly to King Abdul? We need to be the ones jointly figuring out how to handle this with the Saudis."

Tom said, "I just happened to have a couple of interesting developments in the last 24 hours. I just had breakfast, at her request, with Sasha Del Mira, an agent I recruited 25 years ago, and who helped us stop the computer terrorism on the oil business two years ago. I also got a phone call this morning from Prince Yassar, the Saudi Finance and Economy Minister. In his call, Yassar said he has a proposition for me that he thinks can help resolve what he called the 'simmering internal conflicts' within Saudi Arabia. He's flying in tomorrow."

"Man of the Year," Ross said.

"Yeah. Sasha had married a guy named Daniel Youngblood, an oil and gas investment banker whose clients were at the center of the computer terrorism two years ago. A shooter was waiting for them in their apartment in Geneva 18 months ago. He killed Daniel. Then Sasha got him. She hung out in an ashram since then to clear her head. Now she's convinced—you won't believe this—that Saif ordered the hit on her husband and she wants back in. She's willing to have us recruit her again and go undercover to get Saif."

Ross said, "You think the two contacts are related?"

"I don't think so. Sasha didn't mention Yassar, even though she considers Yassar to be like a father to her. After he brought her to Saudi Arabia, he schooled her in Islam, got her tutors in Arabic, indoctrinated her into the culture."

Ross laughed. "I'll say he indoctrinated her. Didn't he bring her there as a concubine for his son?"

"Yeah, Ibrahim. But that's not as crazy as it might sound to us in the West."

Ross shifted in his chair, looking impatient. He said, "Can you trust Sasha?"

"Absolutely. I recruited Sasha all those years ago to keep an eye on Ibrahim, Yassar's son, while she was Ibraham's concubine. Ultimately, Ibrahim got turned by the al-Mujari and was gonna kill Yassar and be installed as the puppet ruler for the al-Mujari. Sasha helped stop the plan by giving our death squad access for a hit on Ibrahim, which went bad, and so Sasha finished Ibrahim herself."

Baldridge said, "Christ almighty. And you say she's like his daughter? Some couple."

"She forgave him and he forgave her, in part because she was able to prove the al-Mujari had Ibrahim all whipped up into assassinating Yassar as part of the plan to bring down the royal family."

Baldridge said, "Sounds like a Shakespeare play."

Tom turned to Ross. "I think we may be able to use Sasha again. I suggest I get a new security clearance in motion for her, just in case. I also think we should reconvene after I find out what Yassar has to say, then decide next steps."

Ross said, "Go ahead on Sasha, and yes, let's get together again after your meeting with Yassar." He paused, thinking. "Keep this on a Need-to-Know basis, limited to the three of us in this room. This is too sensitive for any fingerprints to wind up on it."

After the meeting, Tom sat in his office, thinking. He hadn't had time to reflect on his breakfast with Sasha before his meeting in Ross' office. Now he thought back, seeing her smiling at him across the breakfast table, but distant. Then her eyes growing hard in her determination. He tried to compare it to how she behaved two years ago, during that computer terrorism mess, then realized he'd been in such an emergency mode that he hadn't really taken her in. Maybe that's how it was for her, too, everything happening at warp speed, like an entire life crammed into a few days.

But he knew this woman, only a girl of 18 when he'd first worked her in Nice, 25 years ago. Observing her at those beautiful-people parties Nigel Benthurst threw on his yacht, then that lunch at the Baron David where they'd first met, then a half dozen other meetings before finally pitching her. He'd pitched her that sweltering August day, seated atop the retaining wall along the Promenade des Anglaise, the central street of Nice, over a simple lunch of cheese, bread and burgundy drunk from paper cups. She knew it was coming, welcomed it. By then she knew Ibrahim was dirty with the al-Mujari. As an agent she was a helluva catch. Sleeping with the scumbag who was plotting to kill his father, placed right in the eye of the storm. The perfect source, too good to pass up. And she had nerve. Brains.

That brought back that grungy feeling he'd gotten whenever he'd let himself reflect over the next year or so as she'd fed him intelligence, then ultimately helped him take out Ibrahim. An 18-year-old kid, screwed over by her drug queen guardian, used by Yassar, and then by him. Not the kind of low-life scum he usually recruited as agents. It had made him feel soulless.

And today? Here she was, coming to *him*, itching to get at Saif, including her having history with the guy who could put her inside, make it work. It was too perfect to pass up. *Maybe this could work*. She wasn't some naive kid anymore; now she was a trained pro. A trained pro, yeah, and a woman acting irrationally out of grief over her husband's murder, begging to let him take advantage of that fact.

Talk about a grungy feeling. *Man.* The things you could rationalize doing in the name of preserving our way of life. *What kind of scum am I?*

He picked up the phone, called Stewart in Security to get Sasha's security clearance in motion. Then he sat back, thinking. He didn't know how he could work it out, but if an operation with Sasha went forward, he'd run her himself, just like in the old days. No one else in between, and not for security reasons. He wouldn't be able to live with himself if somebody else screwed up and she got killed because of it. If he was gonna use her under these circumstances, she deserved at least that much.

CHAPTER 5

TOM DIDN'T REALLY THINK IT was necessary to meet in the Caymans, but Yassar insisted, so the next day he boarded one of the Agency's Learjets out of Dulles and was at the Ritz-Carlton on Seven Mile Beach in Grand Cayman by 10:30 a.m. *Must be nice to be king,* Tom thought, *or prince,* walking through the lobby past rattan chairs, the sea breeze coming in through the open end of the lobby, the beach and the blue Caribbean shimmering beyond it fifty yards in the distance.

Upstairs, one of Yassar's entourage let Tom into Yassar's suite, walked him past two bodyguards and sat him in one of two chairs parked on the balcony, angled toward each other and facing the ocean. The man offered Tom something to drink and he asked for a sparkling water with lime. Feeling that beautiful sun, the breeze coming off the ocean, Tom felt like asking for a gin and tonic, but knew with Yassar's Muslim strictures against drinking that was out of the question. The man brought Tom's drink and left.

Five minutes later, Yassar came out, dressed in a Western business suit, tan, as casual as he got. He'd aged in the two years since Tom had seen him, deeper crow's-feet around his eyes, the corners of his eyes drooping more, his jowls heavier. His goatee and mustache were still cropped, but speckled with more gray than before. And while he was still a vibrant, barrel-chested guy, Tom detected the beginnings of a stoop in his frame.

After ten minutes of small talk, Tom started getting impatient. Normally, he'd have said something like, "So, you wanted to talk about 'the simmering internal conflicts' within Saudi Arabia?" but knew better than to push Yassar. As down-to-earth as Yassar seemed, he was still a royal.

Finally, Yassar said, "Thank you for agreeing to meet on such short notice, and in this out-of-the-way place. A Saudi royal visiting the United States always has the potential to attract attention. A few days of vacation in the Cayman Islands are of little consequence to anyone." He smiled and shrugged. His cool, blinking eyes were impassive. "So, let me tell you why I asked you here." He crossed his legs and turned so he could face Tom. "I'm certain you are aware of the internal pressures we've recently been experiencing in Saudi Arabia."

"No one seems to be immune to the Arab Spring phenomenon."

"Tactfully phrased. But our situation goes well beyond that, has greater risks to the stability of our country, and to yours. My royal cousins are unwilling to adapt to some new realities. In fact, with Saudi Arabia and the United States' mutually successful campaign against the al-Mujari two years ago, my cousins have become complacent." He paused.

Tom felt that Yassar expected a response, so he said, "How can we help?"

"Our dialogue with the executive branch of your government is limited at this point."

Tom nodded.

"Our two countries have always maintained a comfortable balance in our mutual best interests. I am afraid that, without some intervention, my cousins, including King Abdul, may veer from the spirit of that balance, and we collectively have very little knowledge of the United States' current thinking about the informal agreements we've previously enjoyed. However, I fear your executive branch may be veering as well."

Why is he talking to me about this? Was it possible the Saudis didn't have anyone else to talk to? Or was Yassar operating on his own?

Yassar continued. "There are some things you can do to help our situation. Naturally, we would reciprocate."

Tom was out of his element, didn't know how to play this. But he figured that fathead, Harmon, the secretary of state, would be about ready to pop the buttons off his vest right now if he were here. Tom couldn't think of anything else to do so he said, "Please go on."

"You may be aware of our plans two years ago to acquire companies to expand Saudi Arabia's interests in the downstream side of the oil and gas business—refineries, pipelines and marketing operations, including gas stations and the like—in an effort to diversify our holdings away from purely the production side—pumping our oil and gas out of the ground. That was the original reason for seeking Daniel Youngblood's oil and gas mergers and acquisitions expertise. That plan was an attempt to increase our profits so that we could fund our social programs without continuing to run government deficits. Needless to say, those efforts were derailed by the al-Mujari's attempts to sabotage the industry. It was a long-term project that would have taken years, perhaps even a decade, to produce tangible results. Based on our current internal situation, we don't have time, and need to resort to bolder strokes. Therefore, I have a proposal for you today that I have vetted with King Abdul and a number of other senior members of the Council of Ministers. If your response is favorable, I believe I could, as you Americans say, 'sell' it within my government."

Tom nodded, thinking, *Here we go.*

"A loan of, say, $200 billion from the United States would allow Saudi Arabia to repay all of our existing external debt and provide us with a fund to enhance our existing social programs over, say, the next ten years in such a way that we can assure the stability of Saudi Arabia's domestic social order as well as maintain the royal family's way of life."

Tom couldn't help himself. "That's a lot of money."

"Yes, but consider this. It is a fraction of the money your government extended to your financial institutions, and to your automobile industry, during the financial crisis."

Tom restrained a smile. Congress had a lot of fun with that one. *They'd love this.* "What's the other side of the coin? And how would you propose to pay it back?"

"We would give you something that you have never achieved on your own and couldn't possibly expect to obtain any other way—a guaranteed supply of oil to meet all your needs at a fixed price. The price would escalate over time, but on a schedule you would know in advance, which would facilitate our repayment of the loan."

"And after that?"

"After that the price would be sufficiently high that we should be able to sustain ourselves, or strike a similar arrangement with you going forward." Yassar steepled his hands and smiled. "It's elegantly simple, don't you think?"

Tom imagined repeating that line when debriefing with Ross and Baldridge, wondering if he could keep a straight face as he said it. He figured he'd have to rehearse "elegantly simple," aloud a few times, letting it roll off his tongue with an affected accent to carry it off. He said, "What if we can't sell the idea on our side? What are the alternatives?"

"That would be unfortunate, but in that case I would bring the idea to the Chinese."

Tom felt a chill. "Understood." Tom turned in his chair to look Yassar square in the eye. "I'm curious. Why bring the idea to me?"

"Saudi Arabia has a long history with your CIA, going back to the days when Allen Dulles was head of the Agency and his brother, John Foster Dulles, was secretary of state. That intimate relationship continued once Saudi ARAMCO was founded. ARAMCO was full of CIA agents while it was owned by the US oil companies, a situation we permitted, even encouraged." Yassar smiled. "And as you know personally, representatives of your Agency continue to reside in our country, and enjoy the benefits of the best of what Saudi Arabia's lifestyle offers. A relationship with your Agency underpins much of the policy between our two nations. And those policies extend beyond changes in presidential administrations."

"And why me personally? You know I'm an intelligence officer and this isn't my specialty."

"I know I can trust you, Tom. I'm sure you can talk to the right people to get something done."

"I can." Tom remembered his conversation with Ross. Ross obviously had had conversations with the Saudis like this himself. "I must ask, how would we go about memorializing our agreement without it surfacing publicly?"

"These things are largely a matter of trust and continuity of leadership. It is Saudi Arabia who should be more concerned about an interruption in continuity of leadership in the United

States than you should in ours. We don't have elections every four years."

Tom nodded.

"But if it is required, I am certain a sufficiently ambiguous 'treaty' or some such document could be created."

"I'll take your concept back to Langley and respond."

Yassar smiled. "I propose a period of a week before I would pursue other discussions. Agreed?" Yassar raised his eyebrows.

"Agreed," Tom said. He waited a moment to see if that was the end of Yassar's agenda.

Yassar turned and looked out at the Caribbean. He said, "We have nothing like this in Saudi Arabia." He turned back to look at Tom. "I would be a rude host if I didn't offer you an early lunch before returning to the United States."

Yeah, he's done. Now it's my turn. "Thank you, I would enjoy that. First, I had something on my mind I'd like to raise with you. Something of mutual interest."

Yassar extended his arms, opened his giant hands as if to embrace the subject and said, "Of course. We can take as much time as you need."

"It's about the al-Mujari. And two men we're concerned about. Saif Ibn Mohammed al-Aziz and his brother-in-law, Qahtani Ibn Mohammed al-Najd." Yassar's face showed no hint of reaction. "I don't know how much of this may have filtered up to your level, but our people on the ground in Saudi Arabia have been working with your field agents on it. In summary, Saif has sponsored an effort to convince a number of your clerics that Qahtani is the Mahdi, who the prophecies—"

"I am familiar with the prophecies. Please go on."

"Our intelligence is that Saif has risen to the level to be the new head of the al-Mujari and positioned Qahtani as the Mahdi to inspire the faithful to enlist in an uprising. A move against the Saudi government may be imminent." Tom stopped, looked at Yassar for a reaction. He got none.

"Anything more?" Yassar said.

Tom clasped his hands together in his lap. "I could elaborate, but that's the succinct summary. That, and the fact that we're concerned and would like to work jointly with you to intervene so any potential..." Tom paused, searching for the right word, "... disruptive internal conflict within Saudi Arabia could be avoided."

Yassar looked at Tom for a long moment before responding. Finally, he said, "This is a situation I hoped that our prior discussion could defuse."

This is bullshit. Tom didn't think he was fully getting his point across by being delicate. "Throwing money at it isn't going to work at this stage. We think you are months, maybe even weeks away from an all-out revolution. Think Tunisia, Egypt and Libya."

"I believe I am current with the state of our intelligence. If what you say is so, we are a step or two behind your efforts. My compliments. What do you propose?"

Tom felt his juices start to flow. "The simplest thing would be to make Saif and Qahtani disappear."

"That presents certain problems for us."

"I'm aware of that, at least without a fatwa."

"Something we have considered. Understand the sensitivity about the prophecies, and the Mahdi. Perhaps with this new information, and some substantiation of it, it might make a difference, but I'm not hopeful."

Tom felt a flash of energy. Had Yassar tried? *Nothing to lose by asking.* "So you've tried to get one—a fatwa?"

Yassar nodded. He said, "But our failure in that regard would not preclude me from sharing whatever information we have to support any effort you might undertake."

"It's sensitive for us as well. You mentioned our executive branch earlier. Any operation we would run would need to be entirely covert, since our current administration wouldn't support it. So we'd need complete deniability."

"You sound as if you have thought this through. Do you have a solution?"

"Possibly. Someone with history with Saif who could get close to him." *Here goes.* "When was the last time you talked to Sasha?"

Yassar turned from Tom and looked out at the Caribbean. He said, "Does this have anything to do with Daniel?"

"The shooter in Geneva told Sasha that Saif ordered the hit before she killed him. She's had 18 months to think it over, and she wants to go in and get him."

"Was this your idea or hers?"

"Hers. I can make it work. At least with your help." Tom paused. "Or willingness to stand aside and let it happen."

Tom could see that Yassar had closed his eyes. Under other circumstances he would have believed him to be meditating, but understood his internal struggle. After a while, Yassar sighed, then said, "I will consider it," almost inaudibly.

"Welcome to the big leagues," Ross said the next morning after Tom debriefed him on his meeting with Yassar. "Yassar must really trust you if he's reaching out to you like this. You're the new fair-haired boy. Don't get hit by a truck."

Thanks.

"How did you answer him?" Ross asked.

"I said we'd get back to him. He wants an answer in a week or he'll take the deal to the Chinese."

"The guy plays hardball. No matter, I'll handle it."

"What're you gonna do? He's talking $200 billion."

"Don't worry about it. That's pocket change compared to the trillions the Federal Reserve loaned to banks here and around the world during the financial crisis. I'll handle it."

"What should I tell Yassar if he calls and asks?"

"Tell him the answer's yes, and I'm working out getting the money. Let's move on. Where's his head on Saif?"

Tom had to swallow hard. Two hundred billion just like that. He filled in Ross on the rest of his discussion with Yassar. Ross thought for a moment. He said, "Sasha's security clearance came back. She's good to go if you can put the operation together."

"That was fast."

"I muscled it through. The more I think about it, the more I like the idea about sending her in. It's clean. She's not one of ours, really. Rusty's assigned a couple of guys to you—communications and weapons for starters. Other than that he's staying out of it for now. We've agreed he doesn't want to know any more than he needs to. Gives him deniability if it goes wrong. Get Sasha locked in, make sure Yassar's fully on board, then put together a team. Let me know what resources you need."

Tom's mind was racing. He hadn't expected Ross to work this fast. "One other thing. I need to run Sasha myself, from over there."

"That's crazy. For something like this I need you here, where I can put my hands on you in five minutes."

"Fleischer will back me up. He's doing half my job now as it is."

"Forget it."

"I need to run Sasha or it won't work."

"You overestimating yourself or thinking with your dick?"

Gimme a break. "Think of her as a Thoroughbred racehorse. She's high-strung. I'm telling you, if I hand her off to someone she doesn't know or trust, I can't guarantee results."

Ross stared him down. "You're not making me feel all warm and fuzzy about your prize mare."

"She's rock solid. She just needs to be handled right."

"Okay, but stay close. I'll need you to talk to Yassar on this other deal. I'm sure there'll be a lot of back-and-forth on it. That's too big to screw up. It's so big I don't even know what to call it. Hell, it's not big, it's potentially life-transforming for us all. Remember what I said earlier."

"What's that?"

"Don't get hit by a truck."

———◇———

Sasha sat in her hotel room at the Willard, waiting. Tom had called a half hour earlier and said he'd be driving directly from Langley. She tried to stay calm, but her heart was thumping in her chest.

Be careful what you wish for, you just might get it.

She heard a knock on the door and felt a stab of nerves. She hurried to the door, saw Tom through the peephole and opened it. He smiled, a reserved one. *Serious.* She smiled back, her face feeling brittle, tense. They moved into the room and sat facing each other. He was back in his khakis and wrinkled sports jacket, the scruffy American again.

She searched his face. He was watching her, his eyes not blinking. "Well," he said finally, leaning forward, "I've got your security clearance. Let's talk this through." She liked the quiet way he said it. She sensed the Tom she knew, the gentleness beneath the rugged exterior. "Do you still want to do this?"

"Yes." She said it automatically, as if the words slipped past her brain without checking in. *Do I?* She felt her pulse rise.

"You know you might get yourself killed, don't you?"

She nodded, now feeling detached from her body.

"Have you consulted anyone about this?"

"No."

"Not Yassar?"

"No. I told you. He'd forbid it."

She saw him observing her, checking, or contemplating. He said, "I spoke to him."

She felt a surge of blood to her face. "When?"

"Yesterday. I met with him off-site. He asked whose idea this was. I told him it was yours, said we couldn't do it without his help or at least his agreement."

"And?"

"He said he'd consider it."

"What do you think?"

"I think you should pack your bags."

CHAPTER 6

ABOARD THE CIA LEARJET, SASHA'S jitters were gone. It wasn't just that they were moving forward, that she was out of that no-man's-land of "Yes or no?" It was more an internal sense that she'd aligned herself with what was right. She thought of Daniel, seeing him smile—his last—as he came through the door in the apartment in Geneva, and thought, *Yes,* that was what drove her. Then she saw his lifeless eyes staring up at her. She pushed the image and the anger surging upward with it inside her to hold in reserve, knowing she'd need that to motivate her later. She turned to Tom across the aisle from her, just the two of them on the plane.

He said, "How're you doing?"

"Better than I've been in quite some time."

He had his business face on, but she could still feel his warmth beneath it. He said, "We're flying straight into Riyadh, then to the embassy. The rest of the team will meet us there. There'll be three of them, supported by another you won't meet for now. I'll take you through their backgrounds and specialties now so when you meet them—"

"Not now, please, Tom. We've plenty of time for that later."

He observed her for a moment, then said, "Second thoughts? Last chance to change your mind. After this there's no turning back."

"No, I'm fine. I'm totally resolved to do this." She smiled at him. "Over the last 18 months I've felt that I didn't exist before I met Daniel. Now I don't even know why I'm here on this planet, except to square this with Saif. I'm not afraid to die in the process. Whatever happens to me doesn't matter. I know you don't like it when I talk like this, but it's just my body, my corporeal form, not me. I feel like I can do anything and it can't touch me. I'm already saved."

"You're talking that crazy Hindu stuff again."

"You only say that because you're stuck here, in a crazy world. I'm not."

"Yeah, whatever you say. Just don't go talking this way with anyone else on the team. They'll think you're on some suicide mission and worry that you'll get them all killed."

"Trust me, I won't do anything to interfere with this operation." She held his gaze, knowing she was showing the intensity of her feelings. "All I keep focusing on is, 'This man had Daniel murdered.'"

An hour later, after she awoke from a nap, Tom said to her, "Good, you're awake." He ordered coffee for both of them, then started briefing her on the rest of the team. She smiled to herself as she listened. He'd never asked if she was ready, just plunged right in.

They arrived in Riyadh at 7:00 a.m. local time. Tom suggested that they freshen up in the lavatory on the airplane, head directly to the embassy and get organized for the team meeting rather than checking into their hotel first. Sasha slid a black abaya on over her jeans and shirt, then put on a hijab headscarf and veil. An embassy car drove them through the center of Riyadh toward the American Embassy. In the center of town, Tom turned to Sasha and said, "I didn't mention one team member while we were on the plane. We have a man on the inside, under deep cover, code named Archer. He's been briefed on the operation and who you are."

Sasha raised her eyebrows, perplexed. *All this trouble and they have a man inside?* "If you want Saif as badly as I do, why don't you have your man inside take him out?"

"We do that and we'll blow his cover. It's taken us five years to get him where he is in the al-Mujari. He's too valuable for that, but he'll be how we get you inside. He won't be at the team meeting. We'll meet him off-site at a safe house later today or tomorrow, depending when he can safely break free." They rode in silence until the car drove through the gates into the American Embassy compound, then into the underground garage. Upstairs in a conference room, Tom set up a map of Buraida on a corkboard, then pulled out a whiteboard and Magic Markers. He sat down across the table from Sasha and checked his watch. "The guys should be here soon."

Ten minutes later a bone-thin man who appeared to be in his mid-30s walked in carrying an armful of papers. He was tall, perhaps 6'5", bald, and with a neck that seemed twice as long as it should be. Tom stood up and shook hands with him across the table. "Great to see you, Ryan." He extended his hand toward Sasha. "Meet Sasha Del Mira. Sasha, this is Ryan Murdoch, our Deputy Station Chief here in Riyadh."

"A pleasure," Ryan said, in a bass voice. His eyes, magnified by his quarter-inch-thick rimless glasses, seemed to bulge at Sasha like cue balls.

"Ryan will be our local liaison to run interference for us on virtually everything—moving our local assets around, intelligence, logistics and transportation. I'm pleased to say I recruited him myself 10 years ago and he's been with us on our Mid-East team ever since. You can have complete confidence in him."

Ryan smiled, sat down and put his pile of papers in front of him. Then he darted a glance at the credenza, got up and walked over to it to pour himself a cup of coffee. He started back toward his seat, then stopped. He walked over to the credenza again, pulled some pushpins from a plastic case and stuck them in the map of Buraida. He took a step back, cocked his head, then nodded to himself before walking back and sitting down.

What an unusual character.

Almost immediately, two men in their late 20s walked in. Both wore conservative gray suits, white shirts and muted ties. Their hair was close-cropped on the sides, slightly longer on the top and sticking up like the bristles on a brush, boot camp style. Tom said, "Sasha, this is Zac Fulton and Seth Green. They're both Army Special Forces, on loan to us, courtesy of Rusty Baldridge, chairman of the Joint Chiefs of Staff. Fellas, Sasha Del Mira."

Zac extended his hand. He was a tree trunk with muscles bulging through his suit and a neck seeming to be as large as Sasha's waist. "Pleased to meet you," he said in a Southern American drawl. Shaking his hand was like grabbing a pound of steak.

Seth stepped forward, wiry and short, with an erect posture like a gymnast. His hair was red and his skin pale alabaster, with freckles like the Archie character from the comic books. "A pleasure, Sasha," he said as he shook her hand.

"Zac is in charge of communications and technology. Seth handles weapons and martial arts. They'll also be your primary support in the field."

Seth smiled, showing a gap between his front teeth. "I'll be giving you crash courses in weapons and martial arts over the next week. Tune-ups," he said, "starting today at noon."

Sasha smiled and nodded, thinking that, after seeing their body types, she'd expected their roles to be reversed.

"Alright, let's get started," Tom said. He had Ryan pass out current photographs of Saif and then said, "This is a single-purpose operation. We locate Saif, get Sasha in and wait for an opportunity for her to take him out, then extract her."

Ryan said, "We aren't sure where he's hiding, but for the moment he's acting pretty cocky, visiting home to see his family frequently, as if nothing's going on, so for Archer to get Sasha in should be doable."

"Yes," Tom said, "but she won't be able to bring in a weapon. So we'll need to shadow her and conceal one someplace for her—or multiple places—after she's with Saif."

"Does the Saudi Secret Police know Saif visits his home frequently?" Sasha asked.

"We don't know. And even if they did, we aren't sure the Saudis are really focused that intensely on Saif yet," Tom said. "Yassar admitted to me that they were one or two steps behind us when I briefed him on our knowledge of Saif's activities."

Sasha shuddered with guilt at the mention of Yassar's name. She couldn't believe she still hadn't called him since she'd left the ashram, especially now that she was actually on Saudi soil.

Ryan stood up and pointed to the three pushpins he'd stuck in the map of Buraida. "We think Saif is staying someplace here in the northeast quadrant of Buraida. He'd want to be near his home"—Ryan pointed to one of the pins, then to the two other pins—"and Qahtani's house and the mosque Qahtani operates from." Ryan then summarized what they knew of Saif's day-to-day routine and his progress in convincing religious leaders of Qahtani's status as the Mahdi. "Overall, we think he's where he wants to be: he's well organized, firmly in charge, has a well-trained force close to him, adequate weapons, close ties to the other Islamic dissident groups around the country and a core group of loyal lieutenants surrounding him. Given the volatile nature of the recent demonstrations, we think Saif could provoke a populist uprising at any time. He's ready, and as you say, Tom, the Saudis aren't."

"I'll be working on that behind the scenes," Tom said, "but in the interim, this operation is our best chance." He turned and looked at Sasha. She set her jaw, feeling the anger, glad for it.

———◇———

After the team meeting, Sasha and Tom were alone, seated next to each other in the conference room. "Seth should be up to get you shortly," he said, still looking at the papers in front of him. Then he glanced up and said, "Well, here we are, just like old times, huh?" Tom's eyes softened and she saw that movie star twinkle they'd had when he was younger.

Impossibly blue. She smiled. "You know, I had a crush on you all those years ago."

He grinned.

"Remember that lunch we had on the retaining wall of the Promenade des Anglaise in Nice?"

He nodded.

"I knew there was more to you than just this sandy-haired, scruffy American, so I wasn't floored when I found out you were CIA, but I thought you were getting ready to make a pass at me."

"Were you disappointed?"

"In a way I think I was."

He shifted in his seat, looking awkward. "Aside from the professional element of it, I was in my early 30s and you were just a baby."

She couldn't help but laugh. "Don't be ridiculous. I was 18, but look at the life I was leading. I'd say that qualifies as an adult."

He nodded and smiled stiffly, then looked away. He turned back to the papers in front of him. For a moment she thought of teasing him, then remembered another moment in their past. It was after she and what remained of the death squad had arrived at the safe house after she'd killed Ibrahim. It was then that she'd seen something in his eyes that she'd missed until that point. Tom had taken her by the arm and walked her into an office. He'd sat her down on a straight-backed chair and taken a seat in front of her. He'd told her how they would get her from the safe house to the embassy, cut and dye her hair, get her out of Saudi Arabia on a US passport as the wife of an oil broker from Houston.

She'd told him she wasn't leaving, that she needed to go back to Yassar to make sure he understood. Tom had just looked at her, speechless. She'd insisted Tom give her the tape of Ibrahim swearing he'd kill his father. It would be the proof she needed. She knew Tom could see her resolve, now not just putting up a good front after her horror at murdering a man, a man to whom she'd served as concubine for three years. She had her mind right, knew exactly what she was doing.

"Okay," he'd finally said, looking resigned. He reached out and stroked her forehead, surprising her. He'd never done anything like that before.

She felt emotion thick in her throat. She tried to say, "Thank you," but could only mouth the words.

Then Tom talked through the scenario of how he would get her back into the Royal Palace to Yassar, talking as much to himself as to her. When he finished they exchanged a few final words about the consequences of what she was doing. Then he turned to her and said, "This is it, you know." He leaned toward her. He reached up and stroked her forehead again, then caressed her cheek. "It's unlikely we'll ever see each other again, and no matter what happens to you, I won't be able to help you." She saw the tenderness in his eyes, and at that moment couldn't understand how she'd never seen it before. He said, "Sasha, I—"

"Don't," she said, surprised she was even able to speak because her throat was burning. Tears flushed into her eyes.

He held her gaze, nodded and smiled, an awkward smile, then looked away.

Sasha now looked over at Tom, engrossed in his papers. She realized he'd just turned from her with that same awkward smile. It struck her like a stab in the heart, forced a sharp breath into her lungs. She had to turn to look out the window to keep Tom from seeing her eyes tearing up. *Oh my God. How could I be such a dolt?* A minute later Sasha had composed herself. She was touched, feeling close to Tom, somehow safer with him now. He cared for her. She turned to him. "Are we friends?"

Tom looked up from his papers. "I suppose we are, in a way."

"I remember back in Nice, then in Saudi Arabia, wondering at times."

Tom didn't respond right away. "Go on," he said.

"I remember a few times in particular. We were in the embassy in Riyadh and you first played the tape of those awful al-Mujari men, Abdul and Waleed, inciting Ibrahim to swear allegiance to Sheik bin Abdur, then goading him to scream that he'd murder Yassar."

She saw Tom watching her, but with a different attentiveness than the way he usually observed her. Was it tenderness?

She went on. "You nursed me through that, propped me up so I could face going back. Back into the Royal Palace, into the bed of a traitor and would-be murderer. I wondered at the time, 'Is he sending me back just so I can gather enough information to bring down these people who are pulling Ibrahim's puppet strings? Does he care what happens to me?' In my moments of doubt I asked myself if you were simply manipulating me for your own goals."

Tom's face was blank.

"I don't know if you're aware that half the reason I was doing it was to get enough information to convince Yassar, who was certain to be unbelieving without proof. But then after I got over my horror that you wanted me to eliminate Ibrahim myself, after I agreed to do it and then changed my mind because I insisted on staying with Yassar afterward, you looked into my eyes and connected with me with the gentleness I always saw in you. I'm sure you had to stand on your head to change the plan at the last minute to send in the death squad instead of having me do it. That's when I was certain that I wasn't just some tool you were using." She felt her emotions welling, not wanting them to. But she wanted Tom to know she was fond of him, even if that's all she could offer.

Tom said, "It didn't matter. You had to step up and do it yourself anyhow when the plan went bad." He smiled at her. "Thanks, I appreciate your saying all that, but I really was just doing my job. Although, I have to admit somehow it was always different with you."

"How so?"

"If you could see the seedy types of double-dealers I work with most of the time you'd understand. Always some kind of payment or exchange. Money or a swap of political favors. To a great extent I pay what amounts to blackmail for information or services. You were different. You were operating out of real commitment, so I handled you differently."

"I did feel that you...cared." As the words came out of her mouth, Tom froze in place like a trapped animal. Muscles tensed, ready to run, but with no place to go. *Why am I going here?* Did she need to hear him say something to confirm what she already knew was true? *Stop this.* She exhaled. "Don't mind me. Maybe it's tension building as I'm preparing to go in. But you should know I haven't forgotten how you've always taken care of me like a friend. And I guess all I'm trying to say is I'm grateful and I think of you fondly, as someone I can trust."

"If that's the definition of a friend, then, yes, I am."

Sasha inclined her head. "You know everything there is to know about me."

"Hardly."

"Still, you know more of my life than most, and yet I know nothing about you."

Tom smiled. "I guess that means I'm good at my job."

"I gather so. But why? How did you wind up in the CIA, and why do you keep doing it?"

Tom took a moment, as if he were uncertain he'd respond. Then he said, "I guess it can't hurt," as much to himself as to her. "There's not much to tell. I started out by making myself up. I left Troy, Michigan, on a Greyhound bus with a copy of *The Great Gatsby*, heading east. By the time I reached New York City, I figured that if Jamie Gatz could make up Jay Gatsby, I could make up Tom Goddard."

"What about before that, in Michigan?"

"Not much to tell. I was a second-string tight end in high school football, my dad drank and my mom had men friends over. When I found out she was taking money for it I got on that Greyhound to New York."

She felt a tug at her heart. "Then?"

"I wandered around New York for a while, waited tables, went to SUNY for two years, then graduated from NYU with a degree in political science. When the CIA came to campus I applied, got the job. It's all I've ever done, and I've been doing it ever since, for 35 years."

"That's it? You simply keep doing it because it's all you've ever done?"

"Well, that's how it was for a decade or so, maybe, but by the time I met you…I'm not gonna get corny here."

"Tom, you're among friends."

He shrugged. "I keep doing it because we're all surrounded by crap. Piles of it. The lowlifes are slinging it at us nonstop. Tearing us down, dragging us into it, trying to destroy everything we work so hard for."

"We?"

"The US. The average guy who keeps his head down, believes in the dream. The kids who bust their butts to go to college, or become baseball players, whatever. Somebody's gotta stand up to the shit that's always flying, deflect it or throw it back."

"You're an idealist."

"Maybe. I don't know. But I do feel like I'm one of the last lines of defense."

"Sounds solitary, even lonely."

"In a way it is. It's a full-time commitment. Hard to have anything or anyone else in your life."

"Are you married?"

"I was. Six years. Ellen. We split up a year ago."

"I'm sorry."

He shook his head. "Don't be. In retrospect it was over a long time before that. Just faded away. Ellen said I was too busy saving the world to have room in my life for her. I'm afraid I wasn't much of a husband, not even around enough for it to end with any fireworks."

She imagined Tom kissing his wife good-bye before leaving for the office one day, coming home and finding her gone, then making macaroni and cheese in the microwave, eating dinner in silence at the kitchen table. It made her feel melancholy. She forced a smile.

"Don't look so sad. It really doesn't matter," he said. He took a deep breath, exhaled. "So, my friend, how about we talk some business before Seth gets here? We've got a lotta work to do."

Sasha reached out her hand to him. He extended his to her. She took his hand and squeezed it. "Okay."

Seth came to the conference room to pick up Sasha at 11:55 a.m., and was taking her through a series of warm-up and stretching exercises in the basement gym five minutes later. He wore black tights and a dark-green army T-shirt. He still looked like a scrawny kid, but his demeanor was totally different than in her introductory meeting. He was all business, barking crisp commands without smiling.

After 20 minutes of warm-ups, he said, "Okay, let's see what you've got." He moved to the center of the mat and took a *zenkutsu* stance, feet slightly apart, one forward of the other, resting on the balls of his feet, arms forward at chest level and his hands balled into fists. Sasha took her stance, moved toward him. He opened one hand and waved her in with his fingers, his eyes steeled. Sasha lunged in and snapped a front kick at his chest. He leaned sideways and deflected her with a knife hand block to the calf that had her seeing stars with the impact. She spun away and bounced on her toes to get the feeling back into her leg. He waved her in again. She stepped toward him, faked a punch with her right and threw one with her left, which he slapped away. She whirled and threw a roundhouse kick. He ducked under it, then swept his leg out into a hooking ankle block and put her on the mat. She lost sight of him momentarily, did a kip up, throwing front hand jab punches as she landed on her feet. She saw a blur in her peripheral vision to her left, never saw the punch that landed square in her ribs and put her on her back again. He stood over her with his right arm poised for a knockout punch to her head an instant later. She held both hands up in a sign of submission.

He moved to the center of the mat and took his *zenkutsu* stance again. "Show me more," he said.

Half an hour later she had trouble raising her arms and she smarted from the blows in at least a dozen places. She was certain when she pulled off her black leotard that she'd have welts and bruises. They took their positions again. This time she waved Seth in toward her. He stepped forward and she went to him, tried to hook his leg with a foot sweep and he put her on the mat again with a short punch to the chest.

He stood back and bowed. Sasha got up, gasping for air, and said, "Looks like I have some work to do."

"Yes, but I'm impressed," Seth said, his face lighting up, showing that gap-toothed smile.

I can hardly breathe, and he's only puffing a little.

"You're in better shape than I expected. You've been working out?"

"Almost every day. Aerobics and calisthenics, but nothing like this."

"No problem. I can teach you some things quickly. You're aggressive, almost too aggressive, but it's easier to dial that back than it is to force you into it if it doesn't come naturally to you. And you lead with your mind and your body follows, in true *Shotokan* fluid style. Not like most of the guys I work with, trained with the macho approach, all muscle. I've got a lot to work with. You'll do great."

Sasha groaned as she stood up. "So that's it for today?"

Seth pointed to one of the treadmills in the corner. "Three miles of roadwork, then some strength training for your core, then stretching."

Sasha smiled. "Okay. Then back to the hotel for a hot Epsom salts bath."

"No, then we break for lunch and hit the range for weapons training."

Tom didn't know how long he sat, staring at the wall, thinking, after Sasha left with Seth to go downstairs for training. Her scent, some hand cream or body lotion, was still on his hand from when she'd reached out to him and squeezed it. Funny she mentioned that lunch on the Promenade des Anglaise, that same afternoon that had come back to him a few days earlier when he'd seen her. Funny the impressions people make on you, how you feel about them, and how it sticks with you over the years. Did she know how he felt about her all those years ago, how it had ripped at his guts to send her back into the Royal Palace, to Yassar, knowing she would tell him she'd murdered his son? Knowing that, however strong Sasha thought the bond was between Yassar and her, Tom was almost certainly sending her to her death.

And here he was, dancing with those same emotions. Now not with some misguided 18-year-old kid who'd been screwed over by anybody close to her, now with a grown woman who lived with her passion for life unconcealed, ready to throw herself in harm's way to do something she felt from her soul. And him sitting here with that grungy feeling again because he was possibly sending her to her death. It was only a few days ago he'd reflected on the same thing and asked himself, *What kind of scum am I?* Now Sasha had forced him to break through his professional veneer that shielded him from a much deeper reason for feeling anguished. He'd fallen in love with her all those years ago. Now what was he feeling? He realized he didn't need to ask himself. Some things just didn't change with time.

He sighed and focused on his papers again. *Enough of this.* He had a job to do.

CHAPTER 7

THE NEXT MORNING, RYAN, TOM and Sasha flew on a chopper to Qassim Regional Airport in Buraida, Ryan and Tom dressed in casual clothes, Sasha in her black abaya, headscarf and veil. Tom told everyone to use code name Archer only. They drove in a beat-up jeep into the center of Buraida and parked in a commercial section behind a halal butcher shop on a back street. They entered the back of the shop and seated themselves around a rough-hewn table in a windowless room smelling of meat and blood. They waited.

"How long?" Tom said to Ryan after about fifteen minutes.

"He's on the way. Could be another five minutes, could be an hour."

Sasha watched Tom as they waited, no one exchanging small talk. She met his gaze and he smiled, then looked over at the wall. She realized she was getting anxious, feeling that sense of unnatural calmness she remembered experiencing as a girl before a riding competition, or when Christina asked her to perform a piano piece she hadn't rehearsed in weeks at one of her parties.

At last, in walked a bearded Arab, wiry, with a trim frame. He wore the dress of an average Saudi—a long-waisted, white cotton shirt with three-quarter-length sleeves, worn over baggy cotton pants. He had deep eye sockets, brown hair shooting off in all directions and carried the smell and dust of the streets in with him. "Sasha Del Mira, meet Archer," Tom said.

Sasha felt rising excitement, inhaled sharply.

Archer sat down, propped his elbows on the end of the table with his arms crossed and hunched his shoulders. He looked at each of them around the table, his eyes penetrating when they made contact with Sasha's. "Things are heating up."

"Tell us," Tom said.

"The UIP founders were imprisoned earlier this week— undoubtedly you've heard. We just got word they were released in exchange for withdrawing all their demands and disbanding their party."

"Were they tortured?" Tom asked.

"Treated like royalty. Air-conditioned cellblocks. Sumptuous meals, even prayer mats. The Secret Police said they might even offer to have their families join them to help them change their minds about the king and his policies."

"Very convincing," Tom said.

"Yes. And if that wasn't convincing enough, the Secret Police told them that the Saudi Arabian Council of Senior Scholars issued a fatwa opposing petitions and demonstrations, including a severe threat against internal dissent."

Tom thought of his conversation with Yassar, wondered if it had anything to do with a renewed effort for a fatwa. He said, "Doesn't sound like it's open season on dissenters, but it does sound like the royals are closing in."

"Yes. It looks like they're going to start rounding people up to keep them out of mischief. Saif is tense. He's got everyone ready to go underground. He's making plans to move his family." Archer paused. "So when do you want to move?"

Tom said, "We need a week to get Sasha prepared. After that, as soon as possible."

"Then I get her in face-to-face with Saif?"

"Yeah," Tom said. "Where is he now? We'll need to hide weapons for her and keep close enough to get her out when we need to."

"Moving around. For the last two weeks he's been at a date farm ten miles outside northeast Buraida."

"Give Ryan the location and we'll get a satellite fix for observation."

Archer looked at Sasha, said, "You sure you know what you're getting yourself into? How long ago was it that you knew Saif?"

"About 20 years ago."

Archer wrinkled his forehead. "That was a long time ago."

Sasha clenched her jaw and leaned toward him. "I know how to handle myself."

"Allah be with you if you don't. How about you tell me about how you know Saif?"

Tom motioned with his head toward the door. "Let's step outside so these two can get acquainted," he said to Ryan. They left.

Not very subtle. "Looks like I'm being interviewed for a job."

Archer shrugged. "You were about to tell me how you know Saif."

"I'd been a concubine to Ibrahim, Yassar's eldest son, for about two years when Abdul and Waleed started working Ibrahim for the al-Mujari."

"I knew them," he said, looking bored.

"Tom recruited me about that time. In the beginning it was just to feed him information about Ibrahim and Abdul and Waleed's influence on Ibrahim. Within a year they'd turned Ibrahim and things changed. At that point Tom played me a tape in which Ibrahim agreed to kill Yassar and be installed by the al-Mujari as their puppet ruler after they'd overthrown the Saudi regime. With Yassar at risk, I agreed to take out Ibrahim as part of a dozen CIA-coordinated hits here and in Buraida on senior al-Mujari lieutenants."

"The al-Mujari remembers that day well. It's a major recruiting tool."

"After the hit on Ibrahim I escaped to a safe house, where I insisted that Tom give me the tape. I returned to Yassar the next day and played it for him. We reconciled. That night, I was kidnapped from my quarters in the Royal Palace and brought to Buraida. I met Saif in Buraida that night."

The memory of that evening flashed into her mind. Coming back to consciousness, wondering where she was and where her captors were taking her. She'd blacked out, then awakened with a piercing headache, her mind fuzzy. She tried to reach up to rub the pain in the center of her chest where she'd been shot by a dart gun and realized her hands were bound in front of her. She took stock of her surroundings: lying on her side on something cushioned, feeling a rocking motion. *Riding in a car.* Her mouth tasted like metal and garlic. *Sedative dart.*

Who was behind this? It had to be Nibmar, the first of Yassar's four wives and Ibrahim's mother. Who else could have the access and power within the Royal Palace to do this? Or motive? *Yes. Nibmar.* Sasha imagined Nibmar's eyes as on the first day she met her. Sasha had seen the steel in them as Nibmar had ordered Sasha to stand at attention in front of her, then had her aides strip Sasha naked. Nibmar stood like a little Napoleon in front of Sasha in a Chanel dress, her prominent nose and pointed chin elevated. Her dark Arab skin was creamy, her daily facials evident. Her British-tutored English was refined on her tongue. The haughty Valide Sultana, ruler of the women's quarters in the Royal Palace, asserting herself. A Saudi mother willing to do anything to assure the comfort and pleasure of her fine Saudi sons. Sasha was now sure those cold eyes showed blood hatred.

She checked the binding on her hands. Plastic electrical connector straps. Sasha moved her feet, finding they weren't bound. They must have been in a hurry when moving her from the Royal Palace to have neglected that. She listened; no one was talking. She felt with her hands and sensed the coarse fabric of an abaya. She inched her hands up to her face, put the plastic strap in her mouth and started gnawing with her front teeth. The plastic was thick and tough, but chewing through it was doable.

Now she heard men joking with each other in Arabic.

Then a female voice, harsh, said, "Stop your foolishness!" It was Nibmar. She must have turned to face the rear, because her voice was now louder. "We are a half hour away. Prepare yourselves."

Another voice from the front, calmer, "Check your weapons, but keep your cool. We expect no problems, but you must be on your guard." Ali's voice. Nibmar's only other child, a son two years younger than Ibrahim, always in his older brother's shadow, a nothing.

Sasha now chewed furiously on the plastic binding strip.

Nibmar said, "When we arrive I will do the talking. We will meet with the man called Khalid in northeastern Buraida at a building next to a mosque he is hiding in. The sheik will not be present. Nor will his right-hand men, Abdul and Waleed, with whom we previously dealt. We understand the sheik has fled to the Yemen, taking Abdul and Waleed with him, following an attempt on the sheik's life and the assassinations of many of his other top lieutenants last night. Khalid has been elevated in the al-Mujari's chain of command and will direct its activities from their headquarters in Buraida while the sheik, Abdul and Waleed are absent. As such we are dealing with someone who can make decisions. Expect Khalid to be surrounded by heavily armed guards. No mistakes, no sudden movements, or you'll be dead. The whore is not essential to our business, only a sweetener for Khalid and his men to enjoy before they dispose of her."

Sasha felt her stomach involuntarily tighten. She didn't know Khalid, but had met Abdul and Waleed many times. And Nibmar doing some secret business with them, and now with this new man, Khalid. It seemed inconceivable. Sasha's heart started pounding. What was going on?

She concentrated. She had a half hour to chew through the plastic binding. As she worked her teeth, she worked her situation over in her mind. The vehicle had three seats, likely a van or some form of military vehicle. Whatever it was, it must have a rear door that she could open from the inside. That would be her escape route.

A moment later the vehicle slowed, felt like it was exiting the highway, then slowed more. It stopped, turned and accelerated again, moving slower than on the highway, bumping on an uneven side road. She continued grinding at the bonds, now making progress.

At last, she heard a snap and felt the plastic break in her mouth. Her breath quickened. She rolled over. Above the back of the seat, she could see two doors at the rear. She knew she'd only have one chance. She took a deep breath, grabbed the back of the seat and hurled herself over it.

"Hey! She's trying to get away!" Sasha heard as she landed on the floor behind the seat. She found the door latch, pulled it up and felt the rush of cold air. She heard shouting inside the van as the door flew open and she threw herself out.

"Ooof!" Sasha landed hard, rolled, got to her feet and limped for the side of the road, realizing she was in a residential neighborhood. Her right knee was in crushing pain, but with each stride she was able to put more weight on it. She turned and saw the van—it looked like an American Chevy Suburban—start backing up toward her. She leaped over a fence between two houses before the van reached her, then ran through a backyard, over another fence and across another street. She heard men shouting, the doors on the van slamming, but by then she was over another fence, through another backyard and crossing another side street. Had she lost them? She heard voices from the direction of the van, then people running on the street a block away. Yes, they were going away from her up another side street she'd crossed.

She rubbed her knee. She'd be fine. She shivered, still winded from her run, and pulled her abaya close around her against the chill of the night breeze. Now what to do? Should she run, leave Saudi Arabia? After the hits in Riyadh the night before, Tom had provided her a passport as the wife of an oil broker from Cleveland to get her out of the country, but took it back when she'd told him at the safe house that she'd decided to return to Yassar. If she could get to the American Embassy in Riyadh she could contact Tom, so that probably wasn't a closed door. Then she thought about Yassar. The fact that Nibmar had history with the al-Mujari, and was going about some new business with them, could mean that he was in worse danger than before. His first and favorite wife up to no good. It didn't make sense. Sasha couldn't think clearly. Maybe the sedative was still affecting her. "Oh, God," she said aloud.

"I hear them coming up the street in the back," she heard a man behind her say. She turned, startled, and saw a young Arab in his early 20s standing in the backyard behind the house where she crouched in the darkness. He said, "Who's chasing you?" He held an unlit cigarette in his hand.

She didn't answer, thinking. She was in Buraida, primarily Shiite Muslim, very fundamentalist and frequently at odds with the Sunni royal family policies.

"Secret Police?" he asked.

"No, but men hired by the royals."

The man nodded as if he understood. He slid the cigarette back into the pack, put it in his pocket and motioned to her. "Follow me," he said, and walked toward a door at the back of the house. Sasha didn't move, trying to decide. "Hurry," he said, and opened the door. She ran inside behind him. He pulled the door closed behind her without a sound. He raised a finger to his lips, and motioned with his head toward the hallway. She followed him into a small room with a desk and cot in it, then closed the door.

"Thank you," she said.

"You're welcome," he said, in English with a British accent, extending his hand. "I'm Saif Ibn Mohammed al-Aziz."

She shook his hand. "Sasha Del Mira." He motioned for her to sit on the cot and took a seat in a chair by the desk. He was good-looking, with high cheekbones, sharp features and curly brown hair. He had no beard, uncharacteristic of most Arab men, and wore a white button-down Oxford shirt and Levis. "Your English is excellent," she said.

"Thank you. I went to university in England. Eton." He seemed proud of it. "We should keep our voices down. I don't want my parents to hear. It isn't considered proper in Saudi Arabia for a man and woman who don't know each other to be alone in the same room."

"I've been here long enough to know." She smiled. "And I also know it's against Islamic law to smoke cigarettes."

He smiled back. "A small luxury I picked up at university." He slid the pack out of his pocket and pulled out a cigarette. "You mind?"

"I'm hardly in a position to object. Thank you again for helping me."

He lit his cigarette. "No trouble. Why were those men chasing you?"

"Let's just say that one of the wives of a prominent Saudi prince had reason to be angry with me, and was doing everything in her power to assure that I stayed out of town."

Saif chuckled. "Ah, yes, the allure of the Western woman. I caught that bug myself in England."

Sasha relaxed, relieved. She'd slipped the story past him with a smirk.

"Now what?" he asked.

"I'm asking myself the same thing."

"I assume you live in Riyadh. What brought you there?"

Sasha felt a twist of discomfort. She'd never been ashamed of anything she'd done in her life, but didn't think telling Saif she was a concubine to a member of the royal family was a good idea right now. Particularly since she'd shot that family member through the heart the night before. "I've had some odd jobs. Work as a domestic, some work in hotels. Nothing particularly interesting." He didn't react, but didn't push her for more. She said, "Mind if I ask why you helped me? You took a risk if it had been the Secret Police after me."

His features hardened. "If it had been the Secret Police, I would have done the same thing. They're simply an extension of the royals. And I've had my own problems lately with the royals." He waved an arm around the room. "You see this room? It's my study now. It used to be the servants' quarters. A married man and woman. That was when my father's business was flourishing. My father built one of the most respected and profitable companies in Saudi Arabia importing oil drilling equipment and supplies. Three decades of firmly entrenched client relationships. But in the last year, while I was away at my final semesters at university, his business took a dramatic downturn."

"What happened?"

"The Saudi royals have been moving in on any industry that happens to be unusually profitable. A number of Saudi princes set up their own oil equipment importing businesses and leaned on my father's customers. Many of them came to my father almost in tears, insisting they had no choice but to move their business to the newly established royal family companies. Otherwise they themselves would have been driven out of business."

Sasha saw that Saif's face had fallen, the energy seeming to drain from him as he spoke.

"That's awful," she said, leaning forward on the cot. She thought of Yassar and the research he was doing at his Finance and Economy Ministry, trying to understand and adapt to the influx of foreign workers willing to accept low wages that were soaking up any available jobs and leaving Saudis out of work. She'd also heard him talk many times about the Saudi merchant class being squeezed out, and realized Saif's father's predicament must be what he had been talking about. Thinking about Yassar brought her back to her own predicament. For the moment she was safe, but where would she go? Getting back to Riyadh was something she could manage, but where to go from there? And what about what Nibmar and Ali were planning? She started turning it over in her mind again.

Sasha saw Saif observing her. She imagined he'd had his share of girls at Eton, and she could see him checking her out. He stubbed out his cigarette. "Where did you just go?" he asked.

"I was just thinking about what you said about your father's company. And then about a man I know who's talked about that issue."

He cocked his head, looking skeptical, and said, "What's the real reason those people were chasing you?"

She sat up straight. "I told you."

"I saw how you tensed when I asked you what brought you to Saudi Arabia. Plus, your answer doesn't make sense. A Western woman, well-spoken, sophisticated, and obviously well-educated, with pampered skin and perfectly manicured fingernails. You're not someone who landed in Saudi Arabia by accident, or who does odd jobs."

She allowed herself a subtle smile. "Thank you, that's very flattering, really, but what I've told you is true."

He laughed. "You're not a domestic and you're certainly not a hotel worker."

Now she sized him up, wondering if she could trust him. "Okay," she said. "So what if I'm not here working as a domestic? What good would it do either you or me if I were to tell you why those men are chasing me?"

"There's only one way to find out. Tell me. If I was looking to turn you in, wouldn't I have just allowed those men to capture you?"

She didn't answer, considering it.

He said, "Oh, come on, this is getting silly. I heard you coming from across the street, saw you take that fence without breaking stride, even in that abaya, then watched you looking around with eyes that were trained for it. I can believe that someone, maybe even a Saudi prince's wife, had you transported here from Riyadh, but your story doesn't add up."

Sasha stared at him, keeping her expression blank, listening.

He went on. "So if I'm right, at the moment you're trying to figure out what to do, where to go." He raised his hands. "And don't worry about me. I don't pose any threat. I'm not the biggest fan of the royals right now, so whatever you have in mind I'm not going to try to stop you, and maybe I can even help you. And that's an offer you should think about, hard. Because if you've been involved with the royals, you're not exactly in friendly territory. For all practical purposes, these northern Shiite provinces might as well be a completely different country."

Finally she spoke. "Have you ever heard of the al-Mujari?"

"I've been in England for most of the last four years, not on Mars."

"It's not just the royals I'm in trouble with. It's also the al-Mujari."

"Keep going."

"So if you were to agree to help me, you might be getting yourself into more than you'd planned. I've been thinking about it and I may need to find one of the senior al-Mujari people before the people that brought me here can get to him."

"You mean one of the senior al-Mujari guys who's still alive, don't you?"

Now Sasha narrowed her eyes. She said, "I understand there was some excitement up here in Buraida last night."

"You might say that. A dozen senior al-Mujari guys killed in coordinated hits. I hear you had some of the same excitement down in Riyadh, too. The locals are blaming the royals, but the more knowledgeable are saying it was the American CIA. Would you happen to know anything about that, Western woman?"

"Ever heard of a man named Khalid? How about Abdul and Waleed?"

Saif arched his head back as if he'd been caught off guard.

CHAPTER 8

SASHA WAS UNCOMFORTABLE CONCEALING THE entire truth from Saif, especially since he agreed to help her. Still, she'd told him almost everything, except the nature of her true relationship with Yassar, allowing Saif to believe she was Yassar's concubine, and completely leaving out anything about Ibrahim, and her knowledge of and participation in the hits last night. She allowed Saif to assume it was her role as concubine to Yassar that had resulted in Nibmar's decision to kidnap her and bring her to Buraida. Sasha explained that she'd overheard Nibmar and her men, while they thought she was still unconscious, discuss some mysterious business they would conduct with Khalid.

"Khalid is hiding in a building next to a mosque about five blocks from here," Saif said, "but you'll never find it by yourself. I'll show you."

"How long have you known Khalid?" she asked while they were driving north.

"A while. Everyone who's critical of the royals in Buraida knows him, and Abdul and Waleed. And that's not an exclusive club." A minute later he said, "That's it up the street." He'd stopped his car about 100 meters from a bedraggled-looking mosque set between simple stucco and brick buildings. "Here, you might need this." He held out a pistol.

Her eyes widened.

"Don't look so surprised. You're in Buraida."

Sasha took the gun and checked it. A Ruger 9mm. She racked the slide, then nodded to him, feeling her heartbeat increasing. "Thank you," she said. Saif nodded back. She got out of the car and started across the street toward the mosque. Saif drove off. Sasha walked toward the mosque. When she neared it she knelt down behind a car and checked her surroundings. She felt her fingers tingling, getting anxious. She closed her eyes and willed herself to calm down, then stood. She saw she was standing behind a Chevy Suburban. She thought she saw movement in the front passenger seat inside, and knelt back down. *What are the odds? But why not? This was where they were headed.*

Sasha sneaked up the driver's side of the Suburban. When she reached the rear door, she eased her head up to peek inside. Sasha felt adrenaline flood through her. Nibmar was sitting in the passenger seat, alone in the vehicle. Sasha felt inside her abaya and grabbed the Ruger. Her heart was knocking as she crept forward, and in one smooth motion opened the driver's side door and jumped into the seat, holding the pistol in Nibmar's face.

"Don't move, don't say anything," Sasha said.

Nibmar's eyes showed fear, then she collected herself, raised her chin and scowled. She took a long moment to turn her head to look over at the building next to the mosque, then back at Sasha, as if to say, *I'm not alone.*

Sasha said, "In your dreams. You're dealing with me now."

"A dead woman. Or should I say, dead whore."

Sasha smacked her across the face. "I don't care if you live or die, but I need you to listen to me for a few minutes." Nibmar gritted her teeth and scowled again. Sasha hit her in the face with the Ruger, then grabbed her by the throat with her free hand and put the muzzle of the handgun against Nibmar's cheek. "I'll shoot you here, then go inside and blast Ali's brains out if you want. Or you can listen to me. Your choice. How do you want to play this?"

Nibmar nodded, her eyes wide.

"Good." Sasha released her hand from Nibmar's throat. "What are you doing here?"

Nibmar froze, silent.

"Okay, let's take this one step at a time. Why did you bring me here?"

Nibmar smiled. "To let them rape and kill you."

"And what else?"

Nibmar raised her chin again. Sasha smashed her across the face with the pistol a second time.

"Whore!" Nibmar screamed, spitting blood.

Sasha's pulse was now thundering in her ears. She pressed the Ruger to Nibmar's forehead. "Tell me or I'll kill you."

Nibmar glared back at her. "You don't have the nerve."

"I did last night with Ibrahim." Sasha grabbed her by the throat again, held the Ruger to her forehead and cocked the hammer. Nibmar shut her eyes and Sasha felt her go limp.

"Murderous whore, you want me to betray my own son."

"Is Ali inside?" She pressed the Ruger harder against her forehead. Sasha felt Nibmar start to tremble, her face going white.

"He and our men are inside the building next to the mosque, dealing with this al-Mujari amateur." Nibmar opened her eyes, defeat in them. "He refused to deal with a woman." Then her eyes showed fire again. "If you harm Ali, I promise you will be raped in hell."

"I already have, bitch. I slept with your son for three years." Sasha's anger was rising. Smashing Nibmar in the face with the gun wasn't enough. Sasha wanted to crush her will.

"Let me tell you about betrayal. I killed Ibrahim because he betrayed Yassar. Your beloved Yassar, his own father. These al-Mujari scum worked on Ibrahim for years, twisted his mind, even while he was at Harvard. I saw it myself. Those worms Abdul and Waleed even showered him with cocaine, got him hooked—"

"Drugs? That's a lie!"

Sasha went on, the gun still pressed to her forehead. "Finally they seduced him by promising he'd be ruler of Saudi Arabia after the al-Mujari took control. The price of entry was to murder Yassar. That's why I killed him, the pig."

Sasha didn't get the reaction she thought: Nibmar leered at her. "You are more of an idiot than I had assumed. And you obviously think me a fool. A fool who's content to be pushed aside by three younger wives, and relegated to managing my sons' harems when I could be the mother of the ruler of Saudi Arabia."

"So you knew Ibrahim was going to kill Yassar?"

"My husband is soft. It is within his grasp to rule, but he is too self-effacing to force his cousins aside to accomplish it. I did not marry him to settle for mediocrity."

Sasha felt a blast of shock. "So you helped the al-Mujari with their plans?"

"Don't be naive. The plan regarding Ibrahim was my idea."

"How could you choose between your husband and your son?"

"Life is choice, hard decisions forced upon us by impossible situations. I have always adapted and made the best of them."

"You're more of a monster than I thought."

"You're obviously not a mother or you wouldn't say that. Particularly not an Islamic mother."

"And now Ali is inside there cutting his own deal with Khalid."

Nibmar glowered. "There's nothing you can do about it. You'll be dead before he becomes ruler of Saudi Arabia."

Sasha was appalled. She wanted to pistol-whip her again. She looked Nibmar in the eye, forced her head against the window, the gun still pressed against her forehead, made a decision. Then she heard footsteps and men's voices in the street and changed her mind. She opened the door and ran into the shadows across the street.

Sasha got lost on the way back to Saif's house, because she kept doubling back to make certain she wasn't being followed. As she finally found her bearings and approached his house, she debated whether she should tell him everything. She decided she could trust him, given that he'd helped her and had even loaned her the gun. She tapped on the window to his study and moments later was sitting there with him.

She told him about Yassar bringing her to Saudi Arabia three years earlier as Ibrahim's concubine, her recruitment by the CIA to feed them information as Abdul and Waleed persuaded Ibrahim to join the al-Mujari, and finally about her role in killing Ibrahim as part of the CIA-coordinated hits the night before on the senior al-Mujari lieutenants.

"I suspected there was more to your story." He didn't seem offended, just contemplative. "So what's the big draw with Yassar? That after killing Ibrahim you would risk everything to go back to him. Are you in love with him?"

"Of course not. He's in his 50s. I'm not even 20 yet. He's like the only father I've ever known. I was raised as an orphan by a guardian. Yassar and she were friends, so I've known him almost all my life. That's a bond we've cemented since he brought me to Saudi Arabia."

"Then if I were you I'd just go back to Riyadh and tell everything to Yassar."

"I'm afraid if I don't do something to stop Nibmar and Ali immediately that it may be too late for Yassar. Besides, I'm sure Nibmar has figured out a way to have me killed if I set foot in the Royal Palace."

"So call him on the phone."

"I'm not sure that will protect him, and Nibmar is devious enough to have packaged a story to poison Yassar against me. I need to act, now."

"So what's your plan? You can't very well go back to Khalid's hideout and storm the place with that pistol."

"I should have killed Nibmar when I had the chance."

"And then Ali? Sooner or later Yassar will get downright annoyed if you keep plunking his family members."

"That's not funny."

"I wasn't trying to be funny. I'm trying to make you see how tenuous your situation is. It seems to me you don't have much future here in Saudi Arabia, Yassar or no Yassar. Why not just call Yassar on the phone, tell him everything, hope for the best and get yourself to the American Embassy so your CIA guy can get you out of the country?"

"That leaves Yassar exposed. You should have seen Nibmar when I was talking to her. She's obsessed. And a sociopath. I think she'll make a move immediately. The al-Mujari was ready before, and I assume they can get ready again, even though much of their top echelon was taken out yesterday. Their plans were already in place, and it looks like Khalid has stepped up to take charge of operations. And even if I were to go to Tom, I don't think he could put together the resources to intervene that quickly. It took him at least a month to coordinate all the hits that occurred yesterday."

"So where does that leave you?"

"Here in Buraida with a 9mm Ruger with eight rounds in the magazine." She stood up.

"Where are you going?"

"Back over there."

"To do what?"

"I don't see that I have much choice. The same thing I did last night."

"How in the name of Allah do you propose to do that?"

"I'll have to figure that out when I get there."

"Sit down. Going over there to snoop around and see if Nibmar and company showed up was one thing. Going back there by yourself with only a handgun to do something about it is crazy. They've got automatic weapons. They'll kill you."

Sasha remained standing. "I have to do something."

Saif looked her in the eye for a long moment, then shrugged and shook his head. He stood up, walked to the closet and opened the door. "I don't know why I'm doing this, but if you won't take no for an answer, at least let's add some additional firepower and plan something." Sasha arched her head back as Saif turned around holding two smooth-skinned green hand grenades the size of oranges. "These aren't the real kind, only concussion grenades. They make an amazingly loud bang and a blinding flash. Anyone in the room won't be able to hear anything for at least 30 seconds, and will be stunned and blinded for a while." He rested them on an end table, then reached back into the closet and pulled out two more, then produced another Ruger and two extra clips. He must have seen the look on her face because he said, "I already told you. This is Buraida." He handed her one of the clips, then walked back over and sat in the chair by the desk. "Sit down and we can talk this through. After last night's hits, the al-Mujari is scattered all over the city. I hear their resources are strained, and they're disorganized. I think we can come up with something that will work."

Saif drove them toward the mosque again.

"Why are you doing this?" Sasha asked Saif on the way there. "This isn't your fight."

"I don't know whether it is or not. I'm ambivalent. I have as good a reason to be angry at the royals as anyone, seeing my father's business destroyed and watching his confidence and energy bleed from him day by day."

"It must be heartbreaking."

"It is." He paused, as if thinking. "But I also love Saudi Arabia, our people, our culture. I'm not ready to believe that violently overthrowing the government is the right thing for us. Particularly if it's to replace the royals with Sheik bin Abdur and his fundamentalist principles and rhetoric. He'd be having us all live in tents again, I'm afraid." He turned to her. "And I'm doing it because I respect your commitment to Yassar, your courage. You believe in something, or somebody, and you're not afraid to fight for it." He started to add something else, but held his tongue.

Sasha felt her emotions rise. She couldn't tell if she was reacting out of exhaustion or tension, but she reached out and placed her hand on his forearm. "Thank you."

Saif eased the car to a stop on an unlit section of a side street a block from the mosque and cut the engine. From there they could approach the building next to it by cutting through the alleys. He said, "I'll leave the key above the visor, just in case one of us needs to run for it. If anything happens, meet at my house. Ready?"

Sasha nodded and got out of the car. She didn't wait for Saif, but, as planned, climbed over a chain-link fence, crossed a backyard and then headed through an alley toward the mosque. Her stomach was fluttering as she crouched in the shadows across the street about 100 meters down from the mosque. She waited, observing. After five minutes of seeing no one, she crossed the street and started walking toward the mosque. The Chevy Suburban was still parked near the front. She stepped into an alley about 25 meters from the mosque and crouched in the darkness. She reached inside her abaya and grabbed the Ruger. *Any minute now.*

After another ten minutes she began to wonder if something had gone wrong, and then heard the explosion and saw a flash like the noon sun a few hundred meters down the street in the opposite direction. She flattened herself against the wall of the building. She heard men shouting and running in the street. A moment later two men carrying automatic weapons dashed past her on the sidewalk in the direction of the concussion grenade. She waited another moment, her heart thumping in her chest, and peered out from the alley toward the mosque. No activity. She took a deep breath, then started walking toward the mosque, at the same time reaching inside her abaya and grabbing the concussion grenade. When she was 10 meters from the door to the building next to the mosque she had to breathe through her mouth to keep from hyperventilating. She passed a narrow alley, saw movement to her right and turned to see the butt of a rifle speeding toward her. She felt a sharp pain in her head and lost consciousness.

Sasha woke up in a dusty room that smelled like perspiration and dry-rotted wood. The right side of her head felt like she'd been hit by a truck. Then she remembered: it had been a rifle butt. She was bound in a seated position to a wooden chair, her arms held flat to her sides and immobile, with duct tape wrapped around her torso and the chair back. The room was dimly lit, but enough that she could see Khalid hunched in one corner with Ali, talking in low tones. Two other men sat on either side of the door with automatic weapons across their laps. *We must be in the building next to the mosque.* Just as she turned her head, Nibmar walked into her range of vision.

"Welcome back, whore." She stopped and bent over her, put her face up to Sasha's, smiling. "You'll notice your feet are not bound again. Last time it was an oversight on our part. Now it's because we'll need you to be able to spread your legs." She spat in Sasha's face, then slapped her, following it up with a backhand to the other side of her face. Sasha saw the two men with rifles sit up straight and Khalid and Ali turn to look at her.

Khalid strutted over and positioned himself in front of Sasha. He leaned over to put his face inches from hers. "Who's helping you?"

Sasha felt her pulse in her temples. "No one."

He stood up, walked over and smacked her in the face so hard she cried out. He said, "Where did you get the weapons?"

"In a backyard shed I was hiding in. We're in Buraida, remember?"

He slapped her again, then walked back over to the corner with Ali.

As he sat down, Nibmar said to Ali, "We'll be leaving as soon as our other two men return." Then to Khalid, "Do with her what you wish, but please make certain she doesn't survive until morning."

Sasha fought back a wave of hopelessness by gritting her teeth and summoning her hatred of Nibmar. She said, "You're a traitor to Saudi Arabia, to your husband and to your religion. No matter what happens you'll die a dried-up, lonely old hag with—"

Nibmar sprang at her and slapped her again, then started throwing wild punches. "Infidel whore! How dare you talk to me about my religion!"

By then Ali had crossed the room, grabbed her by the shoulders and pulled her back. Sasha's chest was heaving. She glared back at Nibmar, then laughed at her. "That's right, Nibmar, your other little mama's boy will come take care of you. This one is even more of a wimp than Ibrahim was." At that point Khalid strode up to her holding the roll of duct tape and taped a piece over Sasha's mouth.

"Silence, cow. You'll have plenty of opportunity to moan later," Khalid said.

Sasha's gaze was shooting around the room as she tried to think of something, anything, to get out of there. She stood up, forced into a hunch because she was strapped to the back of the chair, and ran toward the door. She'd almost reached it when one of the men seated by the door smashed her in the shoulder with his rifle, throwing all of his weight behind it. She collapsed sideways to the floor, the wind knocked out of her. He stood over her as she gasped to get air back into her lungs. He picked up the chair by the back, lifting her with it like she was a ten-pound barbell, walked back to the center of the room and plopped her down again.

She heard a knock on the door. The other man stationed by it looked at Khalid, who nodded, and then the man turned and opened it. Saif walked into the room as casually as if he were stopping by to visit friends, his hands in the pockets of his windbreaker. He nodded to Khalid. *Oh my God.* Sasha felt her limbs go limp, her hopes sink and tears begin to form in her eyes.

Khalid said, "Saif, my friend. So you've reconsidered?"

Saif shrugged and said, "I'm keeping an open mind." He stepped farther into the room and observed Sasha, making no comment.

"That's tonight's entertainment. For later. You can be first if you want. Consider it a signing bonus," Khalid said. He motioned to one of the men by the door, then pointed to Sasha, then to the back of the room. The man walked over, grabbed the chair Sasha was bound to and dragged her across the room. He opened the door in the rear, walked her through a small anteroom, opened another door and deposited her in a room lit with only a single bulb hanging from the ceiling. Before he left and closed the doors, Sasha heard men laughing from the front room.

Sasha let out a long sigh as best she could with the duct tape over her mouth. She inhaled, her nose stinging from the cold air in the room. She felt desperation clouding her brain, tried to pull her wits together. *Think.* She closed her eyes and felt another wave of hopelessness. *Saif.* What had he said in the car? He was ambivalent. He'd either changed his mind and decided to betray her, or had been setting her up all along. But why give her the gun and the concussion grenade if he was setting her up? *What difference does it make? I'm dead.* She hung her head and started to cry.

She cried for a minute or two, then lifted her head and took a deep breath. *Pull it together.* She looked around. A few pieces of furniture, a dusty wooden floor, two boarded-up windows on the left and the single door leading to the anteroom. The only escape was through the windows, and that would be impossible without tools. But she'd noted a window in the anteroom. *Maybe.* First she'd have to free herself. She checked her bindings. The duct tape lashing her to the chair was secure around her arms, keeping her from lifting them. She shifted in the chair, checking it. It was wobbly and old. If she leaped into the air and fell straight down on her back she might be able to smash it. Either that or hurl herself backward into the wall. Once she'd smashed the chair there might be enough slack in the tape that she'd be able to get her arms free. Then if she couldn't get the window in the anteroom open she'd at least be waiting for whoever was the first to come into the room with a piece of the chair as a club.

She stood up and shuffled toward the door, then glanced over her shoulder at the far corner of the room, opting for a run straight at it and a last-minute turn before hitting the wall. Would they hear the chair smash from the other room? Through two doors? Did it matter? She couldn't see any other options. *Quit stalling. Move or die.* Her pulse started racing. She flexed her leg muscles, ready to run.

The door opened and light flooded into the room. *Saif!* He shut the door, holding a finger to his mouth. *What the...?* He sat her back down, then opened a pocketknife and started cutting the duct tape.

"Shuush. This can work," he said, "but we need to move fast." He'd freed her from the chair and now pulled the duct tape from her mouth. "Try not to shoot me, too," he said as he reached into his pocket for his Ruger and handed it to her. "Ali has the other

Ruger. I'm sure Khalid is armed. Two men with AK-47s on either side of the front door." He reached into his other windbreaker pocket and showed her a concussion grenade. "If we both get out alive we'll meet at my house." Then he took off his windbreaker and pulled the pin on the grenade, still holding the safety clip in place. He led her back into the anteroom, stopped behind the door and said, "Eight seconds." Saif let go of the safety clip and it clanged on the floor. He dropped the grenade back into the windbreaker pocket, waited a few seconds, then opened and walked through the door carrying his windbreaker. She heard him say, "I changed my mind about screwing her," as he was closing the door.

Sasha's limbs were buzzing with adrenaline as she moved to the side of the doorway and pressed her back to the wall. She racked the slide on the Ruger, closed her eyes, took a deep breath and held it, waited. *Three, two, one…*

She wasn't prepared for the force of the explosion. The wall shook and the door flew open, and even with her eyes closed she could see the yellow flash. She jumped into the doorway in a firing crouch, the Ruger extended in both hands. Everyone was on the floor, dust and smoke thick in the air. She fired two quick rounds, one into the chest of each of the men on either side of the door. She stepped into the room, now hearing muffled moans, seeing Saif moving. *He's alive.* Khalid was still in the corner with Ali, the two of them also starting to move. Nibmar appeared to be unconscious. Sasha started toward Ali, who rolled over with the Ruger in his hand. She fired, putting him down with a round in the chest. Khalid had now sat up and was looking at her, dazed, coughing. She pointed the Ruger at his chest and fired. When she saw he was still moving she put another round in his head. *Five rounds, three left.*

Move, she told herself. She knew the explosion would bring others. She knelt next to Saif and whispered, "Are you okay?" He nodded, said, "Go."

She didn't have much time. Sasha saw the roll of duct tape on the floor, ran over and grabbed it. She stepped behind Nibmar and taped her mouth, then her wrists. When Sasha was finished taping, Nibmar opened her eyes, not seeming to recognize Sasha or know what was happening. Sasha stepped over to one of the dead guards, picked up his AK-47 and slung it over her shoulder, then strode back over to Nibmar and pulled her to her feet. She was wobbly but she could stand. Sasha smacked her in the face a few times and pushed her toward the door. "Come on, First Wife. I'm taking you back to Yassar so you can tell him about your friends in the al-Mujari. Outside or I'll kill you here." She grabbed Nibmar by the hair and forced her through the door in front of her, checked both directions, then herded her toward the Chevy Suburban. She took a chance the keys were in it—no luck. Not in the ignition or over the driver's side visor. *God!* Time wasted. She'd have to make it to Saif's car.

She had started pushing Nibmar across the street when Nibmar began to resist, swinging her elbows and trying to kick Sasha. Sasha stood her up and smacked her in the face with the Ruger, pushed her forward, but when they reached the alley Nibmar lay down and refused to budge. "Alright, then I'll have to drag you." Sasha hooked her arm through Nibmar's taped wrists, hoping the duct tape would hold, and started dragging her into the alley like a sack of rocks. Now she heard shouts and footsteps in the street behind her. She got another surge of adrenaline and turned back to see two men racing up the street toward them carrying automatic weapons. Sasha dropped Nibmar and slid the AK-47 off her shoulder. She crouched and took aim. One man kept running and died from the first burst, the second dived behind a car 50 meters away. Sasha put her face next to Nibmar's ear and said, "Make your choice. Run or die here." Nibmar got to her feet and started running down the alley just as the return fire from the other man ricocheted off the wall next to them. Nibmar was in front of Sasha when they emerged from the alley into the backyard, so Sasha grabbed Nibmar's hair again and guided her to the chain-link fence, pushed her as she climbed, then threw her over it. Sasha leaped over it herself, then muscled Nibmar toward Saif's car.

She stuffed Nibmar in the passenger seat and drove off, holding the Ruger to her head. *Now what?* At that moment Nibmar swung her arms at Sasha, pushing away the Ruger long enough to allow her to grab the steering wheel. She yanked it and the car swerved and crashed into a truck parked at the curb. Sasha's head hit the steering wheel, dazing her. Nibmar was crumpled half on the seat and half on the floor. The Ruger had fallen from Sasha's hand. She opened the door to look for it on the floor just as a spray of automatic weapon fire shattered the windows of the car. She pressed herself to the ground, grabbed the AK-47 and crawled to the back of the car. She couldn't see where the fire was coming from. She felt her pulse throbbing in her temples, was aware of the soreness in her back, the pain in the side of her head from the rifle butt, now in the front from the steering wheel. She tried to slow her breathing. *Focus.*

She raised herself up to peer over the trunk of the car and saw a starburst of muzzle flame from the shooter. Now she could see his shape crouched behind the fence a block away in the wash of the security lights from the building behind him. She ducked down and crawled forward, around the front of the car, then past the truck she'd crashed into. She peeked out from around the truck's fender. She could still see him. She took a deep breath, exhaled, then rose up and braced the AK-47 on the hood of the truck and fired. She saw the man go down, then she ran back to Saif's car. *No!* Nibmar was gone.

As she stared into the empty front seat of the car, she heard the crunch of someone's foot on the gravel behind her, then a shot shattered the windshield next to her head. On instinct, Sasha rolled, hearing another shot as she righted herself and came up firing at the shape she saw five meters away. The burst from the AK-47 flattened Nibmar in the street. Sasha walked over and kicked the Ruger away from her. She felt for a pulse. Nothing. *Good riddance, bitch.* She picked up the Ruger and ran.

———◆———

Sasha waited in Saif's backyard for an hour before he arrived. "Are you okay?" he asked.

Sasha was so exhausted and emotionally spent that she only mustered a nod. "You?"

"I see you broke my car" was all he said as he opened the back door and motioned her in. "I'll need to borrow my father's to drive you back to Riyadh. It's a good thing you'll be sitting on my right, because I can't hear anything out of my left ear." They tiptoed into his study and closed the door. "You're a mess. I suppose the first thing you'll want to do is take a shower."

"No. The first thing I want to do is find out what exactly went on back there."

"I told you I'd met Khalid. And Abdul and Waleed. Perhaps I downplayed it a bit. They've been trying to recruit me since I returned from university. When I didn't hear or see anything after I set off the concussion grenade, I assumed they'd captured you. I knew it was risky to walk in there, but as you saw it didn't raise Khalid's suspicions. I just prayed to Allah that he had you stashed someplace where I could get to you."

"What would you have done if they hadn't put me in the back room?"

Saif shrugged. "I would have pulled the pin on the grenade and hoped either you or I woke up first."

Sasha let out a long sigh. She realized her hands were trembling, maybe only now appreciating how close she had come to dying. That, and catching up to the reality of what else she'd done in the last two days. She'd killed at least eight people. *God.* Where would her life go from here? *Who, what am I now?*

"What are you going to tell Yassar?"

"The truth."

"Everything?"

"I confessed worse to him this morning. Besides, he's the one who needs to reconcile himself to what Nibmar and Ali were planning. And to what Nibmar had been planning with Ibrahim. I'm sure that will be a blow. And I'm sure I can help him get past it." She felt the purity of her emotions as she said it, but her raw nerves gave her an ominous sense of a dark future.

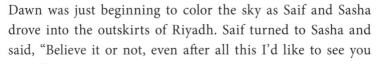

Dawn was just beginning to color the sky as Saif and Sasha drove into the outskirts of Riyadh. Saif turned to Sasha and said, "Believe it or not, even after all this I'd like to see you again."

Sasha smiled, placed her hand on top of his on the steering wheel and squeezed it.

CHAPTER 9

"So, HAVE I PASSED THE interview?" Sasha said to Archer, smiling.

Archer said, "So far." His eyes were dead as he motioned for Sasha to go on.

Nothing. The man's a stone. "It was two weeks later when I saw Saif next. He just showed up at the Royal Palace."

Sasha was there again, walking into the entry hall to Yassar's quarters, from which the Royal Guards had summoned her.

Saif was standing waiting for her. "You look disappointed to see me," he said, shifting his weight from foot to foot.

"No, but I thought you'd at least call first."

"Yeah. And ask for whom? Former concubine to Ibrahim? You're not exactly listed in the directory, and if I called the palace switchboard, you think Yassar would take my call?"

Sasha smiled, then relaxed. She took Saif in. He *was* good-looking, as she remembered him. High cheekbones, curly brown hair, a slim frame and an athletic build. Still no beard. Today he was dressed as a Saudi young man, white cotton shirt with three-quarter sleeves, black cotton pants. She could smell his cologne. She liked that, obviously done for her benefit. The awkward kid coming for the first date. "How are you?" she said.

"Good. Just a chap from the northern provinces hoping a sophisticated girl can show me around the big city."

Sasha rolled her eyes. "Laying it on a little thick, aren't you?"

"I sometimes have a little trouble breaking the ice."

"I'd say that concussion grenade you carried into the room in Buraida already broke the ice in spades." She walked over to him and took his arm. She whispered, "I don't believe I properly thanked you for saving my life. I suppose I was still in shock." She stopped, looked to see that no one was watching, then kissed him. She pulled away, looking into his eyes. "Thank you."

He smiled at her. "Is there somewhere we can go and talk?"

"I have a favorite spot in the gardens." She guided him into a corridor, then to a massive glass-domed botanical garden. They sat on a bench in the shade, the frosted glass on the top of the structure shielding them from the midday sun. The air was cool and damp, smelling of moss and orchids.

He still seemed awkward. "I'm not sure how to go about this here at the Royal Palace."

"It's not any different than anyplace else. You ask me out, we go to dinner, a movie, whatever. Only I wear my abaya and we don't touch in public. Not any different than in Buraida, I'm sure."

"I don't need Yassar's permission?"

"Only mine, and you have it." She paused, then said, "Why did you do it? Come back for me when I was being held in Buraida?"

He seemed surprised by her question. "I already told you. I admired your commitment, your willingness to put yourself on the line for what you believe in. I guess that's something I've been struggling with."

"How?"

"Even after seeing what's happened to my father and how that's also affected my mother, I've had trouble coming to terms with what direction I should take."

"Direction?"

"Abdul and Waleed and their cronies have been trying to recruit me to the al-Mujari. I've been torn, not because of any loyalty to the royals, but because I can't see getting myself pulled along by my nose like most of the other disaffected guys my age I see buying into their rhetoric."

"That's a good thing, isn't it? Not letting yourself get dragged mindlessly into it?"

"Of course. But it also leaves me feeling I'm not taking a stand one way or the other, not willing to believe strongly enough in anything to make a choice."

Sasha tilted her head, telling him to go on.

"It leaves me feeling I'm betraying my father in a way. Like I'm not willing to fight for him. Fight the way you've fought for Yassar."

Sasha was touched. After a moment Saif said, "How did it go with Yassar after you got back from Buraida?" Her stomach tensed, remembering how she'd felt as she faced Yassar to tell him about shooting both Ali and Nibmar. "Not well in the beginning. I'm sure you can imagine how crushing it was for him. Losing his two eldest sons and his first wife within 24 hours."

He took her hand.

She clasped her fingers through his, held tight. "Trust me, it was worse for him. Much worse. Not just facing the loss, but the reality of what they were plotting against him. He's still not himself. I'm not sure he ever will be again."

"Is he okay with you?"

"It's been hard." She looked up into Saif's eyes. "But I think I can be there for him in a way the rest of his family can't. In a way, I'm his oldest child now."

Archer was looking at Sasha impatiently, his elbows still on the rough-hewn table. "I hope you're not going to tell me about the whole 20 years. This is taking forever."

Sasha wanted to blast him, but held her tongue. "He saved my life," she said. "It's often said that people develop strong bonds after such experiences."

"I can imagine. Can't we cut to the chase? He saved your life and you thanked him in the finest way a concubine knows how, right?"

Sasha's anger flared. She leaned forward and spat her words at him. "What are you, an animal? Or is that part of how you're testing me? Either way it's incredibly crude. I should spit in your face. I don't need to take this disrespect from you."

Archer's neck receded into his shoulders. "I apologize," he said. "I *was* testing you. Because you'll need to listen to worse than that if we move forward. Including from Saif."

Sasha took a moment to calm herself, then continued with her story.

After Saif visited three more times, Sasha and he chatting and surreptitiously holding hands in the botanical gardens, walking the grounds of the Royal Palace, taking tea in the court-yard outside the women's quarters, Sasha began to wonder if this was going anyplace. Saif was young, sexy and available. She was 19, had become accustomed to daily sex for three years, and couldn't wait for Saif to put his hands on her. She assumed he felt the same way. *What in God's name is he doing?*

Over dinner the next time in town she put it to him. "I'm beginning to wonder if this is the type of Victorian courtship your stay in England led you to believe I expect."

He looked up from his lamb stew, open-mouthed, then laughed. "I already told you I don't know how to do this."

She smiled at him. "So at Eaton you sat in your dorm room and studied every night? Then read your Koran before going to bed at eight o'clock?"

"Yeah, right." He shook his head. "What I'm talking about is figuring out how to make a move on a woman who's effectively the daughter of a member of the ruling family of Saudi Arabia, here, in Riyadh, the capital, with all the ridiculous rules we have in Islam."

Now we're getting someplace. She reached under the table, found his knee, squeezed it. "So does this mean you're not gay after all?"

Saif's smile faded. He rose up in his chair and waved to the waiter. "Check," he said.

Sasha started to get upset, thinking she'd pushed him too hard. Was his ego that fragile?

Then he leaned forward and spoke in a whisper. "You're the most beautiful woman I've ever seen smoke a bunch of Islamic fundamentalist terrorists with a 9mm Ruger semi-automatic. Want to go up to my room at the hotel and knock me around?"

She laughed. "Only if you've got those little peanuts in the minibar."

Upstairs in Saif's room at the Hyatt, Sasha could hardly stand the tension. She was excited to finally be getting to it. She felt the ache for him in her bones as she took off her abaya. Standing in her street clothes, she said, "I need you to know I'm not experienced at this."

"You're hilarious."

She unbuttoned her blouse, then reached in and unhooked her bra. She walked over to him, her eyes locked on his, strutting, wanting him to see her desire. "I mean it. I've only been with one man before." She stopped in front of him and opened the buttons on his shirt, then held her blouse open and pressed her breasts against his chest. He pulled her to him and kissed her. She felt his command. She sighed, felt her legs weaken. *At last.* He walked her to the bed.

After they made love they napped. She awakened first and watched him as he slept. He was such a gentle lover, so responsive to her, reading her and sensing what she wanted. She felt a surge of desire for him again. He stirred, awakened and smiled at her.

After a few moments he said, "What was it like?"

"What?"

"Being a concubine?"

Her forearms tensed. "Not much of a romantic, are you?"

He shrugged.

She felt a burst of anger and rose up on one elbow, started to pull the sheet up over her breasts, then decided to flaunt them, thrust her chest out. *Enough.* She'd defuse this now or be done with him for good. "If you've got such a problem with it, why are you hanging around? Was this all you were looking for?"

"No, of course not. I've heard about that life, read about it, but it's just not something I've been exposed to firsthand before. It's such an unusual…" His voice trailed off.

"You can say it. 'Profession.'"

"That wasn't the word I was looking for. It's not like you were getting paid."

"Well, to be honest, I received a generous allowance. After three years, I'm rich by most people's standards."

He turned to face her. "Why did you do it?"

She studied his face. He looked troubled, even pained. *He can't get past the fact that I was a concubine.* If that was the case, so be it. "I've got nothing to hide, and I'm not ashamed of anything I've done. At the time I felt I didn't have any other options. With Christina casting me off, I really had no place else to go. In retrospect, I guess the whole concept was so surreal to me that I was suffering from some sense of unreality, and just sleepwalked into it. I never found out how much Yassar paid Christina for me. I suppose it doesn't really matter. I was horrified enough without knowing the amount. But I can remember having a Scarlett O'Hara moment before leaving Christina's chateau to fly with Yassar to Saudi Arabia." She laughed. "Remember that scene in *Gone with the Wind* where Scarlett is standing in the muddy field, a turnip in her hand, dirt under her fingernails and she swears to the heavens, 'As God is my witness, I'll never go hungry again'? Well, that day I felt consummately betrayed by both Christina and Yassar, and I swore I'd make enough money to get out and never let myself need anyone else again."

"What changed your mind?"

"Yassar."

"I'm surprised that you're still so close with him."

"We reestablished our relationship soon enough, after I learned the ways of the Muslim world." Sasha went back again in her mind to the months after she'd arrived in Saudi Arabia, Yassar schooling her in Islam, helping her with her Arabic, explaining to her the mysteries of Saudi culture. Finally, one day she decided to press him, to hear the apology that would allow her to purge her anger at his betrayal and accept him back into her heart. "Why did you do this to me?" she asked, averting her eyes and keeping her head bowed in the manner she'd learned of a submissive Saudi daughter.

Sasha sat cross-legged on a prayer mat on the floor of Yassar's study in the Royal Palace. She faced him where he sat on his own prayer mat in front of a *kursi*, the stand that held his Koran. They had just finished praying, cleansing themselves after her lesson in Islam. She waited for him to respond, still not making eye contact, giving him time. She heard the rustle of his robe as he got up and seated himself in his chair. She didn't move, waiting. He said, "Perhaps I didn't handle things as I might have. I want the best for my son, and I know he needs settling down if he is to be groomed for his role in one day running Saudi Arabia. I confess I was conflicted between that and my affection for you. In a way, Ibrahim is my biggest weakness. One day when you have children you will understand. If I was insensitive to your feelings I regret it."

It was as close to an apology as she would get. *Still Yassar.* She felt a release, a calmness—almost a sensation of her chest being stroked.

Yassar said, "Your experience of the world with Christina prepared you for this. It surpasses that of Ibrahim's." He paused.

She wanted to tell him Ibrahim's experience of the world consisted of bullying those around him, indulging his sexual desires and wasting his life on partying. She wanted to force Yassar to hear it, then press him harder, but resisted the urge to spur him on. *In his own time.*

"As such I thought you could help guide him, keep him out of trouble. And stand up to him with cleverness in a way the other girls couldn't. Undoubtedly you've observed, well…" He trailed off. "Sometimes a father cannot interfere directly with any productive result."

So he knows Ibrahim doesn't spend his time studying the Koran. And about the cocaine, too? She itched to meet his gaze, read what was in his eyes. She resisted.

He went on. "I long ago observed that despite your own lack of fear of the world and your fascination to try everything, you do have an ethical rudder. I need you to be Ibrahim's gyroscope, to straighten him out."

Sasha slowly raised her head, her jaw tense, eyes expectant. She met his gaze.

"Please," Yassar said. She saw the emotion in his eyes. They pleaded to her, not at all the eyes of one of the most wealthy and powerful men in the world. The eyes of a father, of her mentor, now telling her he was sorry, but asking more.

Sasha nodded, but she'd already told him with the tears in her eyes that she'd do what he asked.

For the next two months, Saif returned to Riyadh every Friday night, stayed at the Hilton, and returned to Buraida first thing Monday morning. After the first few weeks, Saif arranged with the concierge to have the same room, so that Sasha and he began to regard it as a little home away from home. One weekend early on, she asked him why they couldn't see each other during the week. He told her he was still looking for a job, that graduates in economics weren't in high demand. "Plenty of opportunities to flip hamburgers, though," he'd said. They both laughed about it, but Sasha sensed his frustration.

One weekend Sasha asked Saif if he could continue to afford the weekly hotel stays. He shrugged it off but she sensed his discomfort. From that point on, Sasha began bringing a hot plate in her luggage and bags of food to cook their breakfasts and dinners. The first weekend he protested, but Sasha prevailed. They'd empty the minibar and use it as their refrigerator.

In England, Saif had been introduced to Bordeaux wines. Sasha had always made certain the Royal Palace's cellar was stocked with the best burgundies. After dinner one evening, they lounged in bed, sipping a Charmes Chambertan.

"Did you have boyfriends in Switzerland?" Saif asked abruptly.

"Boys, yes. Who didn't? But I found the men who attended Christina's parties much more interesting. I had a few crushes."

"Anything serious?"

Sasha looked up at Saif and laughed. "Why are you asking me questions you might not want to hear the answers to?"

Saif didn't respond.

"If you must know, none of the men in Christina's circle ever touched me. I already told you: I'd only been with one man before you." She reached over and stroked his hair.

"What was it like?"

"Saif, I don't want to talk about that."

"I mean, what was it like being with Ibrahim after you learned he was planning to kill Yassar?"

Sasha looked off at the wall, experiencing it in her mind's eye. "Well before that, after Ibrahim had bought into Abdul and Waleed's nonsense, I made up my mind to take my money and get out."

"But you didn't."

"I felt I needed to convince Yassar that Ibrahim was choosing sides against him, against his way of life, before I could leave."

"And?"

"He couldn't hear me, just wouldn't accept it, so I stayed a little longer, then a little longer." She paused, seeing it in her mind, her emotions welling. "When Tom told me that Ibrahim was planning to murder Yassar for the al-Mujari, I couldn't leave. It wasn't long, only a few weeks, that I needed to swallow that horror—sleeping with Ibrahim to keep up appearances, stay close enough, until we could…" She paused. "… until *I* could kill him. That was an abomination I can't describe. The only reason I was able to do it was for Yassar." She felt sickened, remembering it as she spoke. Her face must have shown it, because Saif took her in his arms.

"I'm sorry I asked," he said. "I won't bring it up again."

After a moment Sasha said, "Sometimes I feel like you've got a checklist."

"Checklist?"

"You're ticking off items each week, trying to convince yourself it's okay to get involved with a woman who you consider sold her body."

He sat up in bed. "I never said that."

"Not in so many words. But for months you've been asking me about that life. Today you checked the box on teenage lovers. Then you hit the biggest box in the concubine/assassin column." She was staring him down, her jaw clenched, angry, and yet felt tears coming at the same time.

Saif let out a long sigh. "I don't want to argue."

"Neither do I."

"Tell me you love me," he said.

"What?" She felt her heart melt. *Oh, God, do I?* After thinking about this for so many months, did she want this?

She grabbed his face, pulled it to her and kissed him. "Oh, darling, do you feel the same?"

His smile told her, but she still needed to hear it. "I asked you first, sweetheart," he said. Then: "Yes, I love you.

It felt like an explosion of warmth in her heart. It was the first time a man had told her that. She pulled his face to hers, kissed him. "Oh, darling, I love you, too."

A month later, Sasha sat on the same bench in the botanical garden where Saif and she had talked on his first visit to the Royal Palace. Now the place always made her smile. It was the scent of the orchids here that inspired Saif to choose his nickname for her: Western Orchid. Her mind was twisting with thoughts, her emotions in a tangle. Her instincts told her it was all wrong with Saif. They seemed to be living a shadow life, eating alone in restaurants or in his hotel room, hardly ever going out in Riyadh during the days. She couldn't complain about his attentiveness to her, or the urgency of his lovemaking, but they seemed to be living in a bubble, away from the rest of the world. He'd never taken her to Buraida, never introduced her to any of his friends, or even spoken of introducing her to his parents. She'd reached the point of wanting to introduce him to Yassar, but couldn't bring herself to ask Saif because she sensed Saif wouldn't hear of it.

She realized it wasn't all Saif's doing. Aside from Nafta, one of her fellow concubines, and Yassar, she wasn't close to anyone in Riyadh. So she wasn't in a position to propose dinners or outings with other couples. She felt stuck, one leg in and then one leg out of her former life as a concubine. If there was a lack of complete fulfillment to her first love, it wasn't something she could blame on Saif. She'd brought a lot of baggage to the table.

Two weekends in a row, Sasha and Saif argued. On the first he left on Sunday afternoon, leaving Sasha with half-cooked *kabsa* on the hot plate. On the second, they went to bed on Sunday night not speaking to each other, and Saif got up early on Monday morning and left without awakening Sasha.

Sasha went into the next weekend tentative. On Friday evening before Saif arrived, her emotions were raw. She paced in her room in the Royal Palace as she waited for him, thinking that this wasn't the way it was supposed to be. She'd never had a serious relationship like this before, but this tension wasn't bearable in the long term without clearing the air in some way.

She was grateful that Saif insisted they eat out at a restaurant that night; it was less stressful than preparing the meal herself. They went back to the room and made love, Sasha giving herself to him as freely as ever. Afterward, she propped herself up on one elbow and said, "I've been upset all week. We've been fighting a lot and I can't understand why. Is it you or me?"

"I don't think we can point fingers. I know I've been stressed. Part of the reason is I can't find a job."

"I'd been meaning to ask you about that."

"You haven't in weeks," he said, sounding bitter.

Sasha pulled her hand away, her feelings hurt. After a moment she said, "I've been thinking about it. Thinking about asking Yassar. He has a number of economists on his staff at the Ministry."

"I thought you said talking to Yassar about me was too sensitive a subject, given that I was involved when Nibmar and Ali were killed up in Buraida."

"I've told him all about you, and he's even agreed to allow us to stay together in the Royal Palace."

Saif shrugged. "Great, so that's one step closer to you asking him about me taking a job for him and the people that are running my father's company out of business."

Sasha's back stiffened. "That's not fair. Yassar is doing all he can to support people like your father. He's created a jobs program, he's pushing for unemployment programs to tide people over until they're on they're feet again, and his Ministry is sponsoring educational loans."

"The royals are driving my father into his grave!"

"Is Yassar responsible for anything done by any royal? You can't lump them all together."

"Why not? They run everything. We've become a nation of haves and have-nots."

"You're starting to sound like Ibrahim after Abdul and Waleed got to him."

Saif got out of bed and started pulling his clothes on. "Maybe I am. Maybe Ibrahim wasn't brainwashed like you keep insisting. Maybe he finally saw the inequity and felt he had an obligation to do something about it."

"Starting with murdering his own father?"

That shut him up. He paused, standing beside the bed, his pants halfway up, looking ridiculous. Sasha laughed at him. That made him angrier. He pulled his pants up and turned away from her as he started putting on his shirt.

"So now you don't just have a problem with me, you've got a problem with Yassar?"

He spun around. "What do you mean, a problem with you?"

"The problem you've always had, that I was a concubine. You've never gotten past it."

"Oh, so the subject is off-limits if I want to bring it up, but you can throw it out there any time you want?"

"Admit it. You'll never let yourself be with me in the long run," she said, realizing she was having trouble using the right words, then pushing through it. "You'll never marry me, because you think I was once a whore. That's it, isn't it?"

He turned his back to her and continued dressing.

Sasha's stomach muscles tensed with rage. "Don't you dare turn your back on me! I'm talking to you!"

Saif spun around and glared at her, then turned back to face the wall again.

"Get out!"

Saif had finished dressing. He turned and said, "So now think you can throw me out of my own room?"

"Get out of Riyadh and don't come back!"

"Oh, Little Miss Royal, banishing me from your capital." He leered at her. "I'm going out for a while. When I come back to pick up my things, I'll expect you to be gone." He walked out, slamming the door behind him.

Sasha felt no urge to cry, but only a sense of liberation. *You're damn right I won't be here when you get back.*

Archer said, "So that was it?"

"I only wish it had been. It went on for months like that. In the end, he called me one week and said he was coming to Riyadh, staying at the Hilton as usual, as if nothing was amiss."

It was quiet in the restaurant, one Saif hadn't taken her to before. The lights were low and they were playing American soft rock music on the speakers. It reminded her of one of the radio stations she'd heard in Paris. Trying to be cool, but five or six years behind the times. She figured it out before he started talking: a quiet, well-populated restaurant, where it would be difficult for either of them to start any fireworks.

"How is your steak?" he asked.

"A little overdone, but tolerable."

He looked concerned, more so than usual, as if making a display of it. "You want me to send it back?"

Sasha didn't look up from her plate. She shook her head. She was waiting.

After another minute or two he got around to it. "I think we should talk."

Now she looked up. "I gathered that's why we're here." From the novels she'd read as a teenager, she felt as if her heart should be breaking, feeling some sense of agony. *Nothing.* She met his gaze, still waiting.

"I think you would agree we've had some difficulties."

Sasha decided he should do this in his own time. She should neither push him nor drag it out. She nodded.

"I've been very troubled over the last few months. I love you, you know that, but I just don't think it's working."

Now she felt a sagging sensation in her chest, as if she wanted him to hurry up, not so much for her, but to make it easier for him. She knew they were through, although she felt oddly detached from it.

"I think we have too many differences. Too many incongruities."

The word struck her. She raised her eyebrows. "Incongruities?"

"I mean, we're from different worlds. Not just Buraida and Riyadh, but you're a royal, I'm from the Shiite North, a working stiff, as the Brits would say it." He smiled for the first time.

Sasha smiled back, reached across the table for his hand. He started to pull away, but left it and she placed hers on top of his, squeezed it. "Go on," she said, her eyes soft.

"We have different opinions about things, too. You know I've been torn about my father's business, and what that means in terms of where Saudi Arabia is going." He looked down at his plate.

She waited, and then when he didn't continue, she said, "Saif, I'm not surprised by this. It's okay."

He nodded without looking up, then raised his head and met her gaze. "I think we've reached the point where this isn't going anywhere anymore. Regardless of how we both feel."

Now Sasha felt the pain in her chest, as if someone were stomping on her heart. She realized this wasn't going to be easy for her. Still, she raised her chin and said, "I know." She couldn't help that her voice was trembling and tears started flushing into her eyes. She looked back down at her plate, carved another slice from her steak and put it into her mouth. They ate in silence for another ten minutes. Sasha noticed that the candle on the table had burned out, smelled the wax as the smoke from the extinguished flame wafted upward. She wondered if that scent would always remind her of tonight. She didn't look up at Saif until the waiter came to clear their plates and asked if they wanted dessert. Saif waved him off. Now Saif's face was somber, his eyes misty, too.

They rode home in a cab to the Royal Palace in silence, holding hands. He kissed her, then said, "Good-bye, my Western Orchid."

She hugged him, her mouth pressed to his ear and whispered, "Good-bye, my love."

Tom checked his watch. It'd been forty-five minutes since he and Ryan had left the room to let Archer and Sasha talk. *It's time.*

He walked back to the door and knocked, then entered. Archer was hunched over at his end of the table, looking at Sasha like a stern teacher. Sasha looked pensive, maybe even upset. He saw her eyes were teary. *What's all this?*

Archer turned. "We're just finishing," he said.

Tom walked to the center of the table and sat down. A moment later Ryan entered and sat across from him. Sasha was looking at Tom like maybe she was annoyed. "Everything okay?" he said to her.

Sasha said, "As he said, we're almost finished."

"What she means is, we're getting through everything we need to, but we aren't getting along very well."

Tom glanced at Archer, saw him look at Sasha.

"Right?" Archer said to Sasha.

Sasha said, "Let's just say my new colleague is an animal."

"I've been called worse," Archer said.

"No doubt," Sasha said.

Tom looked back and forth at each of them, figuring he'd let them go on for a while if they needed to. Finally he said to Sasha, "All part of the process."

No one spoke for a few moments. Ryan cleared his throat, said, "Well," and opened his mouth to speak. Tom shook his head at him. Ryan kept his mouth shut.

After another moment, Archer turned to Tom and said, "I won't do it. I won't risk my life for some emotional woman seeking closure with her former lover. She's living in the past. She doesn't know Saif as he is today."

Tom glanced over at Sasha, saw her ball her hands into fists.

Archer said, "Besides, you don't have a plan. You expect me to bring her in to Saif with no idea what happens beyond that. It's absurd."

Tom said, "That's one of the reasons we're here today. To start developing a plan." He assumed that Sasha would have at least started working that out with Archer. *Apparently not.*

Sasha said, "Once I get inside, I'll improvise, as I always do."

"He'll slit your throat, or cast you off to his men to do with you what they please."

"I don't think so," Sasha said.

"I'm under deep cover, my life on the line. I'm not in a position to sit by and see if your sentimental notions of his memories of you as his lover cause him to spare your life."

"I'm not working off of sentimental notions."

Tom's head was going back and forth to each of them as they spoke, like at a tennis match.

Archer said, "I think perhaps you've lost your mind."

"We'll see."

"No, we won't. Because I'm not risking my life for you."

Tom looked at Sasha and said, "This is the one subject we haven't talked about yet. What do you propose to do once you're inside?"

"I just told you, I'm not sure. I'll improvise." Her eyes were intense. "All that matters is that I kill him."

"You're awfully confident," Archer said.

"I get that a lot."

Tom said, "You have to admit it's thin. Risking your own life is one thing, asking Archer to risk his is another."

Sasha looked Tom in the eye. She said, "I haven't told you everything. The shooter said something else to me other than Saif's name. He said Saif wanted me back. He's not going to kill me, or turn me over to his men for sport."

Archer said, "That's moronic. The shooter could have just decided to say that."

"The shooter used Saif's pet name for me. Only Saif could have told it to the man."

Tom said, "Pet name?"

"The shooter said, 'Saif wants his Western Orchid back at his side.'"

———◇———

Tom took note that Sasha was unusually quiet on the helicopter flight back to Riyadh. *Whatever it is, I'm sure I'll hear about it shortly.* After their driver dropped off Ryan, she turned to Tom in the backseat of the embassy car and said, "You could have given me a heads-up."

"About?"

"That I'd be getting cross-examined by Attila the Hun in there."

That's all. "Like I said back there, it's part of the process. He pushed you pretty hard?"

"Like I said back there, he's an animal."

"To do what he's doing, he has to be. Besides, you sold him in the end when you told him about the Western Orchid comment the shooter made, didn't you? You convinced him that Saif wouldn't automatically have you shot on sight."

Sasha nodded.

"He's cleared you, so we're good to go. His name is Rashid al-Abdel. And don't be so hard on him. He's got his own reasons for wanting Saif taken out—all of the al-Mujari, for that matter. His younger brother was recruited as a suicide bomber by the al-Mujari seven years ago. The kid's in paradise now with his 100 virgins. And about six months later his older brother and his wife, daughter and baby son were killed on a bus in Riyadh full of American soldiers by another suicide bomber. So whether you know it or not, you two are kindred spirits."

CHAPTER 10

AMIR SAT IN THE SHADOWS between two houses, feeling the cool of the Saudi night, the breeze on his face. The stars illuminated his line of sight 100 meters to Saif's house, and back up the street another 200 meters. Two SUVs cruised up and stopped fifty meters from Amir, engines idling. A light went on briefly in one of them, but he couldn't get a glimpse inside. Was it the Secret Police?

He wrote a text to Saif: "SP, 100 METERS, MOVING TO YOU," got ready to send it, then decided he needed to be sure. He opened the gate and walked out from between the buildings, heading toward the SUVs, his mouth dry, sweat on his forehead. The breeze whipped up the sand and he could feel it sticking to his face. He kept his eyes straight ahead. Thirty meters now. He thought of the imam, Sheik Qahtani, what he said about paradise and the virgins who would await him. He felt the grenade inside the left pocket of his windbreaker, cradling it like he'd been taught, so it wouldn't sag conspicuously. He held the disposable cell phone in his right windbreaker pocket, his thumb on the SEND button.

Ten meters now. He fingered the grenade, slipped his thumb inside the ring. He thought of his older brother, Syed, from his father's second wife, who had declined when the imam had offered the opportunity to serve. Syed had ridiculed Amir when he'd accepted and gone for weapons training for two months in Madinah Province. Now what would Syed say? Little, insignificant Amir, intervening to protect Saif and preserve their path to glorification.

There is no God but Allah, he prayed.

He was abreast of the nose of the first SUV, facing toward him in the direction of Saif's house. Light gray Mercedes, both of them—identical. He darted a glance inside. *Nothing. Tinted glass.* His breath came in short gasps, waiting to hear a door open, the sound of a man telling him to stop. He passed the first SUV, now abreast of the front door of the second. *Still nothing.* He held his pace.

He was past both SUVs now. No sound, no movement. It had to be the Secret Police. *Send it*, he told himself, still with his hand on the cell phone button. He heard the sound of an engine revving, turned back to see the first, then the second SUV moving away from him toward Saif's house. He hit SEND, saw the SUVs picking up speed. He turned back and forced himself to continue walking at the same pace.

His virgins would wait for another day.

Saif stood in his backyard, admiring the stars, breathing the cool air of the Saudi evening. But for the breeze a perfect evening. He heard the ping of a text message, pulled out his cell phone, saw nothing. He felt rising alarm, then pulled out the disposable cell phone from his other pocket. *SP, 100 METERS, MOVING TO YOU.* Now a burst of adrenaline. He darted behind his house, thinking of Noor and Indira, then his brother, Farid, and his family inside the house. *No time.* Had they come simply to toss the place or was it a death squad? He felt a spasm in his chest, then leaped the fence into the neighbor's yard, running parallel to the street. He kept moving, leaping fences. From three houses down the street he heard vehicles, saw the headlight beams, the sound of tires skidding to a stop in the dirt of the street. Saif turned ninety degrees and headed toward the street when he saw the headlights from two more SUVs approaching from the other direction. He turned around, jumped the fence and headed toward the street behind his, hoping they hadn't the foresight to cover the rear.

Five minutes later Saif started the Land Rover hidden four blocks away and turned it toward the center of Buraida, driving as fast as he dared without attracting attention. Then the thought of Qahtani being targeted at the same time caused him to clench his stomach muscles and press down on the accelerator. Would they go to the mosque or his house? *Both, you fool*, he told himself. He slowed for a moment, then reached under the seat for the AK-47 stashed there. He got to the intersection 200 meters from the mosque and saw four vehicles parked in front, headlights trained on the door. *Too late.* Or had his spotters gotten word to Kassem and Tewfiq, Qahtani's bodyguards?

He turned right and gunned the engine toward Qahtani's house. *Ridiculous*, he decided. He took a left and headed for the safe house in the northeast quadrant of Buraida.

They'd planned for this, but were never sure when to expect it. It was bound to happen now that they had broadened the discussions with the other Islamic dissident groups, the Ikwan, the Islamic Revolutionary Party, and the Muslim Brotherhood. And with their meetings with the clerics and Koranic scholars to convince them Qahtani was the Mahdi, sooner or later there would be a leak, and obviously it had happened. He felt a bolt of alarm as he saw a flash in the rearview mirror. Headlights behind him. Was it a tail or just another car?

He was now a quarter kilometer away from the safe house. He turned off the street, headed north up an alley and pressed the accelerator to the floor, checking the rearview mirror. *Nothing.* He kept going straight, then saw headlights behind him turn down the alley, and then another set. He pulled up behind the safe house. *Fool.* He'd led them right to it. He leaped out of the Land Rover carrying the AK-47 and the sack of grenades from under the seat. He pounded on the back door. Someone flung it open and he ran inside, smelling the oil from weapons. He saw Qahtani, ten other men. They would have to be enough. He waved three men to the front, two of them scared boys whose names he forgot and the other Rashid. Rashid was a steady hand who could calm the boys. The rest of the men he waved toward him. He found Kassem and Tewfiq.

"Stay with the Mahdi," he ordered them.

He turned back to the door, stood inside until he heard the SUVs almost upon them. He waited, feeling his nerves dancing with anticipation. Or fear?

This is it.

He ran out into the alley, holding aloft the AK-47 in one hand, the bag of grenades in the other. He passed through the headlights and crouched behind the Land Rover. He waited for the other six men to pull up behind him, then leaned over the hood and opened fire into the windshield of the first SUV. The Secret Police had angled their SUVs sideways as a firing screen. He saw the far side doors open and then the flashes of return fire. The windshield of the Land Rover shattered and glass flew everywhere. The Land Rover shook from the bullets slamming into it. Saif pulled the pins on two grenades and lobbed one at each SUV, then retrieved his AK-47 and kept firing. The return fire stopped for a moment after the grenades exploded, then resumed, the noise now muffled in Saif's ears from the blast of the grenades. A man next to him was slapped backward like a doll, his head exploding. Saif felt moisture on his face and wiped it away. He smelled gasoline and then the Land Rover's gas tank exploded, the concussion knocking him over backward. He felt for the AK-47, righted himself and started firing blindly through the flames.

There was less return fire now. Only two starbursts of flame from the rear SUV. He threw two more grenades over the top of the SUV. He waited for the first to explode, then yelled, "Now!" and ran toward the SUV. From the corner of his eye he saw four of his men follow him. He prayed to Allah the clip on the AK-47 would hold out. After the second grenade exploded he rounded the rear SUV and saw four men down, three in a pile. Saif walked up to them, his AK-47 trained. He kicked the men. No movement. He turned to his men behind him and waved the all clear.

He looked at the SUV, riddled with bullets, the windows blown out and the tires on this side both flat. "See if it starts," he called out to Omar, one of his men, pointing to the other SUV. Omar climbed into it, then out, shaking his head. Saif heard a sound behind him, spun and saw a man pulling to his knees from underneath two others piled on top of him. He heard the click of the man's assault rifle, then two more in quick succession. *Empty clip, praise be to Allah.* Saif lunged toward the man and smashed him in the head with his rifle butt. The man collapsed to the ground, unconscious.

"One's alive," Saif called out. "Bring him. Hurry!" He ran back to the side of the safe house and shot the lock off the wooden doors next to it. He opened them and ran to the Land Rover parked behind them.

"Bring the Mahdi." Saif climbed into the Land Rover and started it. Kassem and Tewfiq brought Qahtani with them into the backseat. Two men dived in the rear with the prisoner, another in the passenger seat, and Saif drove off. The others would have to disperse, fend for themselves.

As he speeded through Buraida he thought, *Now it's on.* The time for talk and preparations was over.

———◇———

The next morning, Tom was working on his laptop in the conference room when Ryan walked in, looking grave. Tom leaned back from his computer when he saw Ryan's face. "What's wrong?"

"You aren't going to like this." Ryan sat down across the table from Tom. "I just got word from the field that last night the Secret Police hit Saif's house, Qahtani's house and the mosque Qahtani operates from. They didn't get either of them, but a team of two Secret Police cruisers, eight men, followed an SUV into an alley and got into a firefight before backup could arrive. Seven men killed, one either escaped or was taken prisoner. Three other unidentified bodies were at the scene, as well as the SUV they must have been following. Everyone else escaped. We haven't been able to get a hold of Rashid yet, but we think it was Saif and his men who attacked the Secret Police."

Tom's legs felt heavy. He wondered again, as he had after hearing yesterday about the fatwa addressing dissidents, if somehow Yassar was involved in this. Whatever brought it about, Ryan was right. It wasn't good news. This would drive Saif deep underground, make it much more difficult to locate him. It also might be a catalyst for the launch of an uprising. On the other hand, seven Secret Police dead would make Saif a wanted man, probably Qahtani, too.

"I'm calling Yassar," Tom said.

"It would be better if we spoke in person," Yassar said when Tom phoned him at his office in the Royal Palace. "I will come to you." "Fine. I'm at the American Embassy." Tom hung up, seething. He detected from Yassar's voice that he knew more about the Secret Police's attempted raids than he'd admitted. In Yassar's position he would have to know; he may have even ordered them. It made sense. It was too much of a coincidence right after Tom got Yassar up to speed on the seriousness of what Saif and Qahtani were up to. *But why didn't he tell me?* They could have worked together, coordinated it.

Calm down, he told himself, realizing he was clutching the edge of the conference table. He had some explaining to do himself, too. He hadn't exactly been forthright with Yassar, hadn't let him know he was in Saudi Arabia yet, and had brought Sasha with him. He also owed Yassar an answer to the proposal he made in the Caymans. That was too important to screw up, so Tom couldn't show his anger over Yassar going around him and driving Saif deeper underground. He stood up, started pacing, then sat back down, realizing that would only get him more worked up. He realized he'd have to suck it in, smile, maybe even kiss Yassar's ass when he got there, despite the fact that the previous night's events had messed up Tom's operation. He frowned. Not things he was good at. *There's a reason you work for the CIA instead of the State Department.*

A half hour later, an embassy aide walked Yassar into the conference room. Yassar was dressed in his Saudi robe and headdress, his face expressionless. *All business.* They shook hands and Yassar sat down. The aide closed the door on the way out.

"I was unaware you were on Saudi soil," Yassar said in a monotone, drumming his fingers on the table.

"I was gonna let you know in a day or so. We arrived yesterday morning and we're just getting organized."

"Where is Sasha?"

"Downstairs training."

Yassar didn't respond.

Tom said, "I gather she hasn't called you. Sorry, I know you're—"

"That is a matter between Sasha and me. Please do not intrude."

Tom leaned back in his chair and put his hands up as if to apologize. He could understand how Yassar might be pissed at Sasha. He imagined that if he had a daughter, or someone he treated like one, and she hadn't called in 18 months and then dropped in without saying anything, he'd be pissed, too. "I apologize," Tom said. "Let's talk about Saif. I heard from one of our men in the field about the fatwa that was recently issued about dissenters. Was that why the Secret Police raids were ordered last night?"

Yassar hesitated, then said, "The fatwa was limited in its authority, and doesn't extend beyond arresting and holding those who are fomenting dissent. It is an effort to slow things down, reduce tensions while our other efforts to mollify our citizens have time to take effect. We have put steps in place to provide additional financial support for the Saudi people under the assumption we will strike an agreement such as the one you and I discussed in the Cayman Islands, either with the United States or another sponsor."

"Since you raised it, I'm authorized to tell you that we'll accept your proposal. My director is working out the details."

Yassar smiled. "I'm pleased," he said, and then his smile disappeared. "In concept. Obviously I will wait to hear something more concrete within the time frame we discussed."

Message received. "I understand. That's our intention." Tom wanted to move on, because he didn't have more to offer on the subject. He figured he'd see how far he could push Yassar on Saif. "Getting back to Saif, I was told seven of your Secret Police were killed last night. I would imagine that makes Saif a wanted man and our job easier."

"How so?"

"It sounds like our primary job now is just to locate him. Certainly the fact that he and his men murdered seven of your people would justify your disposing of him."

Yassar raised his eyebrows.

"A cruise missile or smart bomb strike is all it would take. I know you have that technology. We sold it to you."

"I thought I was just very clear. Our fatwa does not extend that far. It might be different if we had proof that Saif was responsible for the men's deaths, but we do not. Our men radioed that they were following a car, with no knowledge of who was in it."

"Yeah, but with a little embellishment, this should give you what you need."

"It's too public, and besides, we have our religious leaders to deal with. We take such things seriously." Yassar shifted in his seat. "I have thought long and hard about your plan with Sasha. I see it as perhaps the only workable solution for the moment."

"So then you could give us support for our operation?"

"The most I can offer is that I will look the other way, and do anything I can to throw our people off the track if they uncover your efforts and prepare to intervene."

"And what about Sasha? You won't try to stop her?"

Yassar averted his eyes. "The fact that I haven't heard from her means she is not receptive to what she obviously knows will be my opinion on the subject. The woman has her own mind."

Tom didn't buy it. He thought Yassar would still try to talk her out of it. He had a bad feeling about it, even though he'd looked in Sasha's eyes and seen her resolve.

In the rocky hills 20 miles northeast of Buraida, Saif pulled his kerchief tighter over his face against the windblown sand and dirt. He could taste it, feel the red earth's gritty texture in his mouth. He watched his men struggle against the wind to set up the camouflage screen on poles above the tents of their camp. The camp was a half mile from the paved highway, and a few hundred yards from the dirt side road, down the slope and around the corner under a rocky promontory. Out of sight except from the air, and in another 30 minutes the 40 x 60 foot main tent, a half dozen smaller tents and their dozens of SUVs would be concealed from aircraft or satellite cameras by the camouflage screen as well.

He wanted to help them wrestle with the poles, ropes and spikes, but he decided that might undermine their perception of his command. There were times when he could make a statement by pitching in, but this wasn't one of them. So he watched, occasionally leaning this way or that in sympathy as they tugged and struggled. His disposable cell phone rang.

"Yes?"

"We know where Fahd is."

"Get him and bring him to me," Saif said and hung up. He both dreaded and welcomed the news. Fahd was in his early 30s, the prime of life, with a wife and two children. An otherwise good man, a loyal follower, quiet and barely noticed, who had now distinguished himself as a coward, deserting his surveillance post outside Qahtani's mosque at the time the Secret Police had arrived. He'd fled, apparently in panic, with no warning message, and failed to report with his weapon to the safe house. It was unforgivable, and Fahd must be used as an example, even though it pained Saif.

———◆———

Fahd heard the afternoon call to prayers as he sat on a bench in the dark of the shed behind his brother's house on the outskirts of southwestern Buraida. The heat inside the tiny space was almost unbearable, and yet he felt grateful for it, accepting it as appropriate as partial atonement for his failure. He had no prayer rug, so he knelt on the dirt floor, facing west toward Mecca, and began to pray. After he finished, Fahd felt his way to the bench again in the dim light coming through cracks between the boards of the shed. He sat, leaned forward and placed his head in his hands and wept. He wept with anguish over how his wife, Nilofar, and his children, Ahmed and Toomi, would receive the news, and with relief that he would be able to compensate for his failure without shaming his family. After a few minutes he stood and walked out the door of the shed, squinting against the sun. Then he opened his brother's gate and entered the street. He began walking, knowing they would find him in time, hoping it wouldn't take long. Against his will, his tears began to flow again.

There is no God but Allah, he prayed as he walked.

He heard a vehicle behind him. He turned to see a pickup truck drive up and stop a few feet from him. Two men—his friend, Rashid, behind the wheel, and another man he didn't recognize—were in the cab. Rashid nodded to Fahd. The other man got out and stepped toward him. Something snapped inside Fahd. He felt a pull at his heart and saw the image of the face of his son, Ahmed, then felt fire in his brain. He screamed, "No!" turned and ran. A few moments later the man tackled him. He screamed, "No, no, no!" and thrashed his legs, punched, flailed and scratched to break free and then Rashid was upon him too, stuffing a rag into his mouth, then swinging a board at him. He felt the thud of it hitting his head once, twice, then blackness.

Saif was just leaving the main tent when the pickup truck entered the camp and stopped in front of him. His pulse shot up when he saw Fahd slumped between Rashid and Hassan, his hands bound, mouth gagged and face and head bloodied. Rashid climbed out from behind the wheel, looked at Saif for a long moment, then walked to the other side of the cab and helped Hassan drag Fahd, sobbing, his feet dangling beneath him, toward the tent. Saif reentered the tent and pointed to one corner, where a rug was placed in front of a video camera.

Saif called out, "My brothers. You must all bear witness." He set his jaw and puffed out his chest as he walked into the center of the throng of 150 men in the tent, glaring at anyone who would look him in the eye. He turned, parting the group, and walked to the corner where Rashid and Hassan now placed Fahd in a kneeling position on the rug in front of the video camera. They removed his gag and bindings. Rashid walked behind the camera and turned on floodlights. Saif nodded to Rashid and Rashid walked toward the rear of the tent.

Saif called out, "There is no God but Allah!" as he walked behind Fahd and faced the camera.

"*La ilaha ilallah!*" the men repeated.

Saif leaned down and whispered in Fahd's ear, "Stop braying like a donkey. You are shaming your family. Are you a loyal servant of Allah? On the one true path?" Fahd nodded his head furiously. Saif could see himself in the video monitor placed on the ground beneath the camera tripod. He paced back and forth behind Fahd, making certain he stayed within the frame of the camera. Saif's pulse was now pounding, his arms trembling with intensity. Not his first performance, but his first as commander in war. He channeled Rickman as he paced, looking toward the heavens and rolling his eyes back. He pulled his lips back from his teeth in a grimace, shaking his fists in the air. "My brothers! We are now at war. A holy war against the already rotting flesh of the al-Asad royals, who have defiled the two holiest sites in Islam with their decadent alliance with the infidel West, and who must be pushed from the Saudi peninsula into the sea, and all traces of their existence wiped from our holy soil. The Mahdi has come. He is among us and it is almost time for him to reveal himself to the believers. He has come to redeem us from the infidels, to restore the one true Islam to the Muslim world, to exalt the righteous and punish the infidels.

"The prophecies say we will be victorious if we are virtuous and if we follow the one true path. The path the Mahdi guides us on. There is no God but Allah!"

"*La ilaha ilallah!*" the men shouted.

Saif turned around and picked up the sword that had been placed behind him on the bench. He began pacing back and forth again, waving the sword as he spoke. "Yes, we are at war. The Mahdi will lead us on our virtuous path, instruct us how to destroy our enemies, the enemies of the one true Islam." Rashid led two men who dragged the Secret Police prisoner with them. His eyes showed terror. Saif leaned over again and said to Fahd, "On your feet." Fahd jumped to his feet, then turned to face Saif. Saif handed him the sword. Fahd looked confused, then his mouth fell open and his eyes went wide. Rashid pushed the prisoner to his knees in front of Fahd. Saif said to Fahd, "Now show us you are among the righteous." He grabbed him by the shoulders and turned him around. He yelled to his men, "The death of our enemy will purify our souls. There is no God but Allah!"

"*La ilaha ilallah!*" the men shouted.

Fahd stood over the man, hyperventilating, staring at the sword. His body shook as he let out an animal howl, swinging the sword. The prisoner's head fell sideways and his body toppled after it. The men roared. Saif held his arms aloft and pumped them, urging them on. Fahd turned, with sweat, blood and a look of horror on his face. Saif took the sword from him and said, "Now die like a man and go to paradise with your soul purified by the blood of your enemy." He pushed Fahd to his knees again. Fahd angled his head forward, accepting his fate.

Saif yelled above the men, "We are the warriors of Allah. And as warriors, we cannot tolerate any among us who would shrink from his duty." Saif affected a wild-eyed stare at his men, now spitting as he spoke, channeling Rickman onstage as Henry V. "Shrink from his duty to Allah, to the Mahdi, and to his fellow warriors in the purification of the Muslim world. We are the righteous! There is no God but Allah!"

"*La ilaha ilallah!*" the men shouted.

Saif now grasped the sword in both hands, closed his eyes and turned his body as he swung it back to his right, praying to Allah for a clean kill, instant death and a dramatic finish to the tape with Fahd's head severed in a single blow. He tensed all his muscles, opened his eyes and swung from his hips, his arms hurling the sword forward. Allah rewarded him. The sword swung through. Fahd's head floated in the air momentarily and then flopped on the ground in front of his body in full view of the camera. Fahd's body tilted sideways, then thudded to the ground. Saif felt blood on his face, held the sword aloft and shouted, "There is no God but Allah!"

"*La ilaha ilallah!*" the men roared.

Saif tossed the sword aside and stood with his legs apart, arms raised, to the sound of his men cheering. Cheering to Allah, to the Mahdi and to him.

Sasha rode the elevator from the basement to the second floor of the embassy, trying to frame her thoughts. Tom had just pulled her out of weapons training, over Seth's objection, telling her that Yassar was in the conference room and wanted to see her immediately. She'd thrown her black abaya over her skintight workout leotard, knowing that exposing every contour of her body would offend Yassar's modesty. She was twisted up inside, aching to see Yassar, yet dreading what she expected would be a lecture over her inconsiderate behavior, probably deserved.

Yassar was now in his early 70s, and while he was still as active as ever at the Ministry and in the Council of Ministers, he lived more for the moments with his children, derived his highest emotional rewards through their triumphs and loves. This must be what it felt like to have a real father, one who grew more emotionally needy as he grew older. Even a few years ago, she'd found that Yassar had begun to need more pampering, wanted her to fuss over him. And while she loved him like no one else in the world, that sometimes could be a burden.

Eighteen months. She would really have to sit through an earful. She then felt a rush of shame at thinking that.

Yassar was seated at the table when she entered the room. He stood, his great, graying head a little grayer, his posture perhaps more stooped. He smiled, and she felt a swell of emotion. "Yassar!" She rushed across the room and hugged him, burying her face in his robe against his barrel chest. He stroked her hair, then leaned down and kissed her forehead. She walked him back to his chair and sat him down. She pulled up another chair facing his and sat, her knees touching his.

"My dear, I'm concerned about you. I haven't heard from you since your call from Switzerland after Daniel's murder."

His words were like a spear in her heart. "I'm sorry, Yassar."

"And to learn of this reckless idea of yours about Saif third-hand? With no opportunity to counsel you?" His face looked pained.

I've hurt him more than I thought. "I knew you'd forbid it. That's why I didn't call." Sasha leaned farther forward and took one of his giant hands in hers, kissed it, then looked up into his eyes. "You know how much I value your advice."

"Hardly, based on recent behavior."

It hit home. *God, is he going to pull out all the arrows in his guilt quiver?* Sasha felt her throat start to burn and her eyes tear up.

Yassar looked into her eyes and said, "You know how worried I am about you with what you're planning to do, don't you?"

"Oh, Yassar." She looked away.

"Why must it be you? Can't you let Tom find someone else?"

"I have to." She felt her mouth contort. "For Daniel."

"What if you're wrong? What if Saif does want to kill you? You'll be walking right into it. It's an insane idea." His eyes were earnest, pleading.

"It's the only way I'll feel I've set things right." She wanted to tell him she didn't care what happened to her, but knew that would only make him worry more.

"What about your teachings? What would your guru say?"

"He would pray for me. As I know you will." She stood up and hugged him where he sat. She felt him sigh, his muscles release, resigned to her decision. She'd known it would turn out this way, but knew she must at least allow him his say. She stepped around behind his chair, wrapped her arms around him and pressed her face against his cheek. They stayed in that position a while, neither of them speaking.

Finally, Yassar stood up and said, "I must speak to Tom." He walked directly out of the room. Five minutes later Tom walked in and said, "What did you say to him?"

She didn't respond, just looked at him, puzzled.

"Yassar just told me he's having Assad, the head of the Secret Police, contact me to provide us intelligence on Saif, everything they've got, including ongoing updates. And he'll make as many men available to us as we ask for, within reason."

Dear Yassar, Sasha thought.

After she left Yassar, Sasha returned to her weapons training. Seth sent her on a walking hunt for hostiles through a course within the firing range that was part obstacles, part maze. Pop-up cutouts of hostiles with weapons and unarmed citizens occurred at random, requiring her to either shoot to kill or pull up her handgun. She couldn't stop thinking about Yassar. She'd been fine until she saw him, but now, after hearing his tone, seeing the wounded look on his face, she felt guilty.

She passed through a doorway and another cutout popped up in her peripheral vision. She swung left and fired her Beretta.

"No!" Seth yelled. "That's the second unarmed Saudi you've killed in the last 60 seconds. Time-out." She turned to him and saw his lips pulled tight, his chin lowered as he walked toward her. "This morning you were dead-on accurate, 96%, in your stationary shooting. Now you can't get out of your own way. What happened?"

Sasha looked at the cardboard cutout of a woman carrying a baby, a hole in the center of her chest. "I guess I'm distracted."

"Distracted? By what?"

"My conversation with Yassar."

Seth stepped over to her and stopped with his face six inches from hers. "That distraction also caused you to miss a hostile holding an AK-47. Out in the field you'll have lots bigger distractions than that, and if you don't get your mind right, one of Saif's men will take your head off without you even knowing it."

Sasha hung her head.

"How about you snap out of it and we start this exercise all over again?"

Sasha didn't respond, just took her position at the start of the course. Seth walked past her, stopped at a table, picked up a revolver and handed it to her. "Here, switch weapons, so you don't get too used to the feel of only the Beretta." It was a Smith & Wesson .357 magnum. She handed him the Beretta Cheetah and took the Smith & Wesson from him. It weighed almost twice as much. She swung out the cylinder and checked that the chambers were loaded. "Remember to compensate for the recoil so your second shot isn't high. That's an angry monster. Okay, now go."

CHAPTER 11

SAIF RODE IN THE PASSENGER seat of a jeep next to Rashid, who drove them toward the center of Buraida. Three of his men rode in the backseat. All had AK-47s concealed beneath their robes. Saif checked his watch. *Seven minutes.* He was talking on one of his disposable cell phones with Noor, his wife, giving her the names of the men who would be checking in on the family over the next three days at the safe house he'd moved them to. The conversation was tearing at his heart. He was worried about them with the obvious increase in Secret Police presence following the firefight the other night. He missed Noor's gentle support, her tenderness. He could hardly bear to hear of Indira, his little daughter, he missed her so much. He noted the elapsed time of the call had reached eight minutes, said good-bye and felt a sting of longing. He left the circuit open, handed it to Rashid, who slowed the jeep and tossed the phone into the bed of a pickup truck heading in the opposite direction. Saif smiled. He knew the Americans had sold the Saudi royals equipment that could triangulate to cell phones within ten minutes. In the event they had picked up his disposable cell phone, they would track it to the outskirts of Buraida and beyond until the battery died.

Saif turned and looked behind them. Two other SUVs followed at a safe distance, containing more of his men. Added to their group would be 20 more men who would meet them at the courtyard outside the mosque in Buraida. *Thirty-five in total. More than enough for the job.*

Rashid parked the jeep a block from the mosque. Saif and his men got out and walked, not waiting for the other SUVs. They'd all meet at the courtyard. He checked his watch again. Noon prayers would have ended about five minutes ago. It was a Friday, and execution of *gisas*—Islamic law punishments—always occurred in the courtyard of the mosque after noon prayers. The Islamic Liberation Front's sources said that Mohammed ibn Gafar and Suleiman al-Saad, two members of the ILF who had been convicted of sedition and treason, would be beheaded in the square today.

When Rashid and his men entered the granite courtyard, a line of ten soldiers in their tan uniforms stood with their legs apart, arms in front of them clutching automatic weapons. Behind the soldiers at the center of the courtyard was a rectangular grate over a drain. An unmarked tan van was parked ten meters behind the drain, two more soldiers stationed at the rear of the van. Saif stopped close enough in front of the soldiers to see beads of sweat on their foreheads. He glanced to his right and saw the first group of his other men reach the square. He felt a knot of tension in his stomach, his hands perspiring. A few more men filtered in from the right. He recognized one of them as Rahul, one of the leaders of the ILF. He glanced to his left, saw five more. Just then the mosque doors opened and the worshipers began filing out, many of them stopping in the courtyard to watch the proceedings. After another ten minutes the courtyard was filled. Saif watched as the rear doors of the van swung open and two more soldiers stepped out, then reached up to guide two men out of the van dressed in white robes, blindfolded, with their hands tied in front of them.

Saif heard his pulse throbbing in his ears as he reached inside the slit in his robe and felt for the stock of his AK-47, then slipped his finger onto the trigger. *Wait*, he told himself. The soldiers led the condemned men forward, pressed them into a kneeling position in front of the drain, their heads bowed. The soldiers stepped away. A man in a white robe and a red-checked headdress stepped out of the van, a curved sword still in its scabbard in his hand. As he approached the condemned men he removed the sword from its scabbard, its steel gleaming in the sun.

A loudspeaker from the mosque that announced the call to prayers crackled to life with a blast of static. A voice came on and began reciting the list of the men's crimes. Saif said, "Now!" to Rashid on his right, swung his AK-47 up and fired, flattening the soldier standing in front of him with a short burst, then turned its muzzle to the left and dropped the next one in line. By the time he aimed at the next in line the soldier had already been shot dead. Saif charged forward, seeing the executioner sprinting away across the courtyard. He couldn't see the other soldiers who had guarded the van and escorted the prisoners, so he raised his rifle to his shoulder, aimed and sprayed bullets up and down the length of the van. He kept firing until this clip was exhausted, dropped it and loaded another. By then a group of men had liberated the prisoners, pulling off their blindfolds and rushing them away. Saif pulled a grenade from the pouch at his side, yanked the pin and rolled it under the van.

He turned and ran, yelling, "God is great!" just as the grenade exploded. He heard panicked screams, saw people running from the courtyard, smelled blood and cordite in the air. He couldn't see Rashid but headed back to the jeep, the plan for each man to escape in the vehicle he had arrived in.

Rashid was already revving the engine in the jeep when Saif arrived. The other three men were in the backseat. Rashid gunned the engine and the jeep was speeding down the street by the time Saif pulled the door closed.

God is great, Saif said to himself, his chest heaving.

Saif's shoulders curled over in his fatigue as he leaned forward in his chair, his elbows on the table. His ears still rang from the shootout in Buraida the previous day. He was dead tired, aching and dusty from the 12-hour drive from Buraida to Mecca, and yet exhilarated. He looked around at the other three men seated at the table—Zafar from the Ikwan, Shahid from the Islamic Revolutionary Party and Anwar from the Muslim Brotherhood—fellow Islamic dissident group leaders.

They were seated in a back room of a restaurant in Mecca, across the square from the al-Masjid al-Haram, the Grand Mosque, the holiest place in Islam. A fitting spot for the group to be collaborating on what, Allah willing, would be the future of Saudi Arabia.

"So we are in agreement on our respective geographic areas of responsibility?" Saif said. He looked around the table at each of the men, who all nodded. Anwar was responsible for the western provinces, including Makkah, where they were currently located. Shahid had the massive Eastern Province, the primary oil-producing region, and Zafar the southern provinces. Saif was in charge of the central and northern provinces.

"What about additional weapons?" Zafar asked.

Saif said, "We don't expect any more shipments of artillery. It's too risky at this point. We are getting in more AK-47s and ammunition on a daily basis."

Zafar made a sour face.

Anwar said, "We have two weeks to take as many as we can from the royals' armories. We hit two more last week for more automatic weapons and ammunition."

"If we are too aggressive, it will alert them to the fact that something is imminent," Shahid said.

"All the more reason to be as aggressive as possible, then," Saif said. "It will be our last chance."

Zafar said, "I am still concerned about the SANG. They have a standing force of over 125,000, with additional tribal militia of 25,000. I think we are underestimating them."

The SANG was the Saudi Arabian National Guard, a force independent of the Minister of Defense, US-trained, and a counterbalance to the ruling Sudairi wing of the royal family. Saif smiled and said, "If we play this right, we can have the SANG take on the Royal Army, Navy and Air Force. Royal faction against royal faction."

"And if we don't play it right?" Zafar said.

Zafar was beginning to annoy Saif. Saif had also noticed Anwar and Shahid glance back and forth at each other during Zafar's earlier whining. Saif said, "In that case we still have them all outnumbered. The Navy and Air Force are largely useless to them in street fighting, and most of the Army's armored equipment will be of limited use unless the royals choose to blast all our major cities apart. Look at the pattern of the uprisings in the other Arab nations."

Anwar said to Zafar, "And we have some local SANG troops sympathetic to our cause who sneaked weapons, ammunition, gas masks and provisions into the Grand Mosque compound over the last few weeks."

Zafar said, "But nationwide, we'll be up against a SANG force of 150,000 and the Royal Army of 75,000."

"We had 70,000 demonstrators a week ago in Buraida alone. That's only one city," Saif said.

"All of them armed?" Zafar said. "Trained for combat?"

Anwar said, "Enough of this, Zafar. We have all been building up to this for years. Are you in or out?"

For once Zafar didn't waver. "I am in. My men will be there, but I am only trying to minimize the number who will die."

Saif nodded, then reached over and clapped Zafar on the arm. "As you should, my friend," he said, "as we all should."

Shahid said, "And consider this, Zafar, we'll be moving our camps around, making us very difficult to locate."

"Kind of poetic, don't you think?" Anwar said.

"Poetic?" Saif said.

"Yes, we'll be operating from our tents in the desert, striking on the fly, exactly as the al-Asads did to conquer and rule Saudi Arabia when they were Wahhabi tribesmen 90 years ago."

"I don't care much for poetry," Saif said, "I just want to crush the royals and return Saudi Arabia to the people." *That, and to get this over with quickly.* Saif knew this would be bloody and ugly, wondering if the others in the room had his appreciation for that fact. He'd watched the YouTube videos on his Kindle Fire throughout the other Arab Spring revolutions. Egypt, Libya and Syria had been particularly brutal. Saudi Arabia would be worse. How many months until they were successful? How many months of chaos following that until he was able to establish himself, with Qahtani's blessing, as the new prime minister? Zafar, Shahid and Anwar had agreed that Saif would serve first, for at least four years, followed by a decision among themselves as to who would be next, unless they agreed the country was stable enough for elections. Saif glanced around the table at each of them. With Qahtani in his own pocket and with the people's support of Qahtani as the Mahdi, Saif would serve as long as he chose to.

Rashid was antsy, waiting in the anteroom for Saif to finish his meeting with the other leaders. This all-night drive to Mecca with no prior notice was becoming Saif's modus operandi. Lately he'd even taken to insisting that his instructions to his senior lieutenants be kept confidential from each other, including the locations of their half dozen other camps surrounding Buraida. Saif's increasingly obsessive secretiveness was making Rashid's job of passing information on Saif's activities and whereabouts more difficult by the day. But the bigger reason Rashid was antsy was the confluence of recent events. Yesterday, Saif had given instructions to break down the camp and move half the men to a new camp northwest of Buraida, and half to a camp ten kilometers outside of Mecca. Saif had let it slip to Rashid that the camp outside Mecca held a thousand of their men. It was also the first time Saif had met face-to-face with all three of the other dissident leaders in at least six months. All those meant something big was imminent.

That also meant Rashid was unprepared. He was out of prepaid cell phones to use to report to Ryan in Riyadh. And with millions of pilgrims for the annual Hajj in Mecca, getting around the city to locate a shop with phones in stock might be impossible. Now the business of helping this Sasha woman into their camp didn't seem at all annoying and dangerous. He only hoped Ryan would get word to him that she was arriving soon.

Rashid looked around the room. It was a ragtag group. Rashid had commandeered Talib and Hassan to serve as additional drivers before they left Buraida. Talib was asleep, Hassan dozing. Neither had bathed, and they were covered in dust from the desert, as was Rashid. The roughly 12 other men in the room looked similar, and the air was close from too many bodies and too much garlic emanating from too many pores. *What a life.* If he had family waiting for him at home he wouldn't be here. But that was why he was here at all: his family was no longer on this earth. He moved his chair back, leaned his head against the wall and resolved to get some sleep. The way things were moving, he was certain he'd need the rest.

He heard the door open and saw Saif step out. He motioned Rashid over. "We'll be another hour or so," Saif said. "You and the men get something to eat." He ducked back inside.

Rashid let his breath out, relieved. He told Talib and Hassan to eat, then left to buy some cell phones.

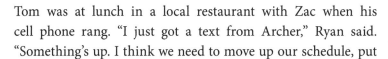

Tom was at lunch in a local restaurant with Zac when his cell phone rang. "I just got a text from Archer," Ryan said. "Something's up. I think we need to move up our schedule, put Sasha in as soon as we can."

"I'm on the way." Tom hung up and waved for the waiter.

Twenty minutes later he was back in the conference room at the embassy with Ryan and Zac.

What've you got?" Tom said.

"Archer says—"

"Just read it," Tom said.

"*SAIF MET YESTERDAY IN MECCA WITH 3 OTHER GROUP LEADERS.*"

Just give me one smart bomb. Take them all out at once, Tom thought.

Ryan continued reading the text. "OTHER LEADERS NOW GONE. NOW SAIF IN TENT CAMP OUTSIDE MECCA WITH 1K MEN. BIG PLANS, SOMETHNG SOON, GET SASHA IN NOW."

"Where's Sasha?" Tom asked Ryan.

"Downstairs training with Seth again."

"Get them up here, now." Then before Ryan could leave, he said, "You got a GPS fix on Archer?"

"Yes."

Tom motioned to Zac. They both left the room.

Never enough time. Tom remembered his last debriefing with Seth, who'd said Sasha was coming along fine, but the more time he had with her the better. He thought of calling Yassar, then realized he couldn't offer any information beyond Archer's text, and so he couldn't very well ask for support based on it.

He thought for a moment, checked his watch, then picked up the phone to call for a chopper.

Twenty minutes later Sasha sat in the communications room facing Zac. "There are six of them sewn into the end seams," Zac said, holding a black abaya in his hands. "This abaya is just like yours." He held the abaya out to Sasha, his fingers on the seam. "Feel it?" he asked. She had her fingers on the seam between his hands, felt a few small lumps beneath the surface of the fabric.

"Yes."

"Feel right here," he said, guiding one of her hands. "Feel that? It's a little squishy, because there's fluid inside the plastic bubble."

She felt it between her fingers and nodded.

"Squeeze it hard and break it. You're breaking a bubble within an outer plastic pouch."

She did it.

"That releases the acid, creating a battery that will last for about twelve hours to power the transmitter."

"It's not detectable?"

"Not by just frisking you, or even feeling the seams on the abaya. You can attest to that," Zac said. "And probably not by any kind of metal detector, although if they have sweepers for bugs, you're hosed." His Southern drawl extended his last word, his smile taking the edge off the point. Sasha didn't take any comfort from it. Hosed meant hosed, no matter how softly or gentlemanly it was put. Zac added, "But we're dealing with men running around in the desert. They're not likely to have that kind of equipment."

"So after I squeeze one of the batteries, I've got a signal that lasts for twelve hours, right?"

Zac said, "Yes, give or take. They operate on five volts, same as a cell phone. Only they're ten times more powerful than a cell phone, so I can pick you up from just about anyplace, even if a cell phone can't get a signal. And you've got six of them.

"And after they've died, what?"

"There isn't much more we can do for you." Now he frowned. "So just pray they don't take your abaya from you. It may be the only way we can locate you."

Sasha's neck went cold.

Saif stood with his legs spread wide apart in the desert camp north of Mecca, affecting a posture of command, much as he imagined Alan Rickman would if playing Lawrence of Arabia or Field Marshal Rommel. He looked out on a patchwork of tents, Land Rovers and other SUVs parked beneath desert camouflage screens held up by poles, everything flapping in the wind that, but for Saif's sunglasses, would have blasted the sand into his eyes. It looked like a military encampment on the verge of the beginning of a war, as it was. It housed about a thousand men. Dozens of other such camps were located around Saudi Arabia, strategically positioned outside major cities, all ready. *But are they enough?* They would have to be.

He walked back inside his tent to the table where his top 20 lieutenants sat. "There is no God but Allah," he said, and sat at the head of the table.

"*La ilaha ilallah!*" his men repeated.

Saif paused, looked around the table into each man's face, dragging it out. Finally he propped himself on his elbows and said, "Soon." He paused for dramatic effect. "I have met with our fellow leaders in the last days, not far from here in Mecca." He turned to Rashid at his right and nodded, expecting and receiving a nod in return. It was a sign to the others that Rashid was his confidant, his top lieutenant. "Our liberation struggle is almost at an end, where we strike out and crush the royals. Then we reclaim our country, our beloved Saudi Arabia, for our people."

Saif stood and began walking around the table. "Each of you has your specific instructions, your individual command, and your own responsibilities to your men. After the Mahdi has been revealed to the people, we and our brothers will strike. We will strike in unison. We have strength in numbers. We will overwhelm the seemingly insurmountable forces of the royals with our passion, our commitment and our willingness to die for our cause. We will sustain casualties. Many of us will die. But we will die for a better future for our parents, our wives, our children. Saudi Arabia can be a great nation again, with all of you leading us into her future." He had finished encircling the table and now stood behind his chair at the head. He raised his arms, spread his legs. "Stand with me now, my brothers, stand for the future of our country, our people. Fight, die, if necessary, to destroy the royals, and return our country to greatness and holiness under the Mahdi."

Saif watched as his men stood, raised their arms and cheered in support of him. It wasn't the resounding thunder of emotion he'd hoped for. *Never mind.* There would be time for that, after many of them had been wounded or seen their brothers die. With the taste of blood in their mouths they could not help but be more passionate.

CHAPTER 12

SASHA, ZAC, RYAN, SETH AND Tom were seated in a private hangar at the airport in Riyadh, waiting for word that the army Black Hawk helicopter that would ferry them to Mecca was finished refueling. Tom had been watching the pilot since he walked into the hangar and sat by himself near the door, looking disgusted. He knew the type. He could see the bars on his uniform, a captain. Grizzled old guy, in his mid-50s, Tom guessed, sitting with his back straight, no paunch on that hard body. Army-issued haircut, short on the sides like the kids Zac and Seth who had been assigned to Tom's operation. Tom figured it was worth going over to talk to the guy, make sure he understood the importance of what they were about to do.

Tom walked over to him and said, "Thanks for helping us out here." He extended his hand. "Tom Goddard."

The man glanced up at Tom, hesitated as if trying to decide if he would shake his hand, then extended his and said, "Jaworski. Captain Steve Jaworski."

Tom sat down next to him. "You in from Dhahran?"

Jaworski seemed annoyed. "That's the only place we keep these big Black Hawks on Saudi soil anymore." Jaworski looked away out the window, as if the refueling process on the chopper was something that needed his attention.

"And I'll bet you're pissed that you got requisitioned to run some errand, huh?"

Jaworski turned back to Tom. "Yeah, you might say that. This hardware is a little expensive for taxi duty, don't you think?" When Tom didn't respond, Jaworski said, "Don't you State Department guys have your own embassy choppers?" When Tom still didn't respond, Jaworski said, "That is, if you really are with the State Department. I don't mind telling you that I don't appreciate being a bag man for some spook escapade without being told who I'm transporting or why."

Tom shrugged. He said, "I'm not in a position to tell you, but I can say it's important enough for my boss to have Rusty Baldridge arrange this through Admiral Raven at Special Ops."

Jaworski's head went back a couple of inches.

Tom motioned to their group seated with Sasha. "The two guys over there with haircuts like yours are on assignment from Raven, too, authorized by Rusty."

Tom could see he had Jaworski's full attention. Jaworski said, "So it's that little black-haired piece of ass we're…" He stopped, searching for the word.

"*Inserting* is the word we use. And my boss calls her my prize mare."

"And your boss would be?"

"The director." Tom smiled. "And now that I've met you, I guess that's why Rusty arranged for you to chaperone us. I feel like we're in good hands. Experienced, pissed-off good hands." Jaworski didn't change his expression. *Jeez*, Tom thought. *This guy never cracks a smile.*

"That all you can tell me?"

"Yeah, except that my little black-haired prize mare is our neutron bomb against a potential Arab Spring uprising against the Saudi government. Consider her precious cargo."

"You expecting any excitement?"

"Nope. But we may not be flying into friendly territory, which is why we asked for a Black Hawk instead of the embassy chopper."

Jaworski stood up and walked outside without another word. Tom could see him through the windows talking with urgency to his copilot and gunner.

Sasha saw Tom and the pilot talking, then the pilot abruptly get up and walk outside. Tom walked back over and sat down next to her. Sasha felt lightness in her limbs. *Nerves.* She closed her eyes and appealed to Ganesha, her Remover of Obstacles, to calm her, keep her safe. She could feel Tom's energy, his leg touching hers. She wondered what he was thinking. Was he feeling anything? She remembered their conversation in the conference room a few days earlier, then told herself that of course he must be. A moment later she felt his hand find hers and squeeze it.

Tom turned to Sasha and said, "How about we step out for a few minutes to stretch our legs?" They walked to the door and Tom opened it for her. The heat blasted her in the face. Her calves ached from tension as she stepped outside. "You okay?" Tom asked.

"Fine. You?"

"I'm not the one who's heading into the dark."

"That's not what I asked, friend."

Tom smiled. "I'll feel better when this is over. And I don't suppose it would help for me to tell you I'm worried about you."

"In a way, actually, it does help."

"Then I guess I've at least contributed something to this operation."

Sasha walked over to him, brushed the hair off his forehead. "You're still scruffy, you know."

"Some things never change." She saw the intensity in his eyes, those blue, blue eyes. She wanted him to let them go, his feelings for her, then in the moment she thought it, she wasn't sure.

"Maybe they do, Tom." She felt a tug of emotion, not quite sure what it was, and then Tom looked away, awkward. After a moment she said, "My God, I'm roasting. Let's get back into the hangar."

When they sat back down with the team, Zac turned to Sasha and asked, "We've been talking. So what's this Hajj?"

Sasha said, "It's an annual pilgrimage that all faithful Muslims are expected to go on at least once in their lives."

"Where do they go?"

Sasha said, "They walk to the Grand Mosque in Mecca, and to other places near Mecca with significance to the Islamic religion, to perform seven different holy rituals."

"Like what?"

"Seven counterclockwise circuits around the Kaaba, the square structure in the courtyard of the Grand Mosque, which all Muslims turn toward in performing their daily prayers. Drinking from the sacred Zamzam Well inside the mosque. Three ritual stonings of the devil, symbolic of the prophet Ibrahim's rejection of the devil's three attempts to convert him to evil."

"They walk all the way?"

"Yes. About 4 million pilgrims each year. That means there can be up to 800,000 pilgrims inside the Grand Mosque and up to 3 million camping in thousands of tents the Saudi government sets up at Mina, near Mecca."

Zac raised his eyebrows.

"The Grand Mosque compound is almost 90 acres."

Tom said, "The Hajj occurs on the eighth through the twelfth days of the last month of the Islamic year, which is a little different each year, because the Muslim religious calendar is shorter than ours by about 11 days."

Sasha got a flash of insight. "Oh my God, I can't believe I didn't think of it." She turned to Tom. "The start of the new year, that's it."

Tom stared at her, waiting.

"The prophecies said the Mahdi would appear just before the beginning of the Islamic New Year. Saif could be planning to start the uprising around the time of the New Year, after revealing to the masses that the Mahdi has arrived."

Tom said, "And according to Archer, Saif is at an encampment only 10 kilometers north of Mecca."

"Which could mean they're planning to start things off in Mecca, with the city full of pilgrims who would undoubtedly respond to the Mahdi's appearance," Sasha said.

Seth said, "That ought to give them hundreds of thousands more committed rebels."

"Try millions," Sasha said. "You're talking about a holy war."

"If you're right, that gives us, what, ten days?" Tom said.

Sasha shook her head, thinking. "Eight days. Today's the final day of the Hajj, the 12th day of the month. The prophecies say the Mahdi will reveal himself on the 20th day."

Tom pursed his lips. "Eight days," he repeated to himself.

The pilot opened the door to the hangar. "We're ready for you," he said to Tom. Tom stood up and led the team to the door. "We'll be in the air for over three hours, so you'll need these," the pilot said. The other two crewmen handed vests to each of them. "These are Microclimate Cooling Systems," the pilot said. "They hook up to portable cooling units in the chopper, mini air conditioners that cool the water in the vests." After they put on the vests, the pilot led them outside to the runway where a US Army helicopter was rumbling on the tarmac. The smell of jet exhaust from its turbines was thick in the air. As she boarded the chopper, Sasha felt oddly detached from the magnitude of what was happening. She wasn't feeling the significance of her part in stopping a major uprising that could result in the overthrow of the Saudi government, along with the worldwide ramifications of that. Right now, to her, it was only about Saif. Finding him and killing him. *For Daniel.* She felt for her anger and was disappointed she couldn't get in touch with it. She wasn't worried. Once she saw Saif, she knew it would be there.

Just before Jaworski had poked his head into the hangar to tell them the chopper was ready, Ryan had forwarded Rashid's latest text to Tom: BROKE CAMP 2 HOURS AGO. COLUMN MOVING TOWARD MECCA. Tom decided not to say anything until they were in the air en route to Mecca, because even though he felt like he'd made an impression on Jaworski, he still believed the crusty old hard-ass needed to be managed. Tom walked out onto the tarmac and stopped in front of the Black Hawk. He waited for the rest of the team to pass him and enter the big side door of the chopper, all the while keeping his head down against the rotor wash. Then he walked around the nose, seeing those nasty 12.7mm GAU-19 Gatling guns sticking out the front of the chopper, afraid of and thankful for them at the same time. When Tom got into the chopper, the copilot was already strapped into his seat, the gunner behind the cockpit in his seat next to one of the side-mounted M240H machine guns. Tom looked back at the team as they buckled into their seats and put on their headphones and microphones. Sasha looked calm, not the tense energy he'd sensed as they walked around outside the hangar. He looked back into the cockpit. The big Sikorsky-made Black Hawk had armor and bulletproof glass that could withstand small weapons fire. After Archer's last message Tom thought they might need it.

Jaworski eased the throttles forward and the turbines whined, then their exhaust roared. The Black Hawk lifted off, hesitated about 200 feet off the ground, then the nose dropped and it shot forward like a sprinter. As they passed over the runways of the airport the Black Hawk gained altitude. They were at about 2,000 feet by the time they started passing the western suburbs of Riyadh, concrete commercial buildings in grays and browns below, sand-dusted asphalt roads crisscrossing through the neighborhoods, then quickly, rolling dunes over the tan desert, then nothing but flat sand. Tom felt the Black Hawk accelerate, heard the pitch of the turbines increase as they picked up speed, and he settled back into his seat as they gained altitude on the way to Mecca.

Three hours later, Tom said into his microphone, "Jaworski, we need a slight change of plans."

Tom saw Jaworski turn his head, then saw him ease back on the throttles. Tom felt his stomach lighten as the chopper nosed up and slowed. "There's a column moving from the camp about ten kilometers outside Mecca toward the city," Tom said, handing Jaworski a piece of paper with coordinates written on it. "I'd like to do a flyover on the way into Mecca. Get in close enough to see their troop strength and what kind of firepower they're packing."

Tom saw Jaworski nod, then glance down at the paper. He handed it to his copilot, then pressed the throttles all the way forward. Tom felt himself thrust into the back of his seat as the Black Hawk rumbled ahead.

About five minutes later, dots that looked like a line of black ants appeared on the horizon of the desert. As they closed in, the ants became a column of jeeps and SUVs driving toward Mecca. Moments later, Tom heard the ping of small weapons fire on the fuselage of the Black Hawk. It must have been from some outlying vehicles a half mile or so off the side of the column.

Damn, too close. Should've figured they'd have sentries stationed. Tom looked back to check on Sasha. He felt his chest constrict as he saw her clutching the sides of her seat, her eyes wide. He grunted and turned forward as the chopper banked hard left, Jaworski going into evasive maneuvers. Then the chopper banked hard right, came dead-on two SUVs in the desert a few hundred yards away. "Battle stations," Jaworski said over the intercom to his crew. He pushed the throttle all the way forward, nosed down at the SUVs and roared toward them. A moment later the Gatlings erupted beneath Tom's feet. He saw tracers heading at the SUVs, then explosions and smoke as one SUV was obliterated, felt the nose tilt left and saw the other SUV disappear in flames and smoke. The Gatlings went silent, the nose came up, and the big chopper banked hard right and came around.

Tom heard the copilot telling his Dhahran base they were under attack and returning fire, reporting their coordinates. Tom looked back at Sasha again. She was still clutching her seat but appeared to be in control of herself.

"Incoming," he heard over the headphones as the chopper banked left, then dived, seemingly out of control for hundreds of feet. Tom's stomach felt like it had dropped to the floor, until the chopper leveled briefly and then climbed so harshly that his vision went down to a pinpoint, like a TV screen turning off when he was a kid in the 1960s. "It's a SAM!" he heard in his headphones, felt the Black Hawk shoot up a few hundred feet, then roll right, then completely over and then right itself again, bank hard left and descend. "Countermeasures!" Jaworski barked. Tom's stomach now felt like its contents might explode into his mouth, then he heard a series of swishing sounds and pops, and saw trailers that looked like roman candles sparkling out from the sides of the chopper.

Tom watched the gunner swing his M240H machine gun around and start firing. He saw the trail of the missile heading in at the Black Hawk, then felt the chopper go upside down, roll sideways, then right itself and speed off to the sound of more pops and flares. He heard more bullets hitting the fuselage, louder, from bigger arms, then a grinding sound. The chopper rumbled as if something was damaged, then leveled off, descended quickly and headed straight back across the desert, skimming a few hundred feet off the sand.

Jaworski came on the intercom. "We evaded the surface-to-air missile but took a hit in one of the engines. They're combat ruggedized and will keep running for a while even after all the oil drains out of them. But we're going down. I'm heading back to the highway into Mecca. Hopefully we can make it. Stay buckled in. I'll let you know before impact."

A few minutes later, Tom heard the grinding noise in the engine growing louder. A moment later the chopper started vibrating. "Get ready," Jaworski said over the intercom. Tom looked back again at Sasha, saw her bracing herself against the back of her seat, hands clutching the harness that crisscrossed her chest, eyes closed. *Probably praying.* He felt his heart thumping in his chest, wondered if they were gonna make it.

He didn't have much more chance to think. It seemed only a moment later that the chopper was vibrating wildly out of control, and he couldn't tell up from down, then saw the desert racing up at him. They hit and the Black Hawk bounced once, then slammed back down and buried its nose in the sand. Tom must have blacked out, because the next thing he knew, Sasha was pulling him out of his seat.

Sasha got over her panic at seeing Tom slumped in his seat, motionless, when she was able to pull him upright. He blinked, his eyes glazed. He had a cut and a lump forming on his forehead. "Are you all right?" she asked, supporting him with one arm around his back, another under his armpit. She felt him regain his balance, saw his eyes clear.

"Yeah. Everyone else okay?"

"Back there, yes." She shot a glance into the cockpit where the gunner was tending to the pilot and copilot. "Up there, I'm not sure."

Tom put his hands on her shoulders and eased her back, then crouched and moved forward into the cockpit. She saw him speaking to the gunner. By the time he came back, Seth and Zac were on their haunches in the doorway to the cockpit, waiting. "Looks like Jaworski has two broken legs, Stilton, the copilot, one," Tom said to them. "They aren't going anyplace."

Tom stepped back into the main cabin while Seth went into the cockpit to help the gunner drag Jaworski and Stilton into the main cabin and prop them against the wall. Zac found a field medical kit and gave Jaworski and Stilton shots of local anesthetic in their legs.

Jaworski told them the radio was out, took Zac's cell phone and then huddled all the servicemen, including Seth and Zac, around him, taking command. They talked for a few minutes. Tom and Sasha hung back with Ryan in the rear of the cabin, staying out of the way. Tom called in to Langley. He didn't think there was much they could do to help them in the short run, but at least they'd be aware of the situation. Ryan called in to the embassy. Between the two calls, Tom figured they might just get some support.

Jaworski waved them forward. He said, "Okay, here's the deal. Stilton and I can't move, so we're staying here, as is Maloney." He nodded at the gunner. "I assume that the base in Dhahran knows our coordinates, because Stilton radioed them in just before we crashed. I called for some backup. Dhahran is five hours away, so I'm not sure how much help that will be."

Tom said, "But you know this is a covert mission. They won't send anyone."

Jaworski said, "Not possible. If we're in harm's way, our guys will show up. And either keep their mouths shut or take the consequences."

Tom felt his guts twisting, hoping Jaworski was right.

"I also called some local Saudi friends in Mecca," Jaworski said. "A Saudi Airborne Army unit."

Tom cocked his head.

"Don't look so surprised. We train these guys to fly our Black Hawks. They're our buddies. I don't know how fast they can scramble, but they'll put three or four of them in the air and be here soon as they can. We'll just have to hold off these desert rats that long. And don't worry about their fatwa crap. If the shooting starts, our Saudi friends will shoot back and explain later."

Tom smiled, not sure if it was from nerves or an appreciation of how this old army jock operated.

"You all need to head out of here ASAP, because we figure these twerps will be on us in another ten to fifteen minutes."

"How far do you figure we are from the highway into Mecca?" Tom asked.

"Maybe two or three miles."

Sasha said, "We'll be safe there. We can blend in with the pilgrims walking into Mecca."

Zac said to Jaworski, "I'll be staying here, too, sir."

Jaworski stared him down. "I understand you're escorting someone important, soldier."

"With all due respect, sir—"

Jaworski cut him off with a wave of his hand under his chin. He said to Tom, "You said she was a neutron bomb. Authorized by Rusty Baldridge himself, right?"

"Yeah," Tom said.

"A lot at stake?"

Tom nodded.

Jaworski nodded back. He said to Zac, "Get going, soldier."

Zac said, "Again, with all due respect, sir, I'm on assignment directly from Admiral Raven, via Chairman Baldridge, instructed to take orders only from Mr. Goddard." Zac looked over at Tom. "And Mr. Goddard insists that I stay."

Jaworski glared at Tom. Tom said, "We can handle ourselves."

Jaworski said, "Okay. Enough talk. We'll hold them off as long as we can. Get help. But above all, get your neutron bomb in place." Jaworski looked at his men, then back at Tom. "Take those coolers with you. Keep them plugged into your vests. They weigh about 13 pounds and they'll slow you down, but they'll save your lives out there. The batteries will give you maybe two hours of cooling. Good luck."

Jaworski looked away. Zac and Seth stepped to the back of the main cabin and retrieved weapons and ammunition. Seth handed Sasha a Beretta and two clips, then automatic weapons—M4A1s—to Ryan and Tom, shouldered one himself and stepped toward the doorway. He saluted Jaworski, who offered a perfunctory one in return. Seth walked back over to Zac and shook his hand, the two of them looking into each other's eyes, stonefaced.

Tom checked to make sure Sasha's cooling unit was plugged into her vest and functioning properly. He nodded to Jaworski as he moved toward the door of the chopper. Then he stopped, put down his cooling unit and reached out to shake hands with Zac. He grunted, "Good luck." Then Tom, Sasha, Seth and Ryan stepped out into the sand. As they headed into the desert, Tom wondered if what awaited them was worse than what was behind them. For Sasha, he was pretty sure that was the case.

———◆———

Saif was in one of the lead cars, a mile or so from where the helicopter attacked the lookout cars about a half mile to the left of the column. Those were Anwar's men. *Fools*, he thought when he learned it was an American helicopter, and that they'd succeeded in shooting it down. Anwar's men must've been trigger-happy and fired first; there was no logical reason for an American helicopter to be in the area, but certainly no reason for it to attack without provocation. By the time he learned that Anwar had authorized 50 vehicles to attack the downed helicopter it was too late for him to intervene. He prayed to Allah that they wouldn't kill any of the Americans. The last thing they needed was to enrage the Americans to the point of bringing them into the situation, even before their uprising started. He remembered how it had gone for Qaddafi, with the Americans working behind the scenes and pushing NATO into the revolution. What would their chances be if the Americans, righteous over American blood being spilled, threw not only their weight but their military muscle behind the Saudi regime?

Back in the Black Hawk, Jaworski had Maloney prop him up next to one of the doorways with an M4A1 and extra ammo, then help him into additional Interceptor body armor covering his legs, groin, neck and throat to supplement his protective vest. He had Maloney prepare Stilton the same way and prop him beside the other doorway. Then he called the young soldier named Zac over.

"What's your name, soldier?"

"Zac Fulton, sir. Sergeant First Class, 101st Airborne Special Forces attached to Special Ops."

"Proud to serve with you, Sergeant. You know how to shoot one of these things?" Jaworski pointed at one of the two M240H machine guns mounted inside the open window of the Black Hawk.

"In a pinch, sir."

Jaworski nodded. "You man this one, Maloney will man the other. Now go back and help Maloney pull out all the cases of ammo, and get yourself suited up in some body armor. It's gonna get pretty hot around here shortly."

The kid hopped to it. After about five minutes, when Zac and Maloney finished suiting up and sliding the ammo cases in place next to the machine guns, Jaworski heard engines approaching from off in the distance. "Alright, listen up. I figure we're dealing with some disorganized, untrained rabble of unemployed plumbers and butchers coming at us with a bunch of SUVs and obsolete Russian AK-47s. Even if they've got some more shoulder-launched missiles, I'm sure these knuckleheads couldn't hit the side of a barn from 100 feet away. Worst case we might be dealing with a 12mm cannon mounted on the back of a jeep, but we'll be able to cut them to pieces with these M240Hs before they can get to us. I don't plan on dying out here in this desert today, so let's show these amateurs how the US Army operates."

Jaworski heard the engines grow louder, saw dust flying up from behind the dunes. He had the safety off on his M4A1, his finger on the trigger, perspiring in the heat. The engine sounds kept coming, sounding like more vehicles than he'd expected. He realized they were smarter than he'd thought, because they were encircling the Black Hawk, or possibly driving around it on the assumption that some or all of their party had started walking off across the desert toward the highway. After another five minutes he figured they were completely surrounded, still with no vehicles in sight. When he saw the first jeep come over a dune, heading straight at them about 400 yards away, he raised his M4A1, sighted it in and exhaled to steady himself. *No sense waiting until they're on top of us.* "Fire at will," he said, and put a burst through the windshield of the jeep. It swerved, turned sideways and coasted to a stop just as automatic weapons fire resonated against the sides of the Black Hawk. He heard Maloney's M240H erupt from the other side of the cabin, then Zac's right above him as two SUVs came into view over the dunes. A moment later both SUVs were riddled with hits and one exploded.

Jaworski's heart was pumping hard, his eyes scanning the desert, still hearing bullets pinging off the Black Hawk but not seeing any targets.

"Incoming!" someone yelled from the other side of the cabin, and Jaworski turned to see the trail of a missile heading at them. He closed his eyes and held his breath, heard a whoosh over the top of the Black Hawk, and saw the missile shoot off toward the horizon on his side of the chopper. Then another missile from his side, clearly heading wide behind the chopper, and he heard Zac's machine gun blasting again and saw the bullets skimming the top of the dunes from where the missile had come. Now two more jeeps came over the dune, then another three, now five or six.

"They're coming!" Jaworski yelled, and started firing into the windshields of each of the vehicles. More came over the top. Two of them got within 100 yards before Zac could stop them with his machine gun. Jaworski changed his clip and started firing again, now seeing men get out of the vehicles and take firing position behind ones they'd already stopped.

His breath was coming in gasps, firing, changing another clip, then he felt the breath go out of him and he was thrown onto his back in the cabin. He groped for his M4A1 and tried to pull himself up, realizing his body armor had stopped the bullets. He leaned forward and kept firing.

He saw the track of another missile coming straight at them, braced himself, felt the heat and blast of the explosion and found himself on his back in the middle of the cabin. He looked to the rear of the cabin and saw it open to the desert where the tail of the Black Hawk had been. Black smoke and dust were everyplace. He looked to the side and saw Maloney get back to his feet and start firing his machine gun again. Stilton was on his side, not moving. Zac was down, coughing, then pulled himself to his knees and grabbed the M240H again and started firing, staggering around as he swiveled the machine gun, shooting at nothing, anything. Jaworski couldn't see his M4A1 so he rolled onto his side and pulled out his Colt service revolver and aimed out the doorway of the chopper. Two men were running at them from an SUV, 25 yards away, and Jaworski raised the Colt and pulled off two rounds. He dropped one of them and Zac got the other.

Jaworski could hear his breath roaring in his ears, the rest of the sounds of the firefight muffled by the ringing in his ears from the missile blast. Zac stopped firing the machine gun and hunched over it to change the ammo belt, then got thrown backward from a spray of bullets. Jaworski winced as he rolled onto his stomach and pulled himself with his arms toward the doorway. He braced the Colt on the floor in both hands and kept firing, but there were too many targets. At least 25 of them were now running from their vehicles, weapons in hand, now that Zac's M240H was silent. *Is this it?* he asked himself. Just as he emptied the Colt he took another hit in the arm, which threw him over sideways. On his back he saw Zac now up again with an M4A1 in his hand. He braced the rifle on the M240H and started firing bursts, raking across the desert and dropping the onrushing men.

Too many, Jaworski said to himself in desperation. He tried to roll on his side and couldn't. His right arm was useless, even though he thought the body armor had held. He rolled his head to look out the window and then he heard the sound of a chopper, low, at an altitude of maybe only a few hundred feet, thundering from behind him, then the sound of its machine guns, big Gatlings, and saw the bullets peppering across the sand, tearing up the vehicles and men.

His breath rushed out in a gush of emotion. *The Saudis!* Another chopper flew over, strafing behind the first, then a third. He saw Zac drop his M4A1 and grab another ammo belt. He loaded it into the M240H and started firing again at the retreating men, at the SUVs that were still moving.

I knew I wasn't gonna die out here in this desert today.

Tom had taken one of the automatic rifles from Ryan and instructed Sasha to stay forward with Ryan while he and Seth walked about 25 yards behind them. "If you hear the sound of engines or weapons being fired, run until you get over a dune where you can lay flat on the desert and try to stay out of sight," Tom had said.

They'd only been walking for about 15 minutes when she heard the sound of automatic weapons behind her. She turned back to see Tom and Seth waving them forward, so she and Ryan started running as fast as they could, carrying their coolers and dealing with the uncertain footing in the sand. The gunfire was constant, punctuated with periodic explosions. She kept checking back, her heart racing, seeing Tom and Seth keeping the same distance from them. After another 15 minutes or so she heard helicopters. She looked back to see four of them with Saudi insignias doing strafing runs, the drum of the rotors and the staccato crack of their machine guns drowning out all the other sounds. After a few minutes the shooting stopped.

Sasha and Ryan turned around and walked back to Seth and Tom.

"Looks like Jaworski's Saudi friends showed up," Tom said.

A few minutes later, one of the Saudi helicopters picked them up and flew them to their base in Mecca. Sasha rode in silence, her hand inside her abaya gripping the Beretta.

CHAPTER 13

DAY ONE. GRAND MOSQUE, MECCA.

LATER THAT AFTERNOON, SAIF AND a team of 100 of his men entered the Grand Mosque and stood by the main gate, which, like all the gates, consisted of two-inch-thick vertical iron bars. Saif and his men were dressed like the pilgrims in *ihram*—white robes of unhemmed cloth—and sandals, their AK-47s, bags of hand grenades and other equipment concealed beneath their robes. More teams entered the other 18 gates. Saif and his team milled around inside the Mutaaf, the marble-floored courtyard in the unroofed section of the mosque, waiting. Rashid led a group of a dozen men surrounding Qahtani to keep him safe in the event of any shooting. Thousands of pilgrims performed the last of their ritual acts on the final day of the Hajj, the Tawaf, walking seven circuits counterclockwise around the sacred Kaaba, the square structure in the center of the courtyard that all Muslims turn toward in performing their daily prayers. The pilgrims' footsteps and calls of "God, God is great" on their circuits rose in a deep rumble. More pilgrims circumnavigated the Kaaba on the first floor and roof of the mosque.

As Saif expected, there was minimal security inside the mosque, with only two slouching policemen near the main gate. At 3:00 p.m., Saif waved his arm to his men and pulled out his AK-47. He pointed it at one of the policemen, a disheveled man in his 50s with watery eyes, whose mouth dropped open as he saw the weapon and raised his hands. Saif heard a few cries from pilgrims, then shouts as a group of them ran out at the sight of the weapons. "Hand me your gun and leave and you won't be harmed," Saif said to the policeman. The man did as he was ordered. One of Saif's men took the gun from the other policeman and they both hurried out through the gate. Saif's men then pushed the gates closed and ran chains through the bars and secured them with locks, holding the gates shut.

He heard shots, then screams and a crowd of pilgrims pushed toward him, running from the commotion. Apparently it hadn't gone so smoothly at one of the other gates, but by now all the gates would be secure, and Saif's entire force of 1,000 armed men would be inside the mosque. Within minutes, Saif's sniper teams would be in position at the top of each of the nine minarets.

Saif walked across the courtyard, half his men and the group still surrounding Qahtani following him, and the other half of his men taking positions near the main gate or climbing the steps to position themselves on top of the walls of the mosque overlooking Mecca. The throngs of pilgrims in the courtyard parted and cowered from him and his men. He entered the main prayer hall, then strode through it, more pilgrims screaming in fear and pushing to the outside of the hall. He left Rashid with the group of his men protecting Qahtani and then climbed the stairway to the security and communications room, now feeling his pulse elevated. He hoped the policemen in the room wouldn't resist; deaths inside the mosque, particularly at this holy time of year, would jeopardize their cause.

He stood against the wall beside the door and called to the policemen inside. "Brothers, we mean you no harm. Open the door and hand out your weapons and there will be no violence. We have come to liberate and purify Saudi Arabia from the poisonous influence of the West, and return it to the original ways of Islam."

He waited. No response.

"We will give you a few minutes to decide. After that, we will enter by force."

Moments later he heard muffled voices inside the room, then louder, arguing. Finally, silence. Saif gave them another minute, then motioned to one of his men, who blasted the lock with a burst from his AK-47, swinging the door open into the room. Two more of his men tossed in concussion grenades. Saif was the first to charge into the room after the explosions, finding four policemen on the floor, two unconscious and two moaning. Saif's men bound their wrists and dragged them all from the room.

Saif stepped back and watched, feeling a warm glow. One of his men took a seat in front of the microphone, pulled out a wad of papers and laid them on the console. Rashid entered with Qahtani and the rest of the men. He saw a few of them smile, nudge each other and raise their weapons in the air. Qahtani stepped forward to Saif, beaming, and embraced him.

"We begin here, today, my brothers," Saif said, "in this holiest of places, in this holiest of times."

—♦—

Sasha had arrived at the Grand Mosque at about 2:30 p.m., after Ryan had received Rashid's text message: 3 P.M., GRAND MOSQUE. IT STARTS TODAY. GET SASHA INSIDE.

Ryan had immediately arranged transportation for the entire team—Zac had rejoined them—into Mecca from the

Saudi military airport where the helicopters had dropped them, but because of crowds of pilgrims blocking the streets they had to walk the last quarter mile to the Grand Mosque. Sasha had insisted on being the only one to enter, saying she was the only one dressed appropriately—all the women on the Hajj wore abayas and headscarves—and that they would attract undue attention by not wearing *ihram* like all the male pilgrims. Tom had reluctantly agreed.

Sasha entered through one of the smaller western gates. She was well inside before she looked back. She felt a lump form in her throat as she saw Tom's gaze still locked on her. She turned again and kept walking to a position in the middle of the courtyard. She watched from there for a half hour until a rebel group subdued the policemen guarding the gate and chained it shut. She worked her way across the Grand Mosque and was standing in the courtyard not far from the entrance to the main prayer hall when the rebels began broadcasting their message from the loudspeakers on the minarets. Whoever was speaking was experienced with it, because his cadence and intonation were the same as the broadcasts of prayers five times a day from mosques all over Saudi Arabia.

As the broadcast over the loudspeakers droned on, she watched as many of the pilgrims listened to the words as intently as they did to the daily prayer broadcasts. "…we advocate a return to the original ways of Islam. We repudiate the infidel influence of the greedy crocodiles of the West, and will expel all non-Muslims from Saudi Arabia. We declare the al-Asad dynasty to be illegitimate due to its pollution by the West, its consequent destruction of Saudi culture and its corrupt and ostentatious waste of the riches that rightfully belong to the Saudi Arabian people…"

Sasha had carried her cell phone and three handguns into the mosque inside her abaya—two Berettas and a Smith & Wesson—and stashed two of the guns with extra clips in cubicles built into the perimeter wall for prayer offerings, not far from where she now stood. She realized the odds of retrieving them were low, but higher than the odds of being able to keep the Beretta she had with her if she were captured or revealed herself.

She stepped into a group of pilgrims and behind one of the four-foot-thick columns around the perimeter walls, and phoned Tom.

"You okay?" he asked.

"I'm fine. They've chained the gates, taken over and are broadcasting their message from the minarets."

"I can hear it. So can half of Mecca. I'm in a hotel suite on the 30th floor across from the mosque."

"Do you have any idea where they might be broadcasting from?"

"Yassar's trying to get me a floor plan of the mosque from the construction company that's doing the expansion work on it. He said there's a communications room not far from the imams' offices, because they're the ones who broadcast the prayers."

"That means it won't be far from the main prayer hall. I'll check."

"Don't go exploring until you hear back from me. I'll call you as soon as we get the plans."

"I'm right in front of the main prayer hall. I'm sure I can find it."

Tom raised his voice. "Don't do anything crazy. If you blunder into something you're likely to get yourself killed."

"I knew the risks when I decided to do this," she shot back, letting her voice show her annoyance.

"Knock it off!" he shouted through the phone. "I told you Yassar's gonna get back to me."

Sasha paused, then decided to end the conversation. "I'll leave my cell phone on vibrate," she said, and hung up.

She fingered the grip of the Beretta under her abaya. If she could get a clear shot at Saif, she could possibly take him out and avoid capture by blending into the crowds of pilgrims. Maybe, but she'd need to get lucky. She started toward the entrance to the main prayer hall.

Saif was in the security and communications room when he heard the crack of weapons fire. A moment later he got a call on his cell phone telling him about an assault. He grabbed his AK-47, told Rashid to stay with Qahtani, motioned to a group of men to follow him and ran up the stairs to the roof. He led his men through the crowd of terrified pilgrims to the outer wall, from which he could see the main gate.

Saif looked over to see a line of 25 or 30 policemen advancing behind riot shields, apparently trying to reach the main gate, cut the chains and force their way in. He could hear the sharp pops of the snipers' rifles from the minarets, the staccato bursts from his men's AK-47s on the walls above the gate. *Fools.* It was insanity, trudging forward in a straight line like British soldiers in the 1700s. Their riot shields were Plexiglas, fit only for stopping rocks, not bullets. Now at least a half dozen of the policemen were on the ground, bleeding.

Then he realized these poor men weren't the fools; it was their commanders, ordering them to their deaths. These men were pawns. He remembered the hapless policeman he disarmed at the gate, his dispirited face, the face of a typical Saudi.

These men are like us. Under the thumb of the royals, stripped of dignity.

After another minute a full dozen lay bleeding in the street, most not moving. Moments later, the remaining policemen began retreating. Mercifully, Saif's men ceased firing as they turned and ran, dragging their wounded colleagues with them and leaving a half dozen bodies behind. It was all over in less than five minutes.

As Saif turned to go, he tasted bile in his mouth. The taste of disgust, of hatred of the royals.

"They were massacred," Tom said to Yassar on the phone. "I can't believe what I just saw. Who ordered this?"

"I have no idea. No one on the Council of Ministers would have approved this. You know our proscription on the use of deadly force without a fatwa."

Some moron captain in the police trying to be a hero?

"What are you gonna do about a fatwa? These guys are dug in at the mosque, and the real party hasn't even started yet. If you can't mount a counterattack, we're all gonna be in big trouble."

Yassar didn't respond right away. Tom gave him some time, imagining him inclining his head, fingering an eyebrow, contemplating. "It is a delicate situation," Yassar finally said. "As you know, *sharia*, our Islamic law, forbids any violence between Muslim brothers. It also forbids any violence within the Grand Mosque. Even plants growing there cannot be uprooted without a religious sanction. Further, it is still during the time of the Hajj, during which additional restrictions apply. I will be one of those presenting to our Saudi Arabian Council of Senior Scholars, our *ulema* who interpret sharia. The only solution is for them to issue a fatwa allowing deadly force in retaking the mosque. Our advisors are counseling us on the line of argument that the rebels are blasphemers because they have violated the holiest site in Islam with violence and have desecrated the sanctity of the Hajj. Still, it may take some time."

Tom felt uncomfortable, wondering if Yassar could get it done. He looked back at the TV, tuned to CNN on mute with the closed captions running, images of the Grand Mosque on the screen. "It's all over CNN, the BBC, the US networks, everyplace. The rebels are getting just the kind of coverage they want."

"Thankfully, world opinion is siding with our government. We have heard from most of the Arab nations, even from Israel, offering their support and confidence in our regime. Many are preparing to say so publicly. Your own President Santorum has called King Abdul to express his support of our government."

Tom was sure that was just tongue-wagging. He checked his watch. Langley had set up a secure line for Tom to talk to Ross in about a half hour. He'd learn more then. An image of Ayatollah Khamenei of Iran flashed up on the TV screen, his words on the closed captions saying, "This is the work of criminal American imperialism."

We're still the Muslim world's pincushion.

Tom said, "We've been monitoring the stuff they're spouting over the loudspeakers from the minarets, and still no mention of the Mahdi."

"I know."

"Wait until they drop that one. By our estimates, that's in seven days. And we think that's when they launch their full offensive. If our sources are right, they'll come at you from all sides, in every province."

"Assad, the head of our Secret Police, is on the way to Mecca now to take command. I will also fly in immediately after my meeting with the Senior Scholars." Yassar paused. "And Sasha, have you heard from her?"

"Yeah. She called a little while ago. She's fine, armed and waiting. Any word on when we can get those plans for the mosque?"

"You should have them in an hour. They'll show everything, including the communications room. What is her plan?"

"You're asking the wrong guy."

Yassar didn't respond.

Tom wondered if he'd offended him with his abruptness. But it was no time for delicacy. This fatwa business had him uneasy. *I hope Sasha gets to Saif soon. This thing might hit the fan sooner than we thought.*

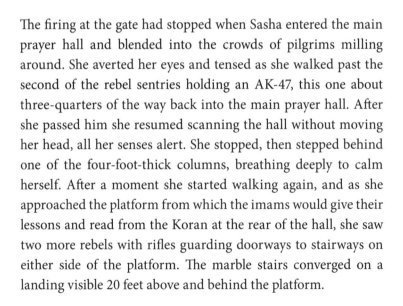

The firing at the gate had stopped when Sasha entered the main prayer hall and blended into the crowds of pilgrims milling around. She averted her eyes and tensed as she walked past the second of the rebel sentries holding an AK-47, this one about three-quarters of the way back into the main prayer hall. After she passed him she resumed scanning the hall without moving her head, all her senses alert. She stopped, then stepped behind one of the four-foot-thick columns, breathing deeply to calm herself. After a moment she started walking again, and as she approached the platform from which the imams would give their lessons and read from the Koran at the rear of the hall, she saw two more rebels with rifles guarding doorways to stairways on either side of the platform. The marble stairs converged on a landing visible 20 feet above and behind the platform.

As she looked up, she inhaled with a short gasp. There, standing at the center of the landing, his legs spread apart, chin raised, stood Saif. His hair was flecked with gray, his eyes seemingly sunken more into his face from the dark circles of fatigue or stress that surrounded them. She thought she could see crow's-feet evident at the corners of his eyes. He wore a close-cropped full beard, also dotted with gray. His frame was still trim, athletic. She expected to feel a blast of anger, but now all she sensed was curiosity at how he had changed, then the urge to throw a derisive laugh at him for how he posed there like he was impersonating some field general.

She exhaled slowly, turning away as inconspicuously as possible, letting her pulse recede. She walked behind another column and leaned her back against it, feeling the cool marble calm her. *Only 30 feet away.* It was a can't-miss shot. She half-closed her eyes as if reflecting, glancing around her. There were at least 50 other women in the prayer hall wearing black abayas. The nearest sentry was 30 feet from her. She could get off three or four quick rounds from behind the column without even being seen, drop the Beretta and melt into what was certain to be a panicked crowd. It was almost too good to be true, Saif standing there, as if preening himself, waiting for someone to come along and send him to his Muslim paradise.

End this, now.

She held the Beretta in her right hand. She reached inside her abaya with her left hand and racked the slide as quietly as she could. She started to glance around to see if anyone had heard, then told herself, *Move. Take the shot.* She stepped out from behind the column and widened her stance. She saw Saif's head jerk toward her in response to the movement from below, and then his eyes lock on hers. She saw the spark of recognition there and in one motion, pulled out the Beretta, braced it in both hands and aimed at Saif's chest.

She fired just as Saif hurled himself to the side—too late. She saw his body rocked by the bullet's impact in the center of his chest. Adjusting her aim as he continued sideways and dropped, trying to flatten himself to the floor of the platform, she pulled off two more rounds, the first hitting him above the heart, the second sending a spray of blood from the side of his head.

A blur of white flashed into her peripheral vision, a robed man hurtling himself at her who grabbed her arm and pulled her to the floor with the momentum of his dive. Before she could throw the man off, right herself and fire again, another man was on top of her. Her gun hand was pinned and then another man was on her back. Her gaze never left the platform, now seeing Saif down but moving.

Next she felt a blast of shock as she saw Saif struggle to his feet and stagger up the stairs.

What? How?

She heard shouts in Arabic of "Get the gun!" and then someone pulled her wrist back to the point of breaking and she felt the gun yanked from her hand. They rolled her onto her back and forced her hands together. One of them secured her wrists with plastic police handcuffs and cinched them up tight. They frisked her and found her cell phone and the extra clip for the Beretta.

Sasha still couldn't believe she'd seen Saif get up. Then it dawned on her. *He was wearing a vest.* She thought about the halo of blood from his head and hoped, but realized that shot must have only winged him if he was able to get up.

After a few minutes a face she recognized came into view standing above her. It was Rashid.

"Who are you?" he said.

Sasha glared back into his eyes. "Tell your little Napoleon it's Sasha. His Western Orchid."

"Downstairs, to the catacombs," he said to the men, and then turned and walked away.

Three men—a giant and a smaller man holding her by each arm, and another who walked in front and seemed to be their superior—led her to the side of the prayer hall and through a doorway. She took each of them in as they led her along a corridor. The two men who held her arms each carried AK-47s slung on their shoulders with straps. The smaller man was skinny and didn't appear to be very muscular. *Easy to take out.* The giant was in his mid-20s, over six feet tall and built like an Olympic heavyweight wrestler, dangerously powerful, but puffy with fat. *Not likely very agile or to have much stamina.* The man in front was in his 50s and shuffled when he walked. He didn't seem to be armed. They reached a door and opened it to a dank-smelling stairway that disappeared down into the darkness. As they descended, she could see ancient granite steps with foot-worn impressions curving their centers. They led her down two levels, then a third and fourth level, into a cold tunnel only six feet wide built of blocks of stone with arched ceilings, lighted by incandescent bulbs within caged housings every 30 or 40 feet.

The air grew colder and damper as they continued to walk, still gradually descending until they reached an old wooden door with iron hinges and hasps. The giant and the smaller man stopped her in front of the door and held her arms with both their hands while the third man pulled a centuries-old ring of iron keys from his robe. He started trying each in turn in the lock. Sasha realized this might be her only chance to try to escape. She glanced to each side, figuring her move, then launched a kick at the man in front of the door. The men holding her arms gave just enough that she was able to snap a heel kick to the back of the man's head. She heard a crack of his neck breaking and he collapsed.

She let out a ferocious yell and spun to her left, dropping onto her left hip. As she'd expected, it wasn't enough to break the grasp of the smaller man on her left, but he buckled as she went down to keep from letting go of her arm. She jumped to her feet again, crashing her head under the man's chin, and this time she broke his grasp. She yelled again and now spun to her right, swinging the giant around enough with her momentum to force him into the wall. He didn't let go, so she hit him with a double-fisted strike under his chin, cracked his head against the wall and when he still didn't let go, she pressed her thumbs into his eyes. She held him there, pressed harder, glancing over her left shoulder to see the smaller man now rolling on his side and reaching for his AK-47. She spun left, now free of one of the giant's hands, and was able to launch a side kick at the man on the floor. She missed, but hit his AK-47 and sent it spinning away from him. She turned back to see the giant coming at her with a punch. She crouched and deflected it with an elbow block, then lashed at him with another double-fisted strike that shattered his nose and rocked his head back.

Finally the giant released his other hand. The smaller man was now halfway to his feet, and she landed a roundhouse kick square in his chest that sent him against the wall. As he rebounded off of it she snapped a solid front kick in his throat. She heard the crunch of cartilage and he fell to his knees, gagging.

She turned back and saw the giant coming at her again, spitting blood, roaring the word "Whore!" She sidestepped him and he lumbered past. She landed a back elbow strike to his kidney and he hunched over. She kicked his legs out from underneath him with a foot sweep and he fell facedown on the floor. It was all she needed. She wound up and smashed a heel kick into the side of his head and he stopped moving.

Now the smaller man was whimpering like a wounded animal and groping on his hands and knees for his AK-47. Sasha landed another heel kick against the side of his head that slammed him against the wall. She jumped onto his back, forced one of her arms around his neck and got a good hold on his throat. She pushed all of her weight on her knees into his back as she pulled upward. It only took about 30 seconds for him to stop struggling. She kept the pressure on his windpipe until her biceps started to hurt, then released him. She stood up, looked down at the man's body, her chest heaving, her breath coming in gasps. She heard movement behind her and turned to see the fist of the giant hurtling at her face. Then everything went black.

Tom was in the living room of his hotel suite, the TV in the background still on mute. He could hear Zac from the bedroom working with his communications equipment, smell oil from Seth cleaning his guns in the kitchen. A representative of the contractor had dropped off the plans to the Grand Mosque and left, which Ryan was reviewing in the living room.

The phone rang. That would be Ross, on a secure line direct from Langley. He wondered if Ross was going to shut down his operation. He didn't like what he'd heard from Yassar about President Santorum calling King Abdul directly.

"What's going on?" Ross said.

"I don't know how much you know, so I'll summarize it." Tom took him through the seizing of the mosque, chaining of the gates, the unsuccessful assault by the police, the estimated 75,000 pilgrims trapped inside the mosque and the rebel's broadcasts from the minarets. He stopped short of telling him about his knowledge from Yassar about President Santorum's conversation with King Abdul, figuring he'd wait to see how much of that Ross disclosed to him.

"What's the current status with Sasha?"

"She's inside the mosque and waiting for an opportunity to get to Saif. It's been 45 minutes since I talked to her. We decided she would work her way to the communications room, from where they're broadcasting their message, in the hope of finding Saif, or at least a lead on where he is."

Ross paused.

Tom waited.

Finally Tom said, "Anything at your end?" He realized that in the hierarchy of things it wasn't necessarily his place to ask that of Ross, but since he was in the field and under a distress situation, he figured it was okay.

"Lots. I've been invited to a meeting in the next half hour in the Oval Office with President Santorum, National Security Advisor Francis, Secretary of State Harmon, Rusty Baldridge, and Admiral Raven, the head of Special Operations Command." Ross paused.

Tom waited for him to go on, not sure where this was going.

"It seems that Francis went around Rusty Baldridge directly to Raven at Special Ops, and talked about wanting to put together a team of his secret counterterrorism forces for a black operation based on intelligence he had received from me in the last week. Instead of telling Francis he already had a black op running,

Raven was cagey enough to keep his mouth shut and just listen." Ross paused again. "I got a call from Raven asking me what the hell was going on. I told him to talk to Rusty." Ross paused again. "Never mind. That's my problem. The point is, I'm going to have to do some fancy footwork to keep your operation under wraps without directly lying to the president."

"Can't you just roll with it and get a Special Ops team assigned? I could use the help."

"What are the odds if your Sasha gets her deal done that it stops this thing before that's necessary?"

"Now that the rebels have seized the mosque, I don't know. Our inside man says the rebels are armed and ready to go. Motivated troops ready to hit strategic targets in every province. We think their timetable for going live is based on the prophecies of the Mahdi revealing himself in eight days. I just don't know."

Ross didn't respond for a moment, then said, "Okay, I'll see what I can do," and hung up.

Tom squirmed, thinking of Sasha, wondering if his operation could get shut down. He'd have to go rogue, and convince Ryan, Zac and Seth to go along with him to avoid leaving her stranded.

Saif stood in the restroom down the hall from the security and communications room. He stared into his face in the mirror after having stopped the bleeding to his ear, injected it with local anesthetic and bandaged it. He now removed his Kevlar vest and examined his chest. Bruises were already starting to show and he felt like he'd been kicked twice by a mule. He hoped few of his men had seen him hit; he wanted as few as possible of them to know he'd been wearing the vest. He put the vest back on. He'd change his shirt so the men couldn't see the bullet holes.

He sighed and stepped back, replaying it in his mind. He had turned his head and looked into the barrel of the gun in her hand and believed that in less than a heartbeat he was going to die. *Sasha.* Her face unmistakable, her jaw set. And when their gaze met, he thought she'd hesitated for a fraction of a second and given him an opportunity to collapse to the floor. Yes, he'd taken two shots in the Kevlar vest, but avoided what might next have been one to the head. As it was, she'd taken the top third of his left ear off. Was he standing here, unnerved, because he'd almost died, or because he'd seen Sasha again after 20 years?

He almost couldn't believe she'd shown up. It had been months since he even considered the possibility, and almost two years since their assassin had targeted her husband. Either their man had successfully delivered his message, or she'd figured it out. Nonetheless, here she was.

And even more beautiful than before.

Her black eyes with even more intensity, her face slim and youthful, that of a woman ten years younger, her skin still luminous.

He splashed some water on his face, dried it. Now he smiled at himself in the mirror. *Sasha.* He remembered when he'd met his wife, Noor. She was a beauty, someone he thought might take Sasha's place in his heart. But no one ever had, and no other woman had ever physically satisfied him the way a good Muslim man was entitled to be. And now, after the difficult birth of Indira, Noor was barren, unable to produce him a son, the male heir he deserved as the man who would lead Saudi Arabia.

He was certain that Sasha, with her vibrancy and health, could still bear him a son.

He knew it would be controversial, a non-Muslim white woman ruling at the side of the new leader of Saudi Arabia. But a bold man took risks. Besides, her allure combined with his charisma would make them a couple that the world would seek out.

Yes, he had almost given up on Sasha, but now she was here. All that remained was for him to convince her. And the mere fact that she was here meant that was possible, even if she'd come armed and had shot to kill.

Now that her men had subdued her in the catacombs, the next step was to apply the appropriate persuasion. There would be time. The situation here at the Grand Mosque would evolve into an extended stalemate. The first order of business with Sasha would be to wear down her resistance with time-tested interrogation tactics. He knew how to do it. Starve her, make her believe that hours were days, then let her stew in her thoughts. He also knew a few buttons he could push that might start her doubting herself. He walked to the door, unlocked it and strode out into the hallway.

Sasha awoke in a room colder than the corridor and lighted only by a single incandescent bulb in the ceiling with a wire cage over it. She was bound by her arms to a wooden chair with plastic police handcuffs like the ones they'd used to bind her wrists.

Now what?

She'd had a clear shot at Saif, and failed. She hadn't considered the possibility of him wearing a vest. She should have thought of that, taken a head shot first, then the chest, instead of the other way around.

In the next moment, she thought of Tom, the rest of the team. How they had almost died earlier in the day in the desert.

She'd let them down. What would they think, after their hard work to get her here, train her, and then learn she'd blown her opportunity? She had a responsibility to them, and to the people they had sworn to protect.

She remembered the signal transmitters in the seams of her abaya, which they'd taken from her when they frisked her. She saw it hanging on a hook on the wall. She stood as well as she could with the chair strapped to her arms and shuffled toward it. At that moment she heard men speaking in Arabic outside the room. She sat back down just as the door opened and someone entered. Sasha's chair was facing away from the door.

"I had given up on you, decided you weren't coming after all," Saif said from behind her.

She refused to turn her head to look at him. Now she felt her pulse rise. "Did you honestly believe I wouldn't respond? I couldn't possibly have changed that much."

He walked over and stopped in front of her. "Time changes people."

"Generally not their deeply held beliefs. Or their willingness to fight for them, or for the people they love."

"Or avenge them?"

Sasha saw the bandage on his ear, then just stared into his eyes, now feeling her emotions rise. *Anger or hatred?* Either would do. "I need to understand."

"What will that accomplish?"

"Closure. And help me decide what to do next."

He walked to the side and picked up another chair, carried it over and placed it with the back toward Sasha. He straddled it and rested his elbows on the back.

Posing again.

He looked down at her wrists. "Plastic straps. Familiar, no?"

Sasha didn't respond.

"These you won't be able to chew through. They're police field handcuffs. If I cut them will you promise to stay put?"

"I'm not making any promises."

"In that case we'll talk this way for now." He let out a long sigh. "So where do we start?"

"Why? Why did you murder my husband, and why did you leave me that message?"

"That was almost two years ago, and I wasn't as firmly in command as I am now. You know our people have been after you off and on for years, since the day Ibrahim and almost two dozen other faithful were murdered."

Sasha glared at him, wanting him to know that she wasn't going to buy any explanation other than the truth.

"So how do you think our senior command reacted to the assassination of Sheik bin Abdur himself, our leader, and almost 40 of our other senior people two years ago with your help? My brothers wanted blood. Both yours and your husband's. I was able to convince them you weren't involved, that it was Daniel who helped the CIA."

Sasha exploded. "So you got them to shift their lust for revenge onto my Daniel?"

"It was going to happen anyway. You're lucky I was at least able to save you."

"Do you expect me to accept that?"

"It's the truth. And if it helps, I thought the whole exercise was unnecessary, since neither of you posed any threat to us anymore."

Sasha was shouting at him now. "Help? How is that supposed to help? Besides, if you didn't agree with it you could've warned me."

"You expect me to choose sides against my own people?" Saif shouted back. "You're the one who's on the wrong side!"

"If I'm on the wrong side, then what was this nonsensical message that you wanted your Western Orchid back at your side?" Sasha was leaning forward, straining against the bonds on her arms, feeling the veins in her neck throbbing.

Saif leaned toward her, still shouting, "It was an invitation to choose the right path, to rule with me and do some good for the people of Saudi Arabia, finally do some good with your life!"

"*Finally*?"

"Yes! After wasting it by either indulging your own desires or letting others use you to indulge theirs. Becoming a whore to one of the royals, then a tool used by the CIA and Yassar for whatever they choose."

"How dare you!" She hurled herself forward at him with her fists raised as far as she could with her arms bound to the chair. Saif sidestepped her, sent her tumbling sideways onto the floor with a shove. As she struggled to get up, Saif put his foot on the chair to hold her down.

He called out to his men and two of them ran into the room. Saif said to them, "Lash her feet to the chair until it's time to take her to the toilet." Then he turned and said to Sasha, "I expected no less. I'll give you some time to think about this rationally, and we'll talk again." He walked from the room.

Sasha's earlier question to herself was now answered. She wasn't feeling anger toward Saif. It was hatred.

Every six hours or so, three men came into the room where Sasha was imprisoned to give her water and take her to the toilet. One man put a prong dog collar around her neck with a leash attached to it. Then the two others cut the straps binding her arms and legs to the chair. The leash man led her while the two others guarded her, armed, keeping their distance as if she were a grizzly bear. They took her to a room down the hall with a hole in the floor that reeked of sewage, where she was instructed to squat. They never took their guns, or their eyes, off her.

The lights went off in her room at an appropriate interval for night and came back on during the day—at least that's what it seemed to Sasha. She wondered if they were trying to make her think she was there longer than she was, but then based on the growl in her stomach, she decided that she had in fact been there for a few days. A few more days without food and she'd become too weak to fight for very long, but they were giving her plenty of water, so she knew she could carry on that way for weeks without dying, if it came to that. But it wouldn't come to that if she could help it.

In the middle of the first day, she'd tried to work herself to the wall where her abaya was hanging, in order to send a distress signal. She tipped her chair sideways, then rolled onto her front and supported herself on her forearms and toes. She was then able to inch forward, caterpillar-style, toward the wall. She made it to the wall in what seemed like about an hour, then collapsed, too exhausted to make a try to get herself upright and reach for the abaya. She rested, anxious every minute about the guards coming in again. She fell asleep, and when she awoke, she wasn't sure how long she'd lain there, but it was dark in the room by that time. She forced her chair upright and then tried to reach for her abaya, but couldn't feel it because she couldn't reach high enough given how tightly her arms were bound to the chair. Dejected, she worked her way back to the middle of the room, forced the chair upright and, as she fell asleep, resolved to try again the next day.

The next day after they brought her back from the toilet, she flexed her arms and legs as they cinched the plastic handcuffs up against them to bind her back to the chair, hoping for enough slack when she relaxed that she would have more flexibility to move. She was right. The next day's trek to the wall was easier, faster. And when she reached the wall this time the lights were still on. She still couldn't reach her abaya with her hands, but she was able to get up high enough on her tiptoes that she could grab the fabric in her teeth. She worked her way up the fabric in her mouth, found a seam and then felt between her teeth for one of the transmitters. She felt something hard. *Got one.* She knew just beyond it in the seam would be the plastic pouch containing the battery acid. She couldn't quite reach it. She settled back down off her toes and the back legs of the chair hit the floor.

Now what?

She could either take one more try at getting up on her toes, or sink her teeth into the abaya and try to yank it off the hook to the floor. That was risky, but maybe the guard coming back into the room might think it had simply fallen off the hook.

Sri Ganesha, she prayed to her Remover of Obstacles.

She got back on her toes, bit into the fabric of the abaya and pulled, then let her weight carry her backward. She heard a tear and then the abaya slid off.

She felt a surge of adrenaline.

She got her hands into the fabric, found one of the transmitters, then the pouch containing the battery acid and squeezed it. She dropped the abaya to the floor, then tilted her chair sideways, rolled on her front and caterpillar-walked her way back to the center of the room. She tilted herself back upright again and breathed deeply. One small triumph for the last few days. At least now Tom and his team would know where she was, or at least that she was still alive.

CHAPTER 14

Day Two. Grand Mosque, Mecca.

SOMEONE CAME INTO THE BEDROOM and shook Tom awake. He glanced at the clock as he rolled over. *4:00 a.m.*

Zac said, "We've got a signal. Its weak, but it's her."

Tom got up and threw on a robe. When he got to the living room of the suite, Ryan, Seth and Zac were sitting around the table looking at the plans of the Grand Mosque.

"Right here," Zac said, pointing. "Off to the side of the main prayer hall."

"Does it mean anything to you?"

"No. Only that she's alive."

Tom went back to bed. He didn't know how long it took him to fall asleep, but he reawakened, perspiring, his mind turning in on itself. He was assaulted by images of Sasha: on the Promenade des Anglaise in Nice when she was 18; a year older, as he sent her back to Yassar in the Royal Palace after she'd killed Ibrahim; two years ago, after Tom realized she was still alive as he'd worked with Daniel on the response to the al-Mujari's oil and gas terrorism; a month ago in the hotel room in Langley when she'd approached him about Saif; and three days ago as he'd watched her enter the gates of the Grand Mosque.

Finally he gave up on sleep and sat up in bed.

Denial.

Men were so great at it, especially him. Burying their feelings beneath multiple layers of work, sports, hobbies, anything it took. But now, here in the dark of night, drenched in sweat, he understood he had to face it. He was in love with Sasha, had been for all those years. Even after it had forced itself upon him in the last weeks and after he'd still pushed it away, he knew there was no more hiding from it. And now he was terrified for the danger she was in, and trembling with emotion that he might never see her again.

In that moment he envied women, with their inability to deny their feelings. Life must be so much easier if you just had to face them instead of forcing them underground and having them compound upon themselves, festering, then rise to the surface and kick you in the ass with a hundred times the force.

CHAPTER 15

Day Three. Grand Mosque, Mecca.

BY NOON ON THE THIRD day after the rebels had occupied the mosque, Tom's nerves were jangled. While he was accustomed to the stress of an ongoing operation, sitting and waiting with nothing happening was like having someone slowly sand his fingertips raw. He'd been unable to reach Yassar for 48 hours and hadn't heard a word from Assad, the head of the Saudi Secret Police, who Yassar said was on the way two days ago. He hadn't talked to Ross in 48 hours, either, and had nothing to report to him. And Sasha's micro-transmitter had died 12 hours earlier, with no new signal since then.

He felt a start as he heard weapons fire. He ran to the window and saw smoke on the far side of the mosque. Zac, Seth and Ryan joined him a moment later.

"It's one of the gates on the far eastern side," Seth said.

"Here, too," Zac said, pointing down to the street at the near side. Tom heard a rumbling noise and saw four armored vehicles with rear-mounted machine guns inching toward two gates with clusters of green-uniformed men behind them.

Royal Army troops. That meant Yassar must've gotten his fatwa. And it might explain why Assad wasn't here. *But why no word?*

Saif was pacing in the command center, talking on the phone with Anwar.

"They're evacuating the city, and the Hajj is now over," Anwar said. "We're losing our opportunity."

Saif saw this as a pivotal moment, one in which he needed to assert his authority. Anwar and the other dissident leaders might not yet see him as the overall commander, but they would learn.

"No. We wait, as planned."

"But that means millions of sympathetic pilgrims will be leaving the city. Many of them men, capable of arming and fighting at our sides."

"They'll fight even harder when they return to their own cities, in defense of their homes and their families."

Anwar said, "This is a mistake."

Saif tensed with anger. "The Mahdi has not yet revealed himself."

"What are you waiting for?"

"It isn't time. Remember our strategy. We orchestrate our moves carefully, like all intelligent field generals."

"I'm beginning to think you're a fool."

Saif tensed with anger, then exhaled to compose himself. "After this is over I will give you the opportunity to apologize for that. For now I expect you to follow our battle plan, execute your orders as we've agreed." He heard shooting, pulled the phone away from his ear. He saw Rashid run into the room, motioning to him. "We're under attack. I must go," Saif said and hung up the phone. "What is it?" he said to Rashid.

"Attacks by the Royal Army on three gates."

They ran up the stairs to the roof. Saif could see all three gates under attack, two on the near side being assaulted by armored vehicles with 50 to 100 men behind each. A gate in the distance on the eastern side was being assaulted by a group of Royal Army troops behind armored barriers. He could hear the crack of his snipers' rifles, see his men on the tops of the walls firing bursts from their AK-47s. He felt his blood rise. These were the royals' elite troops. And his men were holding them, even with many of his troops maintaining their positions at the other gates in case these were only initial assaults. Now he saw the armored vehicles moving toward the gates.

"Where are our shoulder-fired missiles?" Saif asked, just as a whoosh rose up from the top of the wall at one of the gates, then another, the two trails of the missiles shrieking toward their targets. One scored a direct hit on one of the armored vehicles, followed by a ball of flame and smoke that erupted with an explosion that echoed off the buildings across from the mosque. The second missile missed, but took out a swath of the approaching troops.

Automatic weapons fire continued from Saif's men on the top of the walls. Now the firing increased as more of his men swarmed to the gates under siege. The three remaining armored vehicles had stopped within 100 feet of the gates, their machine guns raking the top of the wall with large-caliber fire. He could see smoke from his men's return fire pinging off the armor in front of each of the machine guns, then a gunner going down. Another man climbed behind the machine gun and began firing again as another missile found its mark and destroyed the vehicle.

"We are holding," Saif shouted above the gunfire.

The firing continued for another 20 minutes. By that time the men surrounding the two destroyed armored vehicles were either dead or wounded. The firing from the other two armored vehicles attacking the other gate had now stopped. He could see the men behind them either huddling close to it or dropping to the street from the fire from Saif's men. He glanced toward the far eastern gate. At least 50 Royal Army troops lay in the street, their barricades abandoned. The other men appeared to have retreated.

Now, back on this side of the mosque, the remaining two armored vehicles started moving in. Another shoulder-fired missile was launched, this one from the ground level at the gate. It slammed into one of the armored vehicles, destroying it. Moments later, another missile whooshed from the gate, spinning the last armored vehicle around with a hit in the rear, disabling it. At that point the men behind it who were still alive retreated, running away and disappearing down a side street.

Saif's men ceased firing. He saw a few raise their rifles over their heads and begin cheering, joined by a dozen, then a few dozen more, then heard the voices of hundreds of his soldiers join in.

"We beat them back!" Saif shouted, slapping Rashid on the back. Saif was beaming. He stood up and raised his arms, cheering his men. They saw him and roared back.

"There is no God but Allah!" Saif yelled.

"*La ilaha ilallah!*" the men shouted back.

CHAPTER 16

Day Four. Grand Mosque, Mecca.

SASHA AWAKENED, BOUND TO HER chair in her prison room.

Seven days.

She'd never been held like this before, so she didn't have any experience with it. She was surprised she wasn't more physically weak, but she realized the silence, the lack of knowledge about time, and the isolation were getting to her. She'd actually started to find the visits of the guards to bring her to the toilet a welcome stimulation.

She occupied much of her time thinking of Daniel. Today, she didn't want to focus on their life in Switzerland, even though that had been the happiest time of her life, because it ended in the horror of his murder. Yesterday she had been tormented by the replay of his murder in her mind, as if on infinite loop. She went back to when she'd met him in Milford, Pennsylvania, where he owned a weekend house. But that only reminded her of how she'd come to be there: sent by Yassar to spy on Daniel, learn if the al-Mujari had penetrated Daniel's oil and gas clients' computer systems yet. The duplicity of it brought tears to her eyes. It wasn't much better that she lived with him for months under those false pretenses. She remembered how that had torn at her heart as she was falling in love with him.

"Oh, Daniel."

She hung her head and started to cry. For the first time she wondered if her captors were monitoring the room with microphones. She cried in silence, her tears rolling down her cheeks and dripping onto her forearms. Finally, she didn't care, and gave in to sobs.

She didn't know how long she cried, but after a while she took a few deep breaths and held her head up.

Oh, God.

She wondered why people always said you felt better with the release of a good cry. She always felt physically relieved, but emotionally drained.

Here she was, captive, Daniel gone forever, and she'd been unable to set right his murder.

Saif.

She'd beaten herself up over that failure already. But was it a failure? A failure to kill another man. Even though Saif deserved it, would taking Saif's life have solved anything? Then she reminded herself of the stakes involved. Kill Saif and save hundreds of thousands, maybe millions, by stopping the revolution, or at least stalling it. She remembered what she'd said to Tom in the hotel room in Langley: *Good versus evil.* Guru Kripananda told Sasha she had a pure heart and good intentions, and therefore was already saved, despite the lives she had taken. Maybe the guru was right.

But what about the two men she'd killed in the corridor as they brought her to this room? What about that stain on her soul? Had that accomplished anything?

The issues she'd wrestled with as she'd gone back to India came back to her. Daniel had been the anchor in her life, a rock. Now he was gone. Who was she before Daniel, and who was she now?

She sat, taking in the silence, light-headed for lack of food, but wanting her mind to clear to give her answers. They didn't come.

She didn't know how much longer it was before she decided she needed to move. She shook her head, then tilted the chair on its side. She rolled it on its back, stretching her limbs as much as she could. The lights went out. She realized this was what they wanted, what Saif wanted. *He's starving and sensory-depriving me so my mind will twist in on itself.*

She decided a crawl to the other side of the room would do her good. She rolled onto her front and started out, working toward the wall on her forearms and toes. She realized she needed something to hold on to, to keep her from these moments of self-torment.

Hang on to your defiance, if nothing else. Don't let him get to you.

She reached the wall and had turned around to work her way back to the other side of the room when the lights came back on.

The lights were off and Sasha was asleep when she was awakened by the sound of someone entering the room. The lights came on and she heard Saif's voice. "I've given you some time to think about your position. Hopefully now you'll be more receptive to a dialogue."

So he thinks starving me for a week will change my mind?

"A dialogue about what?"

"My vision for the people of Saudi Arabia. And for you to be at my side as I lead them."

"Vision? What vision? You're a murderer who leads an organization that commits acts of terror on innocent people."

Saif sighed. "We kill infidels who are trying to destroy our Saudi way of life. The way of life of righteous Muslims."

"Righteous Muslims, listen to you. Look who's now a model of Muslim sanctity. I never once in my life saw you answer the call to prayers."

"I am a leader to my people, and I will inspire them to throw off their oppressors."

"You're a thug, and you're spouting platitudes."

Saif sighed again and stood up. He started pacing around behind Sasha. "You talk about me being a murderer. You killed two men and injured another as they brought you here. Why?"

His words hit home. She felt a stab of anguish, but shot back at him despite it, "Don't be absurd. To get away. To get another shot at you."

Saif walked in front of her, leaned toward her face and said, "Where does it stop? The killing?"

"When you're dead."

Saif looked off at the wall, thinking for a few moments. "We have become a nation of privilege, access and influence."

Now it was Sasha's turn to sigh. "That was a tired old argument over 20 years ago. You said you were going to do something about it then, and you've done nothing."

"That's right. And now I am doing something about it."

"Oh? Killing people needlessly? Taking tens of thousands of your righteous Muslim faithful hostage and watching them murdered in the crossfire or starved to death? Assassinating a group of policemen as they come to rescue them?"

"You're completely missing the point"

Sasha sneered at him. "You don't have one."

"I do. We've become a nation of haves and have-nots. Every coveted position is handed out to royal family members, 50,000 princes and counting. It's no different than the class system of the British Empire. The Saudi royals are living in the past. I want you to join me, be at my side as I restore Saudi Arabia to what it once was. In doing so, you and I can recapture what we once had together. When you've come around to see the error of your views, there will be nothing to keep us apart. If you think back, you'll remember and know I'm right."

"*You're* living in the past. You were my first lover. We were together for six months 20 years ago, before either of us knew much of anything about life. Get over it."

"I can see this isn't going anywhere. I'm going to leave you again to give you more time to think. Think about the direction of your life."

"I don't need to think about the direction of my life."

"Yes, you do. You need to examine your life, how you've been used by the Americans to further their goal of dominating the Eastern world for their political and economic ends. To secure the oil supplies for their bloated lifestyle. And how you've supported the corrupt royals' collusion with them to line their own pockets and live off the backs of the average Saudi."

"Are you done with your speeches for today?"

Saif didn't respond. He walked to the door and left.

Saif made the rounds visiting the men. Two of his top lieutenants—Kareem and Zaki—had been against it.

"What if the royals have snipers? You will be out in the open, an easy target."

Rashid had said, "All the more reason to show the men you aren't afraid."

Saif had agreed. "He's right. It will inspire the men."

He left Rashid in command, then walked outside with his shoulders thrust back and his head held high, accompanied by Kareem and Zaki. His wish to impress the men notwithstanding, once he crossed the courtyard he stayed close to the perimeter wall so he'd be shielded from sniper fire.

It was glorious. The sun was bright, but the day not too oppressively hot. The smell of cordite was still in the air, the odor and black smoke from the burning armored vehicles lending an aura of battle drama. The men spotted him as he approached the first western gate that had been attacked by the armored vehicles. They formed a crowd, cheering and waving their weapons, then parted as he strode through them, nodding, smiling and waving his arms. He made a point of congratulating each of his lieutenants who had overseen the defense, hugging and slapping them on the backs. He thought of giving a short speech, then realized he had two more gates to visit.

He was just returning to the main prayer hall after 45 minutes of visiting with his men when he heard the helicopters coming in. He looked up and the air went out of his lungs. The sky was full of them. At least two dozen Black Hawks with Saudi markings were coming in low and fast, as if on a strafing run. He ran through the prayer hall for the steps to the communications room, the rotors pounding so loudly he had to yell to be heard. "To the roof," he shouted to Rashid. He grabbed two AK-47s and ran for the stairs.

By the time he reached the roof, four of the helicopters were hovering just above the ground in the courtyard, and a dozen men had already abseiled from them. He crouched in firing position and started shooting at the soldiers as they hit the ground. With the noise of the choppers, he couldn't hear any others firing, but knew his men were responding, because most of the soldiers collapsed before they could run more than ten yards.

It took less than a minute or two for the first Black Hawks to deposit their men, and the first group of helicopters lifted off and hovered a few hundred feet over the mosque as another four Black Hawks came in. The first Black Hawks provided cover from their side gunners while the second group deposited their men. At least a dozen men from this wave survived and ran to join the few of their colleagues from the first tranche who had made it to shelter behind the four-foot-thick columns surrounding the walkway beneath the perimeter walls.

Saif looked up to see the face of one of the helicopter pilots as he swung his Black Hawk around, lowered its nose and trained its guns on the group of men who had accompanied Rashid and him to the roof.

"Down!" Saif yelled, pushing Rashid into the stairwell and diving in after him. Two of the men made it into the stairwell a few seconds after Saif heard the clatter of the Black Hawk's cannon. The man in the rear, still in the doorway, was cut in half, while the man in front had one of his arms severed just before his head exploded. His headless torso fell onto the first landing where Saif lay.

Saif waited a few moments after the cannon fire stopped and climbed the steps again. He shivered with disgust as he lay down on the bloody threshold to peer out at the sky. Another wave of Black Hawks was coming in as the preceding one lifted off. Over a dozen of the choppers were hovering, continuing to provide covering fire as additional men abseiled from newly arriving ones. Rashid appeared next to him, handing Saif an AK-47, then taking aim with his. He emptied a clip at the tail rotor of the nearest Black Hawk. Almost immediately, the chopper began wobbling, then spinning out of control. It descended out of sight below the edge of the roof into the courtyard below.

Saif crawled out to the edge of the roof and saw the Black Hawk sitting on the courtyard. He raised his AK-47 and sighted in on the tail rotor of another Black Hawk. He expended his clip to no effect. He turned back toward the doorway and saw Rashid firing at the same chopper from a prone position. As he entered the doorway he heard a metallic groan behind him, turned and saw the Black Hawk wobbling and vibrating where it hovered. This one banked to the right and headed east, away from the mosque and disappeared from view.

"I'll tell the men to fire at the tail rotors," Saif hollered, pulling out his cell phone to call his lieutenants.

"No need," Rashid yelled back. He pointed over his shoulder. Two more Black Hawks were now wobbling and spinning, one heading for the courtyard, the other toward the street outside the west wall. Most of the other Black Hawks were pulling up, safely out of range of effective small arms fire. Saif could also see they weren't firing into the mosque itself, only at his men on the roof and the tops of the perimeter walls.

Saif motioned for Rashid to follow him down. He stopped at the communications room, grabbed two more clips for his AK-47 and ran down the stairs. The main prayer hall was jammed with pilgrims huddling and crying, their faces showing fear and horror. Saif pushed his way through. When he reached the doorway to the courtyard, he saw clusters of his men huddled in the doorway and behind the columns in firing position, in a firefight with the remaining Royal Army troops who had managed to shelter themselves behind the outer columns. He could see his men all the way across the courtyard firing from behind columns as well. Then his men began using grenade launchers, shooting grenades almost horizontally, skipping them from one side to the other across the marble surface of the courtyard. The firefight went on for another hour, the Royal Army troops in a continual crossfire, the Black Hawks hovering above but no longer firing. When return fire from the Royal Army troops on the ground had ceased, the Black Hawks, one by one, flew off toward the east. After another few minutes the skies were clear and the only sounds in the mosque were the moans of the wounded and dying, and the prayers and whimpers from terrified pilgrims.

CHAPTER 17

Day Five. Grand Mosque, Mecca.

THE NEXT MORNING, TOM WAS standing over Zac and his communications equipment in the bedroom of the suite. Zac was playing with the dials on a shoebox-sized piece of equipment he called a MantaRay. It had a laptop connected to it with a USB cable. The laptop had dozens of vertical bars with numbers underneath them showing on the screen. He pulled off his headphones and spoke to Tom.

"The MantaRay is from the same company that makes the StingRay that the FBI and police departments use in the US to track bad guys' cell phones," Zac said. "The StingRay can only track location. The MantaRay is much more sophisticated. It lets you listen in on cell phone conversations. It's the same device I use to pick up the transmitters we put in Sasha's abaya. It mimics a cell phone tower and gets phones to connect to it, then measures the signals. I have it pointed at the mosque, and I've got two more units in buildings on either side of the mosque, so with the mapping software in my laptop I can instantly triangulate to the location of any cell phone I pick up. I'm getting hundreds of signals."

"Hundreds? How do you figure that?" Tom asked.

"The rebels are using them to communicate, and maybe even some of the pilgrims were cheating by carrying cell phones with them on the Hajj."

Tom nodded for him to go on.

"But that's not the important point. I'm getting consistent signals from a number of phones, particularly those emanating from the area of the communications room. I think I'm close to zeroing in on Saif's cell phones and being able to listen to his conversations."

Tom smiled and walked back into the living room of the suite just as Yassar called. Yassar apologized for going dark on him and said he'd explain if Tom could join him and Assad in his suite, five floors above Tom's in the same hotel.

"Tom, please come in," Yassar said as one of his bodyguards answered the door. It was only Yassar and Assad in the living room of the suite, attended by two more bodyguards. Yassar motioned and the three bodyguards disappeared into the bedroom and closed the door.

Yassar motioned to an armchair, and as Tom walked toward it he saw the Grand Mosque through the window, more damage apparent than from the view on his floor. He saw pockmarks from small weapons fire and big chunks blown out of the tops of the perimeter wall from the Gatling guns on the Black Hawks. Debris was scattered all over the marble courtyard, and rebel crews dragged dead bodies toward the shade underneath the columned walkways by the wall. Dark stains of blood were evident everywhere. Two of the armored vehicles were still smoldering in the street, as was a Black Hawk that had been downed, the acrid odor evident even inside the hotel.

Man, have these guys gone about this the wrong way.

After they sat down, Yassar said, "Please allow me to apologize. I was out of touch, and Assad did not contact you, because we were dealing with some internecine issues within the royal family. Defense Minister Ali ordered both of yesterday's strikes. In his defense, neither of the assault teams obeyed orders. The ground troops were not authorized to fire until they had crashed through the gates, and then only at the rebels inside the mosque, with instructions to hold pilgrim casualties to a minimum. The helicopter pilots were not authorized to fire at all. As I am sure you saw, the results were disastrous. King Abdul has since intervened and requested that Assad, with my guidance, command the situation at the mosque."

Tom asked, "What if the situation escalates beyond that into a countrywide revolution?"

Yassar said, "Naturally, Defense Minister Ali will command our armed forces, but King Abad has already insisted that Assad and I have direct access to him and input into our strategy and tactics."

Tom nodded.

Assad said, "I would like to get your assessment of where we stand, since it seems your intelligence is superior to ours. I would also like to know the status of Sasha's efforts. But first, allow me to apprise you of the current situation in the mosque." He settled back in the sofa and looked up at the wall as if he were reading from a blackboard. "We estimate that somewhere between 50 and 75 thousand pilgrims are trapped inside the mosque. We have effectively evacuated Mecca, which means that the roughly 3 million pilgrims who participated in the Hajj have left the city, and that anyone living within three blocks of the Grand Mosque has been temporarily relocated."

Tom imagined millions of Mecca residents living in thousands of tents in the desert outside the city, as the Hajj pilgrims did.

Assad continued. "We estimate hundreds dead and many more wounded inside the mosque. Rebels, pilgrims and Royal Army troops. Outside Mecca, we are monitoring approximately 15 radical sheiks who have been elevating their rhetoric in the last week, presaging the coming of the Mahdi at sunup in three days. Our aerial surveillance has located seven rebel tent camps outside six of our major cities and two tent camps in the desert near major oil fields in the Eastern Province, all of which we are monitoring for any activity. All our armed forces are on heightened alert." He looked back at Tom.

Tom arched his eyebrows at Assad's last comments, surprised and impressed with the Saudis' intelligence and readiness.

Tom said, "Thank you. First, regarding Sasha, she's inside the mosque. She has signal transmitters in her abaya, and we received a signal three days ago that put her someplace near the main prayer hall. We haven't heard anything since. Overall, we have no new intelligence beyond my briefing to you, Assad, last week in Riyadh." Tom had never told either Yassar or Assad they had a man inside and decided it was too risky to disclose that at this point, either. "I haven't received confirmation yet from my director, but he told me three days ago that the national security advisor to our president had contacted our head of Special Operations Command to consider making a team of our counterterrorism specialists available to assist."

Yassar said, "Perhaps we should tell you what Assad has been thinking as to how we should proceed."

Assad said, "We're virtually certain they have no medical supplies or trained medical personnel inside the mosque. We're also certain that many pilgrims who were not even injured in the fighting are in need of medical attention. Many are elderly and the five days of the Hajj are physically demanding. We also suspect there are limited or no food supplies inside the mosque. On that basis we propose to contact the rebels and offer a truce so that we may evacuate wounded, remove the dead so they may be buried on a timely basis in accordance with Islamic tradition, and allow the families of any dead, and any sick or infirm pilgrims, to leave the mosque."

"Why do you think they'll release any of the pilgrims? I've assumed the rebels consider them hostages."

Assad didn't reply.

Tom said, "Okay, so let's assume they go along with that. Then what?"

Yassar said, "Then we wait and see, with no further assaults."

Not much of a plan, Tom thought. "Doesn't that just play into their hands?"

Assad said, "How so? If we have to, we'll starve them out."

"Time isn't on our side. You said yourself that the radical sheiks are already priming the pump about the Mahdi. What happens when Saif unveils him and starts blasting his message from the loudspeakers in the minarets? And then that message gets picked up and spouted all over the country? We think that's the beginning of Saif's endgame, and it's only three days away. At that point, holy war."

Yassar said, "If we need to take action against the camps we have located, we will."

"I get that. But I can't imagine you've located them all. And most of the Arab Spring uprisings have started directly within the cities. So even if you take out some camps, assume you wind up with a full-blown revolution in the streets of all your major cities after Saif turns over his Mahdi card. Then what?"

Yassar and Assad looked back and forth at each other. Neither had a response.

Tom leaned forward and cleared his throat. "Assad, I have an idea I've kicked around with my team. How about we go downstairs and talk in my suite."

When Assad and Tom got downstairs to Tom's suite, Tom called Ryan, Zac and Seth into the living room and sat down in front of the maps of the Grand Mosque. Tom pointed to the dotted lines, like passageways, all over the map.

"We saw these and wondered what they were," Tom said, then flipped forward a few pages in the maps, "then we found this page, which has those dotted lines as solid lines, with the outline of the mosque as dotted lines." He looked up at Assad and pointed to the caption on the page.

"Yes," Assad said, "the catacombs."

"You know about them?"

"Of course. They date back to the 8th or 9th century, built when the mosque was first constructed. They're a labyrinth of miles of underground tunnels and rooms beneath and around the mosque, with access from multiple locations inside the mosque."

"Do the rebels know about them?"

"I can only assume so. They are no secret to those who are knowledgeable about the mosque."

"Do they have maps of them like this?"

"Impossible. No one has this level of detail. It's never been produced before, and this mapping was only undertaken as part of the mosque expansion currently under way, to avoid any damage to the underground structures during the construction."

Tom pointed to a spot on the map with Arabic words and numerals next to it. "What's this?"

"That's a gate, through which one can enter the tunnels of the catacombs from the outside."

Tom could hardly believe it. A perfect way to get inside the mosque undetected, and the Saudis knew all about it but still had insisted on making a frontal assault. He smiled, felt his pulse quicken. "Great. So can you see any reason we can't put a team, or a few, inside the catacombs to sneak into the mosque and take out the rebel leadership?"

Assad said, "As Minister Yassar and I said upstairs, our plan is to starve them before taking any action such as that."

"But we've only got three days left before they reveal the Mahdi and launch the full uprising. You aren't gonna starve out anybody in three days. I already told you my director was working on getting a Special Ops team on site here. I assume you can field a few of your own teams, can't you?"

Assad nodded and smiled. "How many men do you think we'll need?"

"Let's work that out once I learn more about what's happening on my side." Tom looked at Zac. "How about you get back in there and see if there's anything new from Langley?"

A minute later they all walked into the bedroom where Zac sat in front of his equipment. Zac pulled off his earphones. "Nothing from Langley."

"Okay, so anything new with your triangulation?"

Zac smiled. "I've got a lock on at least a half dozen phones."

Tom stepped closer and sat down. "Do you think it's significant?"

"Yeah. Four of the phones get regular use, almost exclusively from the communications room. Mostly outbound, but some inbound calls. Whoever is using them is smart enough to turn the phones off when he isn't making calls, but obviously doesn't know we can zero in on them even if they're turned off as long as the batteries are in them."

Tom said, "You have a look on your face like you're awfully proud of yourself."

"I'd say so. I think it has to be Saif. He's rotating phones, because he can't throw them away and use new ones because doesn't have any more."

"Can you tell when they're switched on?"

"Of course."

"So that means we can make an incoming call to him, right?"

Zac nodded.

Tom turned to Assad and said, "How about we get Yassar down here?"

Saif walked across the courtyard toward the entrance to the main prayer hall. Spent shell casings crunched under his feet. He saw a few of his men using clothing lashed to their AK-47s to brush the cartridges into piles because they didn't have any brooms. The sickeningly sweet smell of blood from this morning had given over to the stench of death. Even though his men had been dragging the corpses into the shade all morning, the temperature at noon was already over 100°, and it was no use; the bodies were decaying rapidly. As he approached the main prayer hall he heard moans, because they were using it as a field hospital. Sympathetic SANG troops had stashed a number of field medical kits in the provisions they hid inside the catacombs for his men, but the medical kits were insufficient to allow them to do more than stem some bleeding with compresses and bandages, or to inject the wounded with morphine or local anesthetic to make them as comfortable as possible.

Saif had known it would be like this. Most of his men hadn't. As he got closer to the entrance to the prayer hall, he looked into the faces of a few of them, crouched behind columns clutching their weapons, watching the skies anxiously. They look frightened and exhausted. The same men who had stood on top of the walls and raised their rifles as they shouted in victory after beating back the ground assault.

Even though they'd successfully held against the aerial assault, the carnage had been so complete, the terror with the Black Hawks thundering overhead so consummate, that Saif knew it was futile to try to raise the men's morale with a rousing victory speech. He increased his pace as he crossed through the prayer hall and climbed the steps to the communications room. Rashid, Amal and Zaki were already there. They huddled together in a corner.

"I've made the rounds and seen most of it," Saif said. "Have you got the details?"

Rashid said, "Ninety-three Royal Army troops killed, 19 wounded, 8 surrendered and being held. Forty-seven pilgrims killed, 136 wounded."

Saif closed his eyes and pursed his lips, dreading the tally for his own men.

"Sixty-two of our own men killed, 73 wounded."

Saif said, "How many of the wounded are serious?"

Rashid looked at Amal. "About half," Amal said. "Probably half of them will die within 48 hours without medical attention. Maybe a quarter of them will die anyhow."

"How many of those that will die anyhow are our men?"

"Perhaps a dozen."

Saif felt a wave of dread. "I understand." He took a breath and looked up at Rashid. "Munitions?"

Rashid said, "Plenty of clips for the AK-47s, hand grenades, surface-to-air missiles, and anti-tank missiles."

"Food?"

"Enough for a week for our men."

"How many pilgrims?"

"About 100,000."

Saif felt it like a jab in the ribs. He'd planned this for the last day of the Hajj, with the hope that the number of pilgrims would be enough for the royals to worry about hostages, but few enough to be a burden. Now he had to deal with it, 100,000 times over.

"Leave us," Saif said to Amal and Zaki.

They left.

"What do you think?" Rashid asked Saif.

"I think we're exactly where we should have expected to be."

"And where is that?"

"In a stalemate, with options, and probably in a stronger negotiating position than we deserve to be."

"How so?"

"Because regardless of how you look at the last four days, they probably think we have more men than we do, and feel like we trounced them three times, because we did. They will take huge criticism for doing the damage they have done to this, the holiest of places in Islam, and will be reluctant to do any more. In addition, we have 100,000 people in here who will keep the royals from attacking too aggressively, even though I was surprised by their willingness to fire at us from the helicopters yesterday."

"So where does that leave us?" Rashid asked.

"Time to go downstairs and talk to Qahtani. In three days we can reveal the Mahdi."

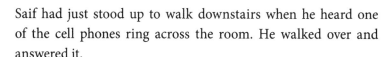

Saif had just stood up to walk downstairs when he heard one of the cell phones ring across the room. He walked over and answered it.

"Hello. Am I speaking to Saif?"

"Who is asking?"

"This is Minister Yassar."

Saif inhaled sharply. "Yes, this is Saif." He felt like he should have said something more, but he was so taken aback that he decided that less was more.

"Very good. I am pleased I was able to reach you. I am nearby, in Mecca, and have witnessed the events of the last four days. I have been authorized to speak on behalf of the Council of Ministers. I regret the violence that has occurred, and am anxious to deal first with the unfortunate casualties, including the innocent pilgrims. I have a proposal for you." Yassar paused.

"I'm listening." Saif tried to keep it low-key. He wondered how Rickman would have played it. But as what character? Henry V? Hans Gruber? Snape?

"First, as a gesture of good faith, we are prepared to turn back on the electricity, gas and water, and—"

"The emergency generators are running, with ample supplies of propane, and the Zamzam Well inside the mosque is an adequate supply of water, one that is even blessed by Allah."

Yassar took a moment to start up again. Saif imagined him stewing over the impudence of a commoner, and a Shiite at that, to interrupt him. Yassar said, "Nonetheless, we will do so. We also propose to provide ambulances, medical personnel and supplies to attend to the wounded and infirm. Further, we will provide body bags, means of transport and personnel to remove the deceased so that they may be appropriately buried according to Islamic religious tradition. Finally, we will provide transportation to remove all the pilgrims who you inadvertently trapped inside the mosque during your occupation of it."

Inadvertently trapped. Very clever. Saif realized Yassar thought he was trying to sell the concept to him. *What a relief to get rid of that baggage.* The mosque itself was the only hostage he needed.

"That is a humane and generous offer. How could I refuse?"

"I am pleased with your response. We are ready to proceed immediately."

"Minister Yassar, I mean no disrespect, but I will insist upon certain procedures to ensure there will be no additional hostilities."

"Of course. I understand completely."

Saif was now thinking on his feet, his mind catching up. "And we will require some additional elements to assure that things proceed smoothly."

"Such as?"

Saif was pleased. Yassar had not hesitated at all, apparently expecting additional demands from Saif.

"The pilgrims are hungry. They will need to eat before they leave the mosque. The first order of business should be delivery of food sufficient to feed 100,000. Consider that they have not eaten for three days, and that a single meal will not be adequate."

"I am not certain—"

Saif cut in, not wanting to give Yassar a chance to push back. "I am certain your people can make the appropriate arrangements.

Assurance of this is a condition to our willingness to proceed. Please contact me again once that has been arranged, and we can discuss the other details. Thank you, Minister Yassar," Saif said, and hung up.

Saif turned and smiled at Rashid. With that much food, his men could stay holed up in the mosque for as long as it took.

Sasha was hanging on, her trips to the toilet and her caterpillar-walks back and forth to the walls providing enough stimulation to keep her from losing touch with reality. She figured now it was over a week, more like ten days she'd been here, although she wondered if that were the case, why she didn't feel weaker. The hunger had passed after about the third day. So, on balance, she was doing fine. And yet she knew she couldn't just sit back and wait for something to fall out of the sky. She needed to do something proactive to change her situation.

Sasha wondered where all this back-and-forth with Saif was going. It wouldn't be long before he'd take another run at her. Above all, she reminded herself to resist. *Play ping-pong. Whatever he serves up to you, just hit it back, as hard as you can.*

Saif's last shot at her had been, "Think about the direction of your life." How she'd been used by the Americans and supported the Saudi royals in fleecing the average Saudi. Coming from a man who had murdered hundreds, if not thousands, and the head of an organization with the objective of multiplying that a millionfold as it took power and persecuted the royals, it rang hollow, even to a psyche enfeebled by captivity, starvation and deprivation. She almost looked forward to his next sortie.

Saif, a man who, barely out of his teens, had loved her, and who seemed stuck in that phase of his life. He, with his preposterous dreams of the two of them having a future together in leading Saudi Arabia. She found it hard to believe that a man could become so puffed up with his own image-making that he actually believed it himself. *Ludicrous.*

And yet, although he wasn't getting to her, her own involuntary ruminations were. Maybe it had been a mistake to spend the six months after Daniel's murder at Swami Kripananda's ashram. For the last few days his message had made it more difficult for her to cling to her hatred of Saif over Daniel's murder. Not that she could ever forgive Saif for it—there was no great rule book that said she had to, even according to Swami Kripananda—but that was part of Swami Kripananda's subtlety. Convert you to the path, then force you to examine your prior actions, cause you to make the right decisions in the future.

She could think about that more once she got out of this alive. No, she realized, she needed to get out of this with her soul, who she was at her core, uncompromised.

She arched her neck back, stretching as much as she could, trying to get the blood flowing. That always helped clear her mind. Today—or was it tonight, she didn't know—she was particularly foggy. She tipped her chair sideways onto the floor, rolled onto her forearms, lifted herself up on her toes, and then started caterpillar walking while the lights were still on.

CHAPTER 18

Day Six. Grand Mosque, Mecca.

TOM SAT IN THE LIVING room of his hotel suite most of the next day, watching the evacuation at the mosque. The first wave was the medical teams, just after sunup. The rebels opened one of the eastern gates, surrounded on the outside by a construction site for the expansion of the mosque. They must have figured it would be harder for the Saudis to pull a fast one on them because of the wide expanse of open territory in front of the gate. About two dozen ambulances pulled in, followed by a dozen buses, and drove across the marble courtyard up to the main prayer hall. He saw white-suited teams pile out of all of them and hurry into the main prayer hall with their cases of equipment and rolling gurneys. They were obviously using field triage, because ten minutes later a half dozen medical evacuation choppers moved in and hovered over the mosque, dropping one by one into the courtyard, having wounded rolled up and loaded, then lifting off. Most of the wounded were evacuated afterward in the ambulances and buses.

Next, flatbed semis drove in to remove the dead, which were laid out in lines on the flatbeds in body bags. Then came a non-stop convoy of buses for the pilgrims. A steady stream of pilgrims who didn't want to wait for a bus started simply walking out the gate. An hour later the rebels opened two more gates to let the pilgrims walk out. It reminded Tom of FedExField after a Washington Redskins game. At 4:00 p.m., when Tom's phone rang for his scheduled call with Ross at Langley, the buses were still coming and going, and the mosque was largely empty.

"What's the status?" Ross said.

"The evacuation is moving according to plan. No hitches, except that at the last minute Saif told Yassar that 'a few thousand' pilgrims had elected to stay in the mosque."

He heard Ross sigh. "'Elected.'"

"Yeah, the way I figure it, that's a little more than two body shields per rebel still left standing."

"What's next?"

"Some of that depends on what's going on at your end."

"Eighteen Special Ops commandos are on the way."

Tom sighed with relief.

"Rusty talked to Raven at Special Ops Command. Raven can't very well say no to his boss, and the way we set it up, the president thinks it was his idea. I told them I was assigning you as case officer in the field to provide intel support. Rusty told the president he'd had Raven authorize a few team members to assist you with communications and logistics."

"Got it. When will they get here?"

"Within 24 hours. You sure this will work?"

Tom hesitated again, thinking, *Are we ever sure?* He said, "I think so."

Ross said, "Where do you stand on the oil deal with Yassar?"

Tom's mind went blank. He said, "I thought you were working out the details."

"You mean you haven't moved it forward? I said I'd sort out the money and told you to go ahead and do the deal. Come on, man, you need to walk and chew gum at the same time. When we met in my office after Yassar pitched it to you, I told you welcome to the big leagues, and I meant it. Get it done."

"How? I mean, I'd be making it up as I go along."

"That's exactly what I expect you to do."

"But I'm no economist or financial guy."

"You think I am? There's no playbook here. It's no different than the way you run a field op. Figure it out. You've got your $200 billion, plus another $100 billion if you need it for negotiating room. Try not to spend it unless you need to. Try to get a livable price escalation and enough oil to keep us driving Cadillacs and SUVs for the next 20 years. Get it done." Ross clicked off.

Tom swallowed hard, hung up, then picked up the receiver again to dial Yassar's hotel suite.

It was dusk as Saif watched his men close the three eastern gates behind the last of the pilgrims and buses to depart. He turned and walked down the stairs from his perch atop the roof over the main prayer hall, heading directly into the catacombs to the room where they held Sasha.

The light in her room was off as a guard unlocked the door and showed him in. When he switched on the light she snapped her head up and blinked. He could see she had been asleep.

Her jaw was slack, her hair stringy and oily, strands of it hanging in her face. Her eyes had no spark of energy, with dark circles beneath them. *Worn down.* He hoped it was a sign that today's talk would go better than the others.

"How are you doing?" he asked.

"Not as well as I was, what, ten days ago?"

Fishing. "More like two weeks." He moved into the room and stood in front of her. He couldn't imagine how she'd managed to get so filthy. There was dirt all over her hands, arms and her pants. He could now see cuts on her wrists from the police handcuffs.

She looked up at him, her eyes glassy. "I hope we aren't going to cover the same territory."

He thought momentarily of walking out, trying again tomorrow, but figured since he was here, he might as well talk to her. He turned, grabbed the other chair and sat down facing her, their knees about a foot apart.

"No, but I realize there's something, or someone, I've left out. Yassar."

He waited for a reaction from her, but she showed none.

"He will have a role in the new government. He's universally respected and trusted, in part because of his reputation for fairness and even-handedness, but also because of his Saudization policies, which are well supported. He's seen as one of the few royals with the common Saudi's interests at heart. In our new government we will need to have a consortium of business, finance and religious leaders—Sunnis and Shiites—and Yassar is the one who can accomplish that."

Still no reaction. He decided to take a different approach. *Appeal to her heart.*

"You had a clear shot and hesitated. Was it because of your feelings for me?"

"I didn't hesitate. I hate you."

"Look deeper. There can be no hatred without love."

"I loved you once."

"Once? Or still? Is a bond such as we had ever broken?"

She didn't respond, seemed to be turning it over in her mind. He waited.

"It's different for a woman," she said. "Once she's taken a man, there will always be a bond."

He inclined his head. *Gently*, he told himself. "So you still feel the bond?"

"I hadn't finished. That bond—that reservoir of emotion—will always be there, however deeply buried. And the betrayal of that is what allows a woman's hatred to be so much more profound than anything a man can ever experience."

Saif felt himself sag with disappointment. He settled back in his chair. "I will speak openly, from the heart, because I sense we're nearing the end of any productive conversations."

Sasha looked away, as if to tell him she didn't care.

"I loved you once, as deeply as I believe you loved me. Feeling your love for me was the most profound thing I have ever experienced in my life. I am certain I could recapture the ecstasy of my love for you if you were to show me just a taste of yours for me." He inclined his head toward her again. "That is all I ask. For you to open your heart again to me for a moment, and let me return it."

She didn't reply. After a few moments she turned her head to meet his gaze. Her eyes grew moist, then a single tear coursed down her cheek.

Saif smiled. *The rain begins with a single drop.* He stood up, kissed her forehead and left, feeling victorious.

Sasha held it in until she heard the lock turn in the door after Saif left, then gave in to sobs. She'd had a moment of panic when

Saif told her he feared that they were nearing the end of any productive conversations. *What was I thinking?* In her disoriented state did she really believe that he would let her survive if she continued to resist him? So she'd done her best to fake it.

She'd tried to conjure a tear for him, but it wouldn't come. She summoned her sense of hopelessness and fatigue, but nothing.

Then she thought of Daniel. Lying on the floor of the apartment with a red circle over his heart, blood pooling beneath him, dying. *No, not dying, dead.* His lifeless eyes staring up at her.

Then, with that image, when that single tear had come it had been difficult for her to keep it from becoming a torrent.

So now she let her tears flow, sobbing unrestrainedly, her body shaking. She cried for Daniel, the guilt she felt for his murder, because without her in his life it never would've happened. Cried for the purest love she'd ever felt being robbed from her only a few short years into what should have been a long journey together into old age. Cried for the waste she'd made of her life, starting as a frivolous young girl, then selling her body as a concubine, culminating in becoming a murderess many times over, and still allowing herself to be manipulated in that role.

She stopped sobbing and hung her head. She'd never be able to convince Saif that she was siding with him long enough to carry it off. He'd wind up having her killed. *I'm as good as dead.* But what difference did it make? Hers was a wasted life anyhow.

CHAPTER 19

Day Seven. Grand Mosque, Mecca.

SASHA HAD JUST FINISHED CRAWLING to the wall. That was enough stimulation to get her emotions back in check and her wits sufficiently about her to regroup.

A wasted life? Saif is finally getting to me.

She forced herself to throw off the thoughts that had just attacked her, like some autoimmune disease. *Quit blubbering and think.* What could she hang on to to steel herself? Daniel was the best part of her. But now that he was gone, what else had she done, what did she have? Yassar. Even Tom. Yes, Tom, who loved her in silence, even perhaps without acknowledging it to himself, but showing it with his actions. Supporting her, looking after her, and out there now with his team waiting for her. And if she was in trouble, prepared to come in after her. That was enough to get her off the floor.

Time to get out of here, and you don't have forever to make it happen.

At the wall, she checked the scratches she marked there each time they took her to the toilet. *Eleven.* Not as many as she would've expected. So maybe she hadn't been here as long as she thought. That gave her a lift. She crawled back to the middle of the room and got her chair upright. She started working out her plan. She didn't know why, but for whatever reason, the last two times they'd come to take her to the toilet, only one armed guard had accompanied the dog collar man.

When they came to get her the next time, she'd be ready.

The lights were on when she heard the key in the lock. She pretended to be asleep. She couldn't tell from the footsteps whether it was two or three men, but when the dog collar man prodded her and she looked up, she saw he only had one guard with him. After the man put the dog collar on her and cut the bindings off her arms and legs, she intentionally staggered and fell getting up from the chair. When he pulled her to her feet with the leash, she forced herself to react sluggishly to the sharp stab in her neck from the prongs, even though she wanted to cry out in pain. She shuffled out of the room, hanging her head and screwing up her eyes as if she were dazed.

She waited until they were down the hall and the dog collar man started to unlock the toilet door. They were in close quarters, the leash slack and the guard only a few feet off to her right. Her heart started to pound, anticipating the moment.

Now.

She spun to the right, reached out to grab the pistol from the guard and wrenched it upward, twisting the man's wrist as she kicked one of his legs out from underneath him. Before the dog leash man had finished turning at the sound, she had the gun against his forehead, saying in Arabic, "Move and you die." She spun again and kicked the guard in the face, sending a spray of blood as she smashed his nose. She turned back just as the dog collar man started to yank on the leash. She backhanded him in the face with the pistol, then smashed him over the top of the head with it and he went to his knees. She pulled the leash out of his hands and turned back to the guard, who was now attempting to struggle to his feet. She aimed the pistol at him and prepared to fire. Instead, she sent the guard crashing to the floor with another karate kick to the side of the head.

She stepped back and pulled the dog collar off her neck, then stuck the pistol in the dog collar man's face. "Wear it," she said and handed it to him. She held the leash in her left hand and pulled him to his feet, glancing at the guard on the floor who was now looking at her, blinking, with fear in his eyes. She pointed the gun at him and said, "Up." She motioned down the hallway toward the room where they'd imprisoned her. Back in the room, she held the gun on the guard and instructed him to bind the dog collar man's wrists and strap him into the first chair.

Then she had him strap his own legs to the second chair. She held her wrists out to him and cocked the hammer on the gun. "Cut the strap," she said to him, keeping the gun pointed at his chest, "carefully." He pulled out the knife and did so; Sasha sighed as the cuffs fell to the floor, tears of relief coming to her eyes. She pocketed his knife. Next she told the man to form a loop with one of the police handcuffs. "Put your hands in it," she said, grabbed the loose end and cinched his wrists tight. Then she strapped his biceps to the back of the chair. She fished into his pockets to find his cell phone.

"Allah will judge you for this, infidel," he said.

Sasha backhanded him across the face. "Shut up, fool. Don't push your luck. It would be less trouble for me to kill you."

She grabbed her abaya from the hook on the wall and dashed out. When she reached the door to the toilet, she picked up the ring of keys. As she ran down the hall, her breath was coming in gasps.

Free!

She ran for about ten minutes, turning right at every intersection in the corridors so she could remember how she had come. She reached a section of the catacombs that wasn't lighted, then pulled out the cell phone to use the lighted face to illuminate her path. She stopped in front of a door. She tested the handle. *Locked.* She tried the keys from the ring one by one and was able to unlock it, then stepped inside a room that appeared to be almost identical to the one she had been held in. She closed and locked the door.

It took her a few minutes of sitting in the middle of the floor, breathing deeply, rubbing her wrists and stretching her neck and shoulders to relax. As she looked at the face of the cell phone, her heart sank.

No signal this far underground.

But she remembered Zac telling her how powerful the transmitters stitched into her abaya were. She felt the seam of her abaya and found another of the battery packs for a transmitter, squeezed it to energize the battery. Still using the lighted face of the phone, she pulled out the pocketknife and found the first transmitter she had used, then cut it out of the seam of the abaya. She squinted and bent over the device and sliced the wires away from its dead battery. She removed the battery from the cell phone and held the transmitter's wires to the contacts. She removed one of the wires, touched it to the battery contact again, removed it once more. *Will the signal work?*

Couric was the name of the guy, mid-40s, who showed up and knocked on the door asking for Tom. He introduced himself as a captain, Special Forces, commanding 18 men from Special Ops Command. He said if Tom's guys wanted in, okay, he welcomed them as long as they were properly armed, and if the Saudis wanted to participate, fine, but it was Couric's show all the way. Tom told him Assad had just left to prep his teams, then turned to see that Seth and Zac had already stepped into the bedroom, grabbing their equipment and weapons.

I guess they want in.

Tom briefed Couric on the situation, then walked into the bedroom and said to Zac and Seth, "I'll need you guys here, at least for now." When he saw their faces fall he added, "Sorry, but we need to monitor what's going on, and Sasha's our first priority." They both started putting their gear back like high school kids being told they weren't starting in that day's football game.

A moment later, Tom saw Zac walk up to Couric where he was studying the plans of the mosque. Zac saluted and said, "Sergeant First Class Zac Fulton, sir. Special Ops Command, attached from Special Forces, 101st Airborne."

"At ease."

"With your permission, sir, I'd like to hook up monitors on some of your men. It'll help me keep track of where your men are."

Couric raised his eyebrows. "How many, and are they detectable by the rebels?"

"A half dozen, and no, the rebels can't have that technology."

Tom saw Zac walk Couric into the bedroom and show Couric his equipment.

"Do it," Couric said when they walked back out. "My men are downstairs."

Couric pulled out his cell phone and made a call. Zac walked back into the bedroom to grab some equipment, then left.

Couric pulled out photographs of Sasha, Rashid and Saif and put them on the table. "My men understand these two are ours," Couric said to Tom, pointing to Sasha and Rashid's pictures. He went back to studying the plans of the mosque. Eventually he said, "I've seen enough. I want to get my men into position. We're moving. It would be better, sir, if you and your team accompanied me so you can see what the lay of the land is."

Five minutes later they were three blocks outside the northeastern perimeter wall of the mosque. Couric's men piled out of the SUVs, Couric saying, "Move, move, move," like they were under mortar fire. It took one of his guys about 30 seconds to open a wire grate on an entrance to the catacombs that looked like something from the 1700s. Couric's men scrambled inside and worked their way up into the tunnel and out of sight.

Couric stood at the entrance to the catacombs and said to Tom, "Well, sir, where the hell are our Saudi buddies?"

"You caught them flat-footed," Tom said, "but they'll be here."

Couric shrugged, looked at his watch.

About five minutes later Tom heard the sound of engines off in the distance. They grew louder, then a dozen SUVs pulled up. Assad jumped out of the first SUV. He strode over to Tom, smiling. He slapped Tom on the arm as if they were old friends, then walked past him to Couric. "I am Assad," he said to Couric. "I have a team of 36 of my best men, all English-speaking, wearing night-vision equipment and body armor, and armed with M4A1s just like yours with holographic sights and sound suppressors, ready to show you the joys of our Saudi underground." Tom was pleased to see Couric flash a smile, receive Assad's hand and shake it. Couric then escorted Assad back to where he'd been standing and the two talked and gestured for a few minutes, apparently about Couric's concept of the operation. Assad then waved one of his lieutenants up and had him speak to Couric, while Zac spoke to Assad, then hooked up transmitters to Assad's three team leaders. A minute later he motioned to his men and they trotted into the entrance to the catacombs, their equipment rattling as they went past.

Assad joined Tom, Ryan, Seth and Zac as they went back to Tom's hotel suite, where Assad called Yassar to join them. Yassar drank tea while Tom sat, drumming his fingers on the arm of his chair. Zac monitored his equipment from the bedroom, Ryan talked on the phone to the embassy in Riyadh, while Seth, apparently not knowing what else to do, cleaned his weapons in the kitchen.

"Now we wait," Assad said to Tom.

A few moments later, Zac called Tom into the bedroom to look at his equipment. Zac switched the laptop to a different screen. It looked like a map, with numbers marking points all over it, and different blinking lights scattered around it.

"I showed this to Couric before I hooked up his men. I input a map of the catacombs," Zac said. "The numbers you see are GPS coordinates, which the MantaRay feeds automatically into the computer from signals it picks up. The blinking green dots you see are those of Couric's men. The blinking amber dots are Assad's men. The blue dot is Rashid's cell phone. The four white dots are Saif's cell phones." Zac looked up at Tom and put his finger on the screen. "And this red dot is one of Sasha's transmitters."

Tom felt a wash of relief. "You sure?"

"Absolutely. See that other red blinking dot right next to it? It's signaling in Morse code."

"Morse code?"

"Yes. It has to be her. It's the only thing that makes sense."

"Who uses Morse code anymore?"

"That's the point," Zac said. "Nobody."

"Then why do you think it's Sasha?"

Zac said, "Because she asked me, in the event of an emergency, what might work if nothing else did. So I taught her Morse code."

"So what's she saying?"

"*Here in the catacombs.*"

"But that doesn't make sense."

Assad, who had joined them, said from behind Tom, "Yes, it does. Please, come back in here." He walked them into the living room and stood over the plans of the catacombs. He pointed. "I'd say she's about here."

What the...? Tom said, "But that's at least 100 yards outside the walls of the grand Mosque, and completely outside the catacombs."

Assad said, "She's in one of the oldest sections of the catacombs. One that the construction company didn't map, because it was outside the area they're doing their work, and so old that they are unsafe to walk in."

Tom said, "Then she must be in trouble." He felt his guts twisting, sweat breaking out on his forehead. He wondered if Zac could see it, then decided he didn't care. He said to Zac, "Can you take this MantaRay thing with you?"

"No, but I know where you're going. I can bring my laptop and it communicates wirelessly with the MantaRay. I can track Sasha as long as I can get a wireless signal on my laptop."

Tom said, "Suit up, guys. We need to go in there and get her out."

Assad said, "I'll put together another of my teams."

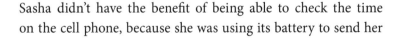

Sasha didn't have the benefit of being able to check the time on the cell phone, because she was using its battery to send her

Morse code signal. She'd send her message five or six times, then pause and think, then signal again. Her mind got clearer with each repetition, or maybe it was just the fact that she had the ability to move her arms and legs.

Enough of this. She put the battery back in the cell phone and used the light from the face to examine the gun she'd taken from the guard. It was an old American army-issued semi-automatic Colt .45. It was a weapon she'd never fired before, but she knew was reliable and had legendary stopping power. She checked the magazine. Eight rounds. She racked the slide to load one into the chamber. She shoved it in the waistband of her jeans, put on her abaya and opened the door. She turned and headed back toward the mosque. She trotted up the ancient corridor, believing Zac had gotten the message, that Tom would figure out what to do. So she focused on what she needed to do.

Hunt down Saif.

Back in Tom's hotel suite, Zac called out from the bedroom, "She's moving."

Tom ran in and looked at Zac's computer screen. "What's she doing?" The red dot was heading back toward the mosque.

Saif paced in the hallway, anxious. Not only had Sasha escaped, but she had managed to take the guard's pistol. It was a distraction at a time when he least needed one. Now that they were announcing the coming of the Mahdi over the loudspeakers from the minarets, they were just one day away from confirming his arrival, the point at which the full revolution would begin.

His top 20 lieutenants were assembled in the communications room. He would address them one final time before he left the mosque and traveled back to Buraida to take his role as commander of all the revolutionary forces. It was a moment that history would remember, and he wanted it to go flawlessly so he could leave a resounding impression upon his men. He smiled to himself, thinking how even a week earlier he had invoked Alan Rickman in order to prepare himself for such a moment. Now, tested by battle, and having shown his men the example of his leadership throughout the seizure and occupation of the mosque, he was his own man. He no longer needed his muse.

He nodded to the guard outside the communications room, then glanced to the top of the stairway to confirm the five men who would escort him were stationed there. He entered the communications room and stood in the doorway until his men saw him and went silent. He glanced around the room, meeting their gazes, smiling and nodding to each of his men in turn. He motioned for Rashid to join him, and Rashid walked to him and stood at his the side.

"My brothers. Tomorrow, at sunup, the Mahdi will reveal himself, and an uprising by the true believers all over Saudi Arabia will commence. In a few minutes I will leave you and travel back to Buraida to lead our fight for freedom. You will stay here and hold the line in this, the holiest of places, and protect our sacred trust, the Mahdi, the Redeemer of Islam."

Saif stepped toward his men, wanting them to see the passion in his face. He took a deep breath and allowed his emotions to swell. "We are all fighting for our country, our culture, our way of life. And for the glorification of the Mahdi. He is the symbol of the way forward in our struggle, the one who will provide our spiritual guidance and bring us the strength to conquer those who would demean or pollute his message. Although I will not be with you here in the mosque, I will be with you in spirit, as will you be present in spirit with all our brothers throughout Saudi Arabia.

"Our brother Rashid will command in my absence. Respect his judgment. Now I must go. Now we truly begin. There is no God but Allah!"

"*La ilaha ilallah!*" the men called back.

Saif stepped out and motioned for Rashid to join him in the hallway. "I will be in touch." He clapped his hand on Rashid's shoulder. "Be strong and don't waver. The men respect you and will follow you. If you are attacked again, at all costs, protect the Mahdi, even if you need to use the pilgrims as human shields. In any revolution, collateral damage is unavoidable."

Saif strode off.

Sasha had decided it was too risky to leave the catacombs by following the same route through which she'd come. When she reached the lighted sections of the tunnels, she made a series of turns so she emerged from a stairway across the courtyard from the main prayer hall. The hot air singed her nostrils, but it smelled and tasted delicious after being underground for so long. She squinted against the sunlight, taking in the courtyard.

She wasn't prepared for the sight. Debris and the wreckage of battle were everywhere. The place was almost empty. *What happened to everyone?* The columns and walls were pockmarked with bullet holes, and bits of stone and marble crunched under her feet as she walked. She pulled her hijab headscarf and veil from her pouch inside her abaya and covered her hair and face. She looked away as she encountered a group of armed men, then passed a cluster of about 25 people who appeared to be pilgrims, mostly men, who sat in the shade near the perimeter wall looking despondent. She reached the main prayer hall and found a few hundred more pilgrims huddled inside, a half dozen armed rebels standing around.

She walked into the crowd of pilgrims and stood, observing. After a few minutes, a group of about 20 armed rebels walked down the stairs together, talking excitedly among themselves, crossed through the prayer hall and exited. After they left she looked back at the stairway and saw Rashid descend, his eyes intense, hurrying someplace. She eased herself through the throng of pilgrims and followed him. He went through a door and descended a stairway into a different section of the catacombs. She glanced back as she pulled the door shut to assure she wasn't being followed. When she reached the bottom of the stairs, he leaped out in front of her from the shadows and thrust a pistol in her face. Sasha slowly reached up and pulled the veil away from her face. He nodded and lowered the gun.

"Saif," he said, and motioned with his head. "I know where he's going." He started walking down the corridor. Sasha reached into her abaya, gripped the Colt .45 and followed.

———◆———

Seth speeded the SUV around the mosque, while Zac directed him from the other front seat, watching the blinking lights on his computer screen. Tom glanced at the M4A1 in his hand, wondering what it would be like to fire the thing, then trained his eyes on the minarets for any snipers exposing themselves, as Seth had instructed him. Seth had given him a 60-second crash course on the automatic rifle, showing him the safety, the switch for single round and automatic fire, and how to change the magazine clips. Seth had outfitted them all with M4A1s, Kevlar vests, pouches of extra clips, and grenades and tear gas canisters for the grenade launchers mounted underneath the barrels of the rifles. Seth and Zac had looked grim and serious as they climbed into the SUV. Tom imagined that his face was probably about as white as Ryan's. Nonetheless, Seth had been unable to talk either of them out of coming with them.

Assad still hadn't returned with his team by the time they were ready to leave, so Tom made the decision. "Let's go," he said. "I'll call Assad just before we enter the catacombs, tell him where we went in."

They had passed through the construction site and were bouncing through an unpaved road when Zac said, "Stop here." He held the computer screen over toward Seth. Tom could see it from the backseat. "Take a look at this."

He pointed at the screen. The blinking green dots, Couric's men, were near the center of the mosque. Assad's men, the amber dots, were across the courtyard from Couric's team. "The blue dot is Rashid's cell phone, and the red dot is Sasha's transmitter, and they're together now, moving through the catacombs again."

"What's that white dot?" Tom asked.

"That's one of Saif's cell phones, and he's on the move, too."

Seth said, "It looks like Rashid and Sasha are following him." With that he threw the SUV into gear again and started driving. "We're on a path to intercept them."

Zac said, "There should be an entrance to the catacombs in about 100 yards."

A minute later they stopped in front of a triangular stone structure jutting up from the sand. Seth pulled a tire iron out of the back of the SUV and pried the lock off the iron grate in front of it. Tom called Assad, got his voicemail, and left a message saying where they were and that they were going in. Zac took one last long look at the screen of his laptop, closed it and tossed it into the SUV. Seth poised at the top of the steps, his flashlight in hand, and said to Tom, "You and Ryan stay back, well back. Let Zac and me handle this." He started down the stairs into the catacombs, his lips pulled tight.

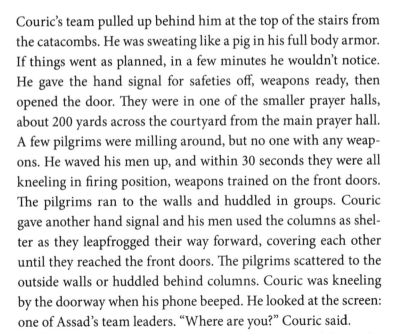

Couric's team pulled up behind him at the top of the stairs from the catacombs. He was sweating like a pig in his full body armor. If things went as planned, in a few minutes he wouldn't notice. He gave the hand signal for safeties off, weapons ready, then opened the door. They were in one of the smaller prayer halls, about 200 yards across the courtyard from the main prayer hall. A few pilgrims were milling around, but no one with any weapons. He waved his men up, and within 30 seconds they were all kneeling in firing position, weapons trained on the front doors. The pilgrims ran to the walls and huddled in groups. Couric gave another hand signal and his men used the columns as shelter as they leapfrogged their way forward, covering each other until they reached the front doors. The pilgrims scattered to the outside walls or huddled behind columns. Couric was kneeling by the doorway when his phone beeped. He looked at the screen: one of Assad's team leaders. "Where are you?" Couric said.

"Aboveground across the courtyard, 100 yards from the main prayer hall. Our other two teams are in position as well, one to the left and one to the right of the main prayer hall, 200 yards and 300 yards away."

"Stay put," Couric said. "We're going in first." He signed off. Couric turned to his team. "I want you four snipers in position outside these doors to take out anybody firing from the minarets. Space yourselves. Go." The four men ran outside. Couric said to the rest of his team, "Sound suppressors in place. Anybody with a weapon gets taken out. Let's get as close as we can before we let them know we're here. Tear gas first, then stun grenades, then we go in." He unhooked his gas mask from his belt, slid it on, then stepped out into the walkway around the perimeter wall, feeling the familiar tightness in his stomach, his pulse rise. He started jogging toward the main prayer hall, hearing the equipment of his men jangling behind him, their boots clomping on the marble. He was about 50 yards from the doorway to the main prayer hall when he encountered his first rebel, flattening him with a burst from his M4A1 and then breaking into a full run, his breathing amplified in his ears by the gas mask. When he was about 25 yards from the door, he crouched and fired a tear gas canister into the main prayer hall. He held his position as two, then five of his men passed him and fired their own canisters inside. He started running again, the rest of his men following.

Still no return fire.

Just as he thought it, he heard the growl of AK-47s opening up from across the courtyard, saw starbursts of flame from the shadows behind the columns across the courtyard. He heard his men behind him return fire and the AK-47s went silent.

"Move!" Couric yelled. The whole team was now sprinting toward the prayer hall doors. A half dozen then positioned themselves behind columns, their weapons trained to the rear, the rest of the team with weapons trained on the prayer hall. Gagging and coughing men started staggering out.

"Stun grenades," Couric yelled. A half dozen of his men lobbed in grenades, followed by concussions and flashes that blew out windows, and then without the necessity of a command, most of his team hurried inside.

Couric heard more firing from across the courtyard, saw trails of smoke from tear gas canisters. *Assad's guys.* One of Assad's teams ran up behind Couric's and took covering positions behind columns, facing out into the courtyard. He saw a few rebels on the roof, pointing AK-47s down at them. Two of his men stood up and took them out with bursts from their M4A1s. Couric now heard firing inside the main prayer hall. He crouched by the door, then peered inside. The air was still thick with tear gas, but he could see well enough to observe a dozen men lying on the ground, bleeding, robed men and women pressed against the walls, their arms covering their heads. His team had moved all the way into the hall, some crouching behind columns, intermittently firing. None of his men were down. *We're kicking their asses.* He turned and waved to one of Assad's team leaders and the man sent in his team. Couric looked back at the men he'd left to guard the rear, then turned and went in, his eyes focused on the stairway to the rebels' command center.

Saif had just reached the first storeroom, one of the ancient rooms in the catacombs where the sympathetic National Guard troops had stashed munitions, food and other provisions for Saif's men, when he heard the muffled sound of gunfire from above, and then a half dozen loud explosions. He felt a flash of alarm.

For a moment he thought of turning back, then realized it was more important for him to get to Buraida, for the good of the movement. He left two of his men to stand guard outside the storeroom and brought the other three inside. He directed his men to take gas masks and extra clips for their AK-47s. He thought he heard a sound outside the door, whipped his head around to look.

Sasha could see shadows on the walls of the corridor from Saif and his men as she ran behind Rashid, her gun now in her hand. They reached a turn in the tunnel and Rashid motioned for her to stop. He peered around the corner, turned back and whispered, "Two guards outside. Saif and the others must be in the room. It holds munitions and other supplies."

Sasha pulled off her abaya and threw it on the floor, then loosened up her arms. "Let me see, please," she said. He stepped back and she looked around the corner. The first guard was only 15 feet away, his AK-47 in both hands in front of him. If he turned his back she could reach him and disable him before he or the other guard knew anything, but the other guard, maybe 25 feet away, was more of a problem. She didn't see any way out of it: she'd have to kill them both. She pressed her back against the wall, closed her eyes.

When does it stop?

She heard Rashid's feet as he moved past her, opened her eyes to see him leap out around the corner and crouch with his pistol in his hand. He fired twice, then three more times. Sasha leaned around the corner to see both guards on the floor, then a man extend his body halfway through the doorway with his AK-47 and fire a burst. Rashid dived back as the bullets ricocheted off the walls. Sasha heard footsteps running down the hall, then another burst from an AK-47, more ricochets off the wall. She peered out again to see Saif and three men running away down the corridor. Rashid ran to the first downed guard, grabbed his AK-47 and started firing at them. Rashid hit one man, who fell and then returned fire. Rashid flattened him with another burst.

Sasha ran past Rashid and reached a turn in the corridor. She felt her heart pulsing in her neck, her arms stiffen with tension as she ran. *Now it's just Saif and two men.*

Tom heard shots in front of them in the corridor, then bursts of automatic weapons fire, silence, then more. He was having trouble keeping up with Seth and Zac. Seth, the weapons and martial arts guy, he expected it from, but Zac, this big guy who'd turned out to be some techie dweeb, was now all of a sudden an animal intent on raw meat. Both he and Seth would stop at each turn in the corridor, scan with their weapons, and Tom and Ryan would catch up to them. Then they'd tear off again, leaving Tom and Ryan 25 yards behind them by the time they reached the next turn.

When they entered the lighted section of the catacombs, Tom heard more bursts of automatic weapons, saw Seth and Zac pick up the pace, and hurried to keep up. Now he could see flashes from around a turn in the corridor. After another 20 yards he could see chips cracking off the walls with ricochets, smell the cordite, even the smell of crushed stone from the bullets raking the walls.

He was running flat out now, breathing hard, feeling life-threat, then thinking of Sasha, knowing she must be in the thick of this. It drove him to run faster.

Seth and Zac pulled up again, crouching at an intersection in the tunnels, checking to the left from where the flashes were coming. Now the guns went silent, now more firing, then the sound of running footsteps. He reached the corner where Seth and Zac sneaked a look, saw them murmuring and motioning to each other. Tom stuck his head around the corner and saw a few men dart across the corridor 100 feet in front of him in a tunnel that ran perpendicular to the one he was looking down.

Someone else ran past. *Sasha!* He ran toward her, hearing Seth yell, "Tom!"

Just before Tom reached the intersection, Rashid ran past him after her, a pistol in his hand. Tom fell in behind him and ran.

Sasha was sprinting flat out, calculating: *Two men plus Saif. Each with AK-47s. I've got eight rounds in this Colt.*

If they turned around and fired, she'd need to react quickly, fall to one knee and fire from that position. They kept running; she kept on after them.

Then something whizzed past her. She saw the flare of a small explosion, smoke, and then the biting odor of tear gas. She kept running, then another tear gas canister hissed past her and exploded 20 feet in front of her. She ran into the cloud of gas, and now felt like her nose, eyes and lungs were on fire. She could barely see, but she kept on, glimpsing Saif and his men turn into another corridor. She followed them. The air was clear in that section, but the stinging in her lungs was still horrible and screamed at her to stop, but she pushed on.

She heard footsteps behind her. She turned back to look; it was Rashid, with a man in the shadows behind him carrying an automatic weapon, then two more men carrying automatic weapons. She turned back and continued to run.

She was gaining on Saif and the men. Now they were only meters in front of her, and then they took a left down another corridor. A few seconds later one of them trained his AK-47 around the corner and started firing. Sasha dived into the corridor to her right, then heard return fire from Rashid and the men running with him. She heard another whoosh, the pop of a tear gas canister exploding and then the smell of the gas. She got down on the floor and looked around the corner. She saw a man dash out of the corridor from which the man had just fired the AK-47 and continue in the direction they'd been running.

Saif!

She heard more return fire from behind her, then men running. More fire, more running, as if the men were leapfrogging each other. Two men passed her, carrying American weapons and wearing gas masks. They stopped and looked left, down the corridor from which the fire had come. She heard more fire from down that end of the corridor from an AK-47, saw rock splinters from the bullets ricocheting off the wall. She got up and raced after Saif. She heard the continued exchange of fire from behind her, then the thunk from the grenade launcher, another explosion of tear gas. Her ears were ringing, but she could still hear Saif's footsteps in front of her. Her own breathing resonated in her ears.

She reached another corridor, wondering if this maze ever stopped, still hearing Saif's footsteps in front of her, running on pure adrenaline. Now her lungs were burning, not from the tear gas, but from sprinting for so long, and after so little food. Her body was beginning to wear out. But now she could see Saif 40 meters in front of her. It lifted her. She ran on.

She saw Saif disappear into the darkness in the corridor, then a few seconds later emerge, running straight back toward her.

A dead end. She had him trapped!

He opened a door and ducked into a room, slamming the door behind him, only to have it bounce off the doorjamb and swing back open. She slid on one knee into the doorway, her pistol raised, her gaze darting around the room, taking in everything. *Well lit. Big, with stacks of old furniture: bureaus, chairs, desks. Two more doors. The smell of dust.*

She slipped in, crept forward.

"Sasha, my Sasha!" Saif called out from the far side of the room. "You still have another chance to make the right choice. Drop your gun and join me."

"I am no longer your Sasha."

"You will always be, as long as I am breathing."

"Then you're still a ridiculous little boy."

She heard a metallic ping and felt her pulse shoot up as she saw a green-skinned concussion grenade hurtling toward her. Saif jumped up from behind a desk with his AK-47 aimed. Sasha dived behind a bureau as the burst from Saif's weapon raked the wall above her. She curled into a ball on the floor, squeezed her eyes shut tight and stuck her fingers into her ears.

The explosion knocked the bureau over onto her, but it absorbed most of the blast. She saw stars, not sure if from the concussion or from the bureau hitting her. She jumped to her feet, the Colt raised, seeing Saif run through one of the doors into an adjoining room.

Another dead end or is he getting away?

She ran toward the doorway, hearing another burst from Saif's AK-47. She pulled up beside the door, glanced in, her heart pounding. The room was similar. *Furniture. Stacks of boxes. Another door across the room.* That door hung open with the area around the lock riddled with bullet holes.

Had he escaped or was he still inside?

She inched into the room. She crushed something underfoot, and Saif came up at the sound, firing from behind a stack of chairs to her left. Sasha dived to the floor, taking cover behind piles of boxes. Saif's rifle went silent and she heard the sound of another clip hitting the floor, then looked up to see the grenade, this one a black pineapple, heading toward her.

A shrapnel grenade. No!

She ran straight at it and leaped feet-first, executing a *yoko tobi geri*, a flying side kick that launched the grenade off the bottom of her foot back toward where it had come from. She landed on her feet, then dived over a stack of boxes just as the explosion shook the room, the breath coming out of her when she hit the floor on her stomach.

Sasha pulled herself to her knees, waiting, listening.

Nothing.

Had the grenade killed him? She got to her feet, air coming back into her lungs, crouching with the Colt in both hands in firing position, still listening.

She heard a clang.

Oh my God, another!

She saw a black shrapnel grenade rolling across the floor toward her.

Move!

She pushed a row of boxes over on it, then dived sideways, her eyes focused on the far doorway. She landed on her stomach, the Colt poised in her outstretched arms. The explosion blew the boxes apart, threw papers and dust into the air, but she was unharmed. Saif leaped to his feet from behind some furniture and charged for the doorway.

Sasha took aim and fired, once, twice, a third time over his head into the wall.

"Warning shots!" she yelled, barely hearing her own voice over the ringing in her ears from the grenades. "You'd be dead if I wanted to hit you." She ran to the doorway and glanced into the room. *More storage, but no door.*

"You're trapped. Surrender."

Saif didn't respond for a moment, then said, "I'm throwing down my weapon." She heard the clatter of his AK-47 hitting the floor. She peeked into the doorway, saw him with a revolver aimed at her, yanked her head back.

"I expected as much," she called out. "I knew I couldn't trust you to be unarmed."

"And why should I trust you? You've been trying to kill me for days."

"I just fired three warning shots."

"And I could have taken the shot just now and killed you, too."

Sasha realized he was right. But he'd fired at her earlier and tried to blow her to pieces with grenades; she still didn't trust him. And yet, she was sick of killing. She wanted him stopped, in custody, and was prepared to accept the possibility of dying to make that happen. Her faith was strong enough to make her unafraid. She'd go in and get him, and whatever happened, so be it.

"I'm coming in with my gun down."

She hesitated, then offered a silent prayer to Ganesha and lowered the Colt to her side. Then she raised her chin and eased herself into the doorway. He held his revolver pointed directly at her, his eyes glazed with fear, breathing hard, but smiling.

Sasha stepped into the room and stopped only 10 meters from him. "What do you think killing me will solve?" she said.

"Only to help me escape."

"I thought you loved me." She spat the words, sneering at him, feeling the cold steel of the Colt in her hand at her side, focused.

"I do, but I love my country more than you."

"Then you're a fraud. You don't really believe in love. You're just as you were, when you had me as a silly young girl. You were afraid of showing your emotions then, keeping me and them holed up in a hotel room, just as you are now. That's why you'll never be a whole person. Don't talk to me about love. I know what love is. I had it with my Daniel, until you had him murdered."

"My, but you're a romantic for one who started her adult life by making her money on her back."

"See what I mean about not believing in love? You're so immune to the concept you can't see your own cynicism."

"As I said, I love my country. I believe in it, in the Saudi people's potential to reclaim it."

"You don't believe in your country. You only believe in what you want for yourself. Power. Your own ambition, your self-deluded notion that you might have a place on the world stage. You once had potential, but you were never able to rise above feeling sorry for yourself about the injustice to your father, your own inability to succeed."

"I am a committed leader to my men, revered by them, as I will be revered as a leader to my people."

"You're nothing, a nobody. A bitter little man who's jealous of what others have and wants to destroy it. Like you destroyed my Daniel."

"I no longer have time for such philosophical ramblings."

Sasha heard voices from the other rooms, men calling out.

"You don't have much time for anything. They're coming for you."

"I'm going to kill you," Saif said, squinting over his gun, taking aim.

"Maybe. Maybe not. But for what? You're trapped, and unless you surrender, you're going to die." She felt her pulse throbbing in her neck. "You aren't trained for this. And you don't have the nerve to look me in the eye and pull the trigger."

Now she heard footsteps in the next room. "Sasha!" she heard someone call.

Tom's voice!

"Drop the gun, Saif," she said. "I won't kill you unless you make me."

She saw movement to her left, realized it was Tom stepping into the doorway, an automatic weapon in his hands. Saif turned, aimed at him. Sasha swung her arm up and pulled the trigger twice, remembering to adjust for the recoil of the big .45 for the second round so it wouldn't make her miss high. Saif lurched over backward to the floor as if yanked by the neck. Sasha motioned with her hand at Tom for him to stop, then ran over to Saif. His eyes were open, staring straight up at her, but no life was in them. He had a hole in his forehead from her first round. She felt for a pulse anyhow, found none. She dropped the Colt to the floor and then walked over to Tom. She threw her arms around his neck and held him.

"Thank God you're alive," Tom said. "I thought I'd lost you."

CHAPTER 20

SASHA SAT IN THE BACKSEAT, eating a bag of peanuts, the only food they'd found in the SUV where Tom and his team had left it next to the entrance to the catacombs. "My kingdom for a Bar Louis cheeseburger," she said to Tom, leaning into him, feeling safe with his arm around her. He'd been hovering over her like an attentive husband since he'd walked her out of the room with Saif's body. Ryan, Seth, Zac and Rashid stood outside, as if they were allowing Sasha and Tom some quiet time together.

"Bar Louis?"

"Hotel Fauchère, Milford, Pennsylvania, where I met Daniel. Best cheeseburgers on the planet."

Tom nodded. "How do you like them?"

She closed her eyes, imagining it. "Medium rare, gruyère cheese, bacon, some bermuda onion, not much ketchup, a little mustard—"

"With fries?"

"Of course, the truffle oil fries—are you tormenting me?"

He laughed. "Just trying to keep your spirits up. It'll be another 20 minutes before the chopper gets here. They'll have something to eat, but I can't promise you a cheeseburger."

Ryan walked up, leaned over and put his head in the open door. "I just got word. Couric and Assad's teams are mopping up. They've taken about 500 prisoners and they think rebel casualties are about 300. After Couric's team took their command center, the rebels just folded. The mosque seems to be secure, but it looks like a number of the rebels escaped into the catacombs. Assad's sending in some additional teams to make sure."

"Is the word out about Saif?"

"We've made sure it's hit the newswires with the news about the rebels being overtaken at the mosque, including some photos of his corpse leaked onto the Internet."

"No mention of our Special Ops guys, I hope."

"No, Assad's men are the only ones identified." Ryan thought for a moment, said, "Let's see if the word on Saif is enough to contain the uprising."

"Maybe if it just stalls it for a while, the Saudis will come up with some real reforms to make it go away. They have to realize now that these guys are serious, and some extra food stamps aren't gonna get it done."

A few minutes later, a Saudi Black Hawk picked them up. Sasha was too tired to even eat the food they'd prepared for her. She nodded off to sleep, her head resting on Tom's shoulder.

Tom wanted to call Yassar, but his first priority was getting Sasha on the chopper and back to Riyadh. Once on the Black Hawk, he waited until Sasha fell asleep, then slid his shoulder out from underneath her and rested her head against the back of her seat. He moved all the way to the back of the cabin and called Yassar. He had to hold one finger in his ear and yell into the cell phone, because Yassar, having been briefed by Assad, was also on a chopper on the way back to Riyadh.

Tom told Yassar that Sasha would be fine with some rest and food, then asked him, "Where do you think you stand?"

"Our Secret Police tracked the cell phone of Zafar from the Ikwan. I spoke to him for a half hour before I left Mecca, and he's agreed to set up a meeting with his fellow leaders from the Islamic Revolutionary Party and the Muslim Brotherhood."

"I'm surprised. Either you're very persuasive or they're back on their heels with the news of retaking the mosque and killing Saif."

"And with the disappearance of Qahtani."

Tom thought for a moment. *No Qahtani, no Mahdi, no holy war?* He said, "What about the al-Mujari?"

"We do not negotiate with terrorists." Yassar paused, as if for emphasis, then went on. "I have a meeting with King Abdul when I return to Riyadh. I have not yet made specific promises to the dissident groups, but I will make certain that the king understands the necessity of delivering on essential reforms."

Tom was impressed. The old guy had been around a long time, obviously in part because he was a cagey infighter, and knew when and how to sell his message. Tom had reached an agreement with him on the oil deal. That would give Yassar's Saudization plans a big shot in the arm, and give Yassar leverage to push for major reforms. Arab Spring in Saudi Arabia could turn into a peaceful summer. He finished his call and went back to check on Sasha. She was still asleep. He walked over and sat down next to Rashid.

"I can bring you back in from undercover," Tom said. "You've done enough. I'll get you a new identity, move you someplace safe."

"I've been thinking about it. This could be a real opportunity. With Saif gone, there will be a void at the top of the al-Mujari, and I was anointed by Saif as his next-in-command."

"Anybody see you leave to try to get to Saif?"

"I don't think so, and anyone who was with him in the catacombs is dead. If I go back in I'll have a shot at being their leader."

"You need to be sure you're not suspected, or you could be killed."

"I'm aware of that. It's a chance I'm prepared to take."

Tom just looked at him, wondering, *Does a guy who's convinced he's got nothing to lose ever get to the point where he really doesn't care about getting killed?* He said, "I don't need to tell you how important that would be to us, but you need to think that through, because if you think what you've been living for the last few years was tough, this would be another thing entirely."

Rashid just nodded.

Tom felt the old excitement, like in the days when he recruited and ran his own agents. He'd warned Rashid, so his conscience would be clear. When they got to Riyadh he'd start working out the details. He got up and sat back down next to Sasha.

As soon as Tom dropped Sasha off at the hotel in Riyadh, he went to the embassy and spoke to Ross on a secure line.

"Nice job. Any complications?" Ross said.

"A few, but not worth mentioning now."

"Where does the situation stand overall?"

"Yassar's in a dialogue with the three main dissident leaders, and he's willing to lean on King Abdul about reforms, hopefully enough to get this thing defused. He'll have plenty of money for it. I did the oil deal with Yassar. It's $250 billion for as much oil as we can't produce ourselves for 30 years, with a price escalation of 4% per year. How did you swing the money?"

"I told you earlier. The Federal Reserve. They don't report to anybody, and I've known Bernanke for years. He jumped at the opportunity. Two to three hundred billion for an assured supply of oil at a reasonable price for the indefinite future. Who wouldn't?" Ross paused. "What about the sheik, Qahtani?"

"The Saudi royals disappeared him, I'm sure never to be heard from again."

"And your man inside the al-Mujari?"

"Looks like he'll be staying put as a senior member of the organization."

"That'd be quite a coup for you."

"For all of us."

The next morning the embassy car took Sasha directly to the Royal Palace. Two Royal Guards nodded with recognition and allowed her to pass into Yassar's private quarters. She knocked on the door to his study, then entered. Yassar hadn't arrived yet, but one of the servants had left a silver tray with a pot of tea and two cups and saucers. She sat down in the chair across from his armchair, taking in the faint aroma of its leather, the wool of the rug, and Yassar's familiar scent.

Five minutes later Yassar walked through the door.

"Yassar," she said, feeling her emotions rise. She crossed the room to him, threw her arms around him.

He hugged her, then pressed her head to his chest.

"Are you all right, my dear?"

She leaned back and looked into his eyes. "Yes. A little banged up, but I'm fine."

His eyes looked tired, his face drawn. She felt guilty, certain some of the stress that had caused it was over her. *Dear Yassar.* She ushered him into his chair, then knelt beside the table in front of him and poured them both tea. They kept away from the subject of the events of the last weeks, talking about the plantings he was planning for the gardens, his eldest daughter's ambitions to attend college, how the younger children were doing.

A half hour later, he said, "I gather you'll be leaving soon."

She smiled. He always seemed to know her mind. "Yes, I still have some things to think through."

He nodded and sipped his second cup of tea.

A moment later she decided the time was right. She stood, walked to him and kissed him on the forehead. "I'll be in touch, I promise."

Sasha didn't show up at the embassy until late that morning. Tom, Zac, Seth and Ryan were assembled in the conference room. She noticed duffel bags on the floor.

"Going someplace?" she asked Seth.

"Our job here is done. Back to our team, new assignment," Seth said.

"Right away?"

"We're already late," Zac said. "We were just waiting to say good-bye to you."

"I'd have been crushed if you hadn't waited." She hugged and kissed them both. Her voice quavered as she said, "Thank you. I knew you were back there. I knew you wouldn't let me down."

They left.

"And I'm staying here," Ryan said.

Sasha hugged and kissed him good-bye.

Sasha dozed for the first hour of the flight with Tom on the CIA Learjet. She felt overwhelmed by the last weeks, and by the reflections forced on her by the circumstances. Admittedly, circumstances she'd thrust herself into, but as it always seemed to go in her life, ones she needed to adapt to rather than try to control.

She'd wondered who she was without Daniel, and now realized she hadn't needed to; she was the same person as always, just clear about it, and now just unclear about what direction her life would take.

Tom said, "You're awake. I was beginning to think you'd sleep all the way home." Then, before she could respond, he added, "Well, maybe not home, but back to the States."

"I'm not sure where I'll make my home now." She turned in her seat to face him. "There's nothing for me in Switzerland anymore, and even though I know that Yassar will always make me welcome in Riyadh, it's hard for me to consider Saudi Arabia my home. I feel as if I need to start over someplace new."

"Maybe you can start over in the States. Think about it up in Pennsylvania over that cheeseburger. After you unwind for a week or so I could even stop up there and help you sort things out." He wore a hopeful smile.

"I'd enjoy that." She smiled back at him. "But I want to change my life, Tom."

Tom nodded.

"I know that nod. Don't humor me. I mean it. I've had enough time to reflect, at Swami Kripananda's ashram, and imprisoned in those catacombs. I've learned how to kill people and it's a skill I'm not interested in continuing to cultivate."

"You've only ever done it out of commitment, when it needed doing. But I can understand how it catches up to you."

"Yes, it does. In those final moments in the room with Saif I was resigned to what would happen. I only knew I didn't want to kill again, at least not out of revenge."

"Then why did you?"

She looked at him, wrinkled her brow, puzzled. "He would have shot you if I hadn't."

"So, it sounds like your dilemma is still unresolved."

She shook her head. "It is resolved. I only killed him because I had no choice. It was you or him."

"Yes, but before I showed up it was him or you."

"And that was a choice I'd already made."

Tom's eyes widened as she saw him grasp her meaning. If he hadn't been at risk, she'd have died rather than kill again.

She said, "I already told you I've been saved." She reached across the aisle for his hand. "And I don't want that life anymore."

"Okay, get some sleep, you've just been through a lot. We can talk about it in Pennsylvania. I hope your place serves more than cheeseburgers, though. I'm more of a Delmonico steak kind of guy."

Sasha got up, squeezed past him into the window seat next to him, then sat down and rested her head on his shoulder.

AUTHOR'S NOTE

A siege and occupation of the Grand Mosque in Mecca, Saudi Arabia, the holiest place in Islam, actually occurred in 1979, undertaken by a fundamentalist Muslim dissident group. Thousands of pilgrims participating in the annual Hajj were taken hostage. The siege lasted two weeks. It ended after assaults by Saudi security forces, the Saudi National Guard and the Saudi Army all sustained heavy casualties, following which the Saudis enlisted the aid of the GIGN unit of the French military to retake the mosque. The efforts to retake the mosque included assaults through the underground catacombs in and around the mosque.

The mosque seizure was led by a man named Juhaiman ibn Muhammad ibn Saif al Otabi, who maintained that his brother-in-law, Mohammed Abdullah al-Qahtani, was the Mahdi, the Redeemer of Islam, whose coming was foretold in many of the prophecies of Islam.

The dissidents broadcasted their demands from the mosque loudspeakers, which included ceasing oil exports to the US and the expulsion of foreign civilians and military personnel from Saudi Arabia.

ACKNOWLEDGMENTS

Thank you to Manette for your comments and suggestions on the outline and manuscript, and for your love and support throughout the process.

Thank you to Peter Maloney for your comments and advice on the Saif and Sasha backstory sections of the manuscript.

Thank you to David Downing for your terrific editing and for your suggestions and comments on the manuscript; it was a pleasure working with you.

And thank you again to the team at Amazon Publishing.

Excerpt from *Trojan Horse*

Trojan Horse

Sasha Del Mira #1

A THRILLER BY

DAVID LENDER

Copyright © 2011 by David T. Lender

All rights reserved. No part of this book may be used, reproduced or transmitted in any form or by any means, electronic or
mechanical, including photocopying, recording, or by any information storage or retrieval system, without the written permission of the publisher, except where permitted by law, or in the
case of brief quotations embodied in critical articles and reviews.
For information, contact dlender@davidlender.net.

PROLOGUE

July, Twenty Years Ago. Riyadh, Saudi Arabia. Omar pressed the button that activated the lighted face of his watch, cupping his hands so he wouldn't be detected. *Today is a good day to die,* he recited the mercenary's creed in his head. 0158 *hours.* The others would start to arrive momentarily. He pulled out the American-manufactured night-vision goggles and stood in the shadows across the street from the outside perimeter wall of the grounds of the Royal Palace. He felt the chill of the Saudi night. He was grateful for the warmth provided by his German kevlar vest and British army fatigues beneath his robe, the traditional Saudi dress he wore as a disguise. Still, his Russian army boots were ridiculously obvious; the disguise wasn't about to fool anyone.

He scanned the street from where he knew the others would be joining him. Still no one. His mouth was dry. He fingered the Uzi clipped to his belt on his left hip, the .45 automatic Colt holstered on his right hip. Then behind the Colt the .22 caliber Beretta with its silencer extending through the hole in its holster. Omar was the only one of the team of twelve who carried a Beretta. He was to be the shooter.

Two men walked toward him, shielded by the shadows against the wall. He motioned to them and they gestured back. It was time. The other nine appeared like a mirage in the desert. Each was armed with Uzis and .45 caliber automatic Colt pistols;

two carried American M-203 grenade launchers. All were eclectically uniformed and hardwared to defy nationalistic identification if killed or captured. They waited silently against the wall, listening for the passage of the patrol jeep. It lumbered by, bearing two heavily armed guards.

Omar raised his hand: the "Go" signal. He felt his pulse quicken and the familiar butterflies and shortness of breath that preceded any mission, no matter how well planned. The twelve-member squad crossed the street to the white stucco perimeter wall of the palace. Four faced the wall and leaned against it, shoulder to shoulder. The others performed a series of acrobatic maneuvers and materialized into a human pyramid. The top man silently secured three rubber-coated grappling hooks with attached scaling lines to the top of the wall. Omar was over the top and down the other side in less than fifteen seconds.

While the others followed, Omar pulled off his robe. His heart pounded. He pulled five bricks of C-4 plastic explosive from his pouch and stuck them to the wall in an "X" configuration, aware that his palms were clammy. He wiped them on his robe and again focused on his work. He inserted an electrical detonator in each brick of C-4, and wired them to a central radio receiver that he inserted into the center block of the "X." By the time he finished, the rest of the team had cleared the wall and removed their robes. They stashed their robes in zippered pouches buckled to the backs of their waists.

Omar squinted at the wall of the palace, illuminated by floodlights, fifty meters away. This area had no first-floor windows. His eyes adjusted to the light, and he looked for guards he hoped wouldn't be there. He focused on a second-floor window at the junction of the east and north walls. *Be there*, he thought. *Just be there.*

Sasha didn't awaken at 2:00 a.m. as she had intended: she hadn't slept at all. She glanced to her right at Prince Ibrahim, illuminated in the light from the display of the digital clock. His body moved up and down with the rhythm of his breathing. Sasha had earlier treated him to some extended pleasures in an effort to assure he wouldn't awaken at an inopportune moment. She smelled the pungent scent of the evening's energies, felt the smooth silk of the sheets against her naked breasts: sensations that under other circumstances would cause her to revel in her sexuality. Now she felt only the flutter of apprehension in her stomach. She thought of the business to be dispensed with.

The Royal Palace was stone quiet at this hour. Sasha listened in the hall for the footsteps of the guard on his rounds. A moment later he passed. A renewed sense of commitment smoothed a steadying calm down her limbs. *It's time*, she told herself, and she slid, inches at a time, from the sheets to the cool marb*Yassar will never forgive me.* She breathed deeply, then felt exhilaration at the cool detachment her purpose gave her. She stood, naked, shoulders erect and head back, observing Prince Ibrahim, the man she had served as concubine for three years. *But you don't deserve to see it coming.*

Backing from the bed, Sasha inched toward the closet. The prince stirred in his sleep, inhaled and held it. Sasha froze in place. She felt her stomach pull taut and she held her own breath. The cool marble under her feet became a chilling cold, the silence an oppressive void. *This mustn't fail.* The prince resumed his rhythmic breathing and she exhaled in relief.

One more cautious stride carried her to the closet. She reached into it for her black abaya, the Muslim robe she wore in the palace. She cringed at the rustle of the coarse fabric as she put it on. The prince didn't stir. She picked up her parcel from the closet floor, crossed the room and slipped out the door.

At the corridor window, she removed the clear plastic backing from one side of a 2x5 centimeter adhesive strip. The acrid odor of the cyanoacrylate stung her nostrils. She slid the strip between the steel window frame and the steel molding around it, precisely where the pressure-sensitive microswitch for the alarm sat.

She took an electromagnet from her parcel and plugged it into an outlet, unraveling the cord as she walked back toward the window frame. She placed the magnet against the corner of the window frame behind the alarm microswitch and clicked on the electromagnet.

The force of the magnet jolted the molding against the window frame. She endured a count to thirty until the adhesive fused the microswitch closed, then switched off the magnet. She turned the window latch, took a deep breath, shut her eyes, pushed. The window opened. *No alarm.*

The face of the man she knew only as the squad leader popped into her view from his perch atop his team, who had formed a pyramid on the wall below. She stepped back from the window. In an instant he was inside, raising his finger for her to be silent, and then turning and attaching one of the grappling hooks to the window frame. *Never mind shushing me,* she thought, *just make sure you know what you're doing.* Within sixty seconds the other eleven members of the squad stole inside. The rope was up and deposited on the floor and the window closed and latched.

The black-haired girl backed herself against the wall, her palms against the marble. Omar stared into her jet-black eyes, saw her fierce spirit. *That was close,* he thought. *She nearly blew it. Late.*

He sensed her excitement in the heaving of her chest, but she appeared otherwise to be in complete control of herself. She raised her chin defiantly. He looked into those penetrating black eyes again. *Black steel*, he thought, and felt a fleeting communion with her. She motioned with her eyes in the direction of Prince Ibrahim's chamber. He nodded.

Sasha stood with her back pressed against the wall and watched as the team leader made hand signals and head motions to his men. He ordered a group to stand guard, then led most of them down the labyrinthine passageways that rimmed the outside perimeter of the palace toward Prince Ibrahim's chamber. She watched the team leader disappear from sight around the first turn of the corridor. For some reason Sasha was seized by the premonition that something was wrong. She pushed herself out from the wall, trotted toward the prince's chamber.

One of the team members, who had spread themselves in pairs in firing position, grabbed her by the wrist as she passed. A bolt of adrenaline coursed through her. She clenched her teeth and shot a glare at the man. His widened eyes showed fear. She jerked her arm away and continued. She was now aware of the exhilaration of life-threat and the calm purpose that drove her.

He'll never forgive me, again crashed through her consciousness. It sucked the strength from her, but she kept on. She reached the next turn, the last before Ibrahim's chamber and saw the team leader ten feet from the door. At that moment three Saudi guards bustled around the next turn in the corridor. She felt hot blood rush to her face and a charge of anger erupt from her chest. She saw two of the squad members three meters beyond the team leader rear their heads back like horses at the sight of fire, then crouch over their weapons.

Shots hissed from the two squad members' silenced Uzis. The three Saudi guards were hurled backward in a spray of blood amid the crack of bullets ricocheting off the marble walls. Their bodies hit the floor with thuds. Two more Saudi guards materialized at the same turn, M-16s aimed from the waist. Bursts from their guns flashed stars of flame from their barrels and flattened the two squad members. The squad leader froze, the hesitation of death, five feet from the prince's door. An instant later twin bursts from the Saudi guards' weapons slammed him backward into the wall.

Sasha forced herself to bury her panic within her. Next she was aware of the rush of her own breathing and the momentary sense she should conceal herself behind a tortured wail. Instead, she stretched out an arm and raised a hand toward the guards. They lowered the muzzles of their automatics and nodded to her in recognition. She pressed her back against the marble wall, her feet inches from the pool of blood that oozed from the team leader's body.

"More!" she called in Arabic and motioned with two fingers back down the corridor toward the window she had opened. The men nodded again, crouched over their weapons and trotted toward the turn in the corridor. She squinted at the two guards as they passed, seeing the panic in their faces, and resisting her own urge to flee. She slid down the wall, noting the Beretta and silencer protruding from the team leader's holster.

This mustn't fail, she told herself again. She yanked the Beretta from the team leader's belt and gave the silencer a jerk counterclockwise to make certain it was anchored in place. Then she held the gun at arm's length with both hands and fired one round into the back of the first guard. She saw the startled look of terror in the eyes of the second as he turned. She aimed the gun at his chest and pulled off two more rounds.

Three gone, five rounds left. She ran up to the two fallen men with the gun outstretched. The second one down didn't move, the first did. She put another round in the back of his head. She spun and darted toward Prince Ibrahim's chamber, gulping air in huge breaths as she thrust herself through the door. The glow from the digital clock outlined the shape of the prince, who sat upright in bed, staring directly at her. She raised the gun at his chest. "Pig!" she said in Arabic.

"Sasha, I don't understand," the prince stammered.

"Then you don't deserve to," she said, and pulled the trigger. He lurched backward onto the pillows. A circle of red expanded on his white nightshirt directly over his heart. Sasha stepped forward, lowered the Beretta and fired another round into the prince's skull just behind his right ear. Then she dropped the gun.

Her brain told her what to do next—run for the window at the end of the corridor, throw down the rope and escape—but her body wasn't nearly as composed as the voice in her head. Her breath came in gasps, her stomach churning at the smell of the blood puddled on the floor as she passed the bodies toward the first turn in the corridor. She shot a glance over her shoulder. *Still no other guards. Thank God.* She heard a crackle of static from a portable radio on the squad leader's belt and heard the words, "We are blown! We have casualties and are aborting! Prepare transport! Minutes one!" Seconds later she heard shots and screams from someplace. An alarm sounded and the corridor lights flashed on. As she reached a turn in the corridor, one of the squad members must have triggered the C-4, because a yellow-white glare flashed as bright as the sun. A shock wave whooshed down the corridor and threw her over backward to the floor.

Sasha jumped to her feet and ran down the corridor. She saw six squad members near the window, leaping out and down the rope each in turn. By the time she reached the window they were all down the rope. She leapt over the top without looking down. As she slid down the rope she listened for the sound of the three BMW 535s she knew the squad would have waiting for their escape. They were her only hope. But she couldn't hear them. She could only hear the pounding of her heart in her ears and the ringing from the sharp blasts of the guns and that malevolent C-4 blast. She knew she was beginning to think again and not just act on instinct and adrenaline and the passion of what she believed in, and she realized she might survive, and that even with the disastrous intervention of the Saudi guards, and her split-second improvisation, the plan hadn't gone so horribly awry.

Sasha ran for the hole in the perimeter wall. At ten meters away from it she heard the staccato bursts of Uzis from two of the death squad members stationed at either side of the hole. She saw two more men running in front of her and now they were in the ten-foot-deep crater where the wall had been. She could see one of the black BMWs on the other side. She heard bullets whiz past her head. The dust from the explosion that hung in the air tasted musty in the back of her throat. She felt the rubble of the wall beneath her feet and lost her balance, then dove into the crater. She landed on her stomach and wheezed for breath but the air wouldn't flow into her lungs.

Sasha could still hear the sharp retort of those Uzis and then even they went silent. Her eyes were wide open again and she couldn't breathe but her legs were starting to work and she tumbled down on top of somebody or something, she couldn't tell which, and then two men were dragging her by either armpit up the other side of the crater and she could see the open door of the BMW in front of her, hear the engine racing, and felt herself being thrown headfirst inside. She smashed her face on the floor and felt another body dive in on top of her and then the car was moving. Soon it was moving fast and she realized that not only was she alive but that she was going to make it out of there. And in that same instant a flash of anguish shot through her brain: *But where do I go from here?*

The crack of automatic weapons awakened Prince Yassar. He reached for his telephone, but there was no one to call, so he placed the receiver back in its cradle. Over the next five minutes he alternately sat and waited for someone to come, then got up and took a few halting steps toward the door to his outer suite, uncharacteristically uncertain. Should he fling the door open into the corridor and investigate for himself? Then a stiffly formal sergeant knocked sharply and entered the room. Prince Yassar observed the sergeant's stony face. He expected bad news and felt as if the weight of it were pulling his jowls toward the floor. He stroked his forehead. *Sweaty.*

"Prince Yassar, sir," the sergeant said expressionlessly, staring as he said the words, "Your son, Prince Ibrahim, has been murdered."

Yassar felt the words burst in his chest like a hollow-point round. He closed his eyes, knowing already that it was true. *She tried to warn me.* His sigh emerged as a moan.

Yassar glanced from side to side as if to find a way to escape. He hung his head in resignation, then glared up at the sergeant. *Why are you telling me what I already know? What I already have imagined in my worst fears?* He felt that he wanted to strike the little man.

"There were no other civilian casualties," the sergeant continued, still with no expression in his voice, on his face. Only that vacant stare. And the measured tones. "But five guards were killed in the corridor only meters from Prince Ibrahim's chamber, and three of the provocateurs"—Yassar noted with rising anger the ridiculously mispronounced French word—"were killed in the corridor. That, and twenty-three other soldiers are dead in the courtyard, most from the explosion. Everyone else is accounted for and safe, except one of the prince's concubines."

Yassar opened his eyes. They felt like black pools of moist agony. And rage. He realized the strength had been sucked from his limbs and now tried to move his arms, wanting to strike at this pompous man. But all he did was motion for the soldier to continue. "It is Sasha. She is gone," the sergeant said, "and we found a disabled microswitch on the window used to thwart the alarm, as well as an electromagnet and a grappling hook and rope. It would appear the death squad had help gaining access to the palace."

Yassar tried to stand and still could not. His legs trembled and he placed his hands on his knees to steady them, leaned forward, then slumped backward onto the bed.

"We found a gun on the bed. We found footprints in blood leading into the bedroom and then out again," the unbearable fool continued. "And we did not find Sasha."

Yassar felt the words like the twist of a knife in an already mortal wound. He closed his eyes again. *Sasha? How could Sasha do such a thing?* He felt his face contort. He raised his head and looked at the man, this man who would say such things, feeling the conflict of his anger against what he knew in his heart to be true. Sasha, whom he had taken under his patronage, treated like a daughter, and who had honored him like a father. Sasha, who had heeded his need for her to both minister to and keep his beloved, yet wayward, son in line. *This cannot be true.* But his shoulders curled over.

The sergeant continued his unemotional droning as if he were pushing through a checklist. "The perimeter of the palace is now secure and no intruders are believed left inside. Except for the three who were killed, the remainder of the assassination team appears to have escaped."

How can this mechanic, this mere functionary defile the memory of my son with his prattle? Yassar felt his strength returning as his anger rose. He sighed, then lifted himself from the bed, seeming to bear the weight of his dead son as he did so. He wanted to crush the man's head like a melon for having the audacity to bring such a message with such methodical reserve. The sergeant reached out and put a hand on Yassar's shoulder. Anger boiled in Yassar at the touch. He whirled, all the strength that had been drained from him in the last quarter hour focused in a single fist that he lashed toward the sergeant's face. A roar emerged from his breast, the single word, "No!" And then with the same ferocity of effort he stopped the blow just inches from the man's face. He hung his head so the man could not see the tears he knew he could not stop. He reached forward blindly, unclenched his fist and placed his hand on the man's shoulder. He squeezed it and pushed the sergeant toward the door. "Go. Please, go," he whispered. He heard the sergeant back out and shut the door.

Yassar turned back into the room. Then a dark sensation rose in him, one he had never felt before in all his years of adherence to the faith in his pursuit of the path of Allah: newborn hatred. *I will avenge this act. I will find out who has done this and chase them down. And Sasha. I will find her and destroy her.*

ABOUT THE AUTHOR

Photograph by Manette Loudon, 2007

David Lender is a former investment banker who spent twenty-five years on Wall Street. After earning his MBA at Northwestern University's Kellogg School of Management, he went on to work in mergers and acquisitions for Merrill Lynch, Rothschild and Bank of America. His first three novels— *Trojan Horse*, *The Gravy Train*, and *Bull Street*—turned Lender into an e-book sensation. He lives in northern New Jersey with his family and a pitbull named Styles.